The Stranger Inside

Amanda Cassidy is a freelance journalist, commissioning editor, former Sky News reporter, and an *Irish Times* bestselling author. She has been shortlisted for the Irish Journalist of the Year Awards, the Headline Media writing awards and more recently has been shortlisted for the CWA John Creasey New Blood Dagger for her debut novel, Breaking. She's a frequent contributor to national radio, print and television and holds a BA in French and Italian from Trinity College Dublin. When she's not on a plane, you'll find her in her cottage in Dublin where she lives with her husband and three young children. Amanda can be found @amandacasssidy on X (Twitter).

Also by Amanda Cassidy

Breaking
The Returned
The Perfect Place
The Stranger Inside

AMANDA CASSIDY

THE
STRANGER
INSIDE

CANELOCRIME

DK | Penguin Random House

First published in the United Kingdom in 2025 by

Canelo, an imprint of
Canelo Digital Publishing Limited,
20 Vauxhall Bridge Road,
London SW1V 2SA
United Kingdom

A Penguin Random House Company
The authorised representative in the EEA is Dorling Kindersley Verlag GmbH. Arnulfstr. 124, 80636
Munich, Germany

A CIP catalogue record for this book is available from the British Library.

Print ISBN 978 1 83598 287 7
Ebook ISBN 978 1 83598 286 0

Cover design by Henry Steadman

Cover images © Shutterstock

Printed and bound in Great Britain by Clays Ltd, Elcograf S.p.A.

Look for more great books at
www.canelo.co | www.dk.com

To Karl—for all the beautiful life chapters we wrote together.

Prologue

The sound of the dogs comes again. Growing closer.

Wispy branches rake their thorny nails across her face as she runs through the thick darkness, fighting her way through the forest. Running blind, breathing hard. Overhead, a helicopter rotor whirs between the dark treetops.

The woman's mind is alive. Fear and adrenaline propel her forwards. She has to remain focused.

A brief hesitation and then she pivots, splashing through the gloop of a narrow stream, the water reaching barely above her ankles. Her injured foot snags and she swallows down a scream of pain. The muddy snow cloys and tugs, slowing her down.

She'd heard something once about water throwing dogs off a scent. But who is she kidding? She doesn't know the first thing about being a fugitive – she'd never even had a parking ticket before all of this. She just knows she cannot stop.

There's something ahead of her. Sanctuary perhaps. The night air is alive with the scent of sweet decay. Her body thuds into a solid barrier marking the periphery of the forest. Momentarily winded, she retches silently into the dirt as the blackness closes in.

The woman squats low for a moment, listening, trying to catch her breath. She's completely trapped but there's no one here who will save her but herself.

The static of walkie-talkies echo in the bleary midnight dim.

No.

No.

Every inch of her body is sweating. The back of her knees are slick with it. Her spine, her hands. The snowfall has left her cropped hair standing up in sodden tufts.

She's come too far to stop now.

Her nails scrape desperately along the mossy timber of the high fence surrounding the woodland, trying to gain some purchase. There's heavy undergrowth along sections of it, conspiring to trip her up. The torchlight is approaching, skimming the landscape, jerky and low.

She's been to this place before, in better times, and she knows it's surrounded by sheer drops.

Something surges in her. She just needs one notch, one dent in the slimy wood.

One fucking chance.

Because someone has to pay for what happened. Someone tore her family apart and she needs to know why.

Her fingers grasp a jutting crack along the unyielding barrier. It's just enough. She pulls herself up with everything she has left. Her muscles scream, her eyes close tight as she scrambles painfully up. At the top she clambers over, then risks a glance back.

Her pursuers are so close that she can now make out their shadows between the trees. Florescent uniforms shouting at her to stop. Sirens in the distance.

Below her on the other side is only darkness. She breathes it shakily in. A fleeting memory comes at her. A fairground, colourful neon lights, the tinny music of a Ferris wheel in the wind, wiping coral beads of wet candyfloss from a tiny face… It clouds over again, disappearing into nothing, like the fog of her breath dragged into the night.

There's no other option.

Ciara closes her eyes.

She pictures her little girl.

She lets herself fall.

Chapter 1

Before

Ciara Duffy barely registers the urgent beeping from the smoke alarm. Her mind is fixated on the image of the dead patient.

Shit.

She jumps up, knocking over a glass of wine and swipes the pan of blackened mince off the stove, throwing it heavily into the sink. A charry sizzle from the running tap against the pan creates an angry hiss of steam. A half-diced onion sits forgotten on the chopping board.

Sally and her little friend Evie glance over, eyes wide. They'd been practically comatose for the past half hour in front of YouTube Kids. It's just her versus the two nine-year-olds for the entire evening.

Ciara rubs a hand over her face as exhaustion stretches around her like a fog. She can't stop thinking about what happened. Not for the first time, she regrets agreeing to her daughter's plea for a sleepover. She's just come off a double shift at the hospital, it's put-the-bin-out night, and it hasn't stopped raining since lunchtime.

Plus Morgan's away. Again.

The idea of facing a long weekend solo-parenting, while also trying to write this upsetting statement to the medical council about the circumstances surrounding a patient's tragic death calls for more wine.

The beeping continues, even after she opens the windows.

Ciara touches the tips of her fingers to her temples. The clutter of the tired kitchen surfaces reflect her chaotic thoughts: a small fruit bowl with a solitary, sad-looking apple; a pile of unopened utility bills; an old candle, its wick encased in wax; a half-finished project on Spain that Sally has been working on for school. The window frames bloom with dark spots. With a sigh, she awkwardly hauls herself onto the kitchen counter, cursing her rather-too-generous frame, and reaches towards the ceiling. She pulls the batteries out and the noise stops. But her worrying doesn't.

The statement she has to write is due on Monday. Though her work as a midwife at St Trinity's is mostly joy-filled, there are times that she wishes she'd chosen a much less emotionally draining job. *Like an influencer. Or a travel reviewer.* Being paid to go to exotic places and lie on beaches drinking cocktails all day.

'Mom, we're *literally* starving to death,' Sally complains, her voice slicing through Ciara's reverie. 'And freezing.' Sitting on the floor in the open-plan living area, she pulls the blanket from the couch around her to make her point.

Ciara sighs again at her daughter's adopted American twang borne, no doubt, from too many hours of US sitcoms she was plonked in front of by babysitters while Ciara was at work. Another thing to feel guilty about.

As she attempts to climb down from the countertop her toe catches on one of the cupboard handles and she curses under her breath. She tries and fails to reconcile her current life with the one she'd envisaged.

'Okay, lovie,' she calls to her daughter as she examines the disgusting remains of the spaghetti Bolognese. Instead, she makes a quick Nutella sandwich for each of them and uses a shape cutter to create star-shaped sandwiches, to tide the girls over.

The shops are just a five-minute dash away. Maybe she could salvage dinner, get this task over with, and try to enjoy the weekend with Sally.

It's the thought of picking up another bottle of Friday night wine that really cements her decision.

Ciara glances at the two blonde heads eating in front of the screen. They'd barely notice she was gone, would they? The alternative is pulling on both the girls' raincoats and wellies, dragging them to the shops and them pestering her for treats for the midnight feast she'd stupidly mentioned when she picked them up from Aimee's earlier.

She'll only be gone ten minutes. Fifteen minutes, tops.

Warm thoughts of a glass of merlot soothe her. Besides, it's the weekend. She'd worry about her life once Monday had swung miserably around once again.

Ciara pulls out the iPad and opens the iParent app. They use a version of it at work to keep an eye on the newborns in the hospital nursery while she's busy with her mum patients. It's like a baby monitor, where maternity nurses can see their little charges via an app on a phone.

It jumps to life, and the girls are framed on the screen. Then Ciara swipes through the colourful array of apps on her iPhone, everything from the school noticeboard and the family calendar, to the one that's supposed to track her fitness and food intake. That one she's barely used.

It takes her a while to find the little icon – purple, with a baby emoji framed in a small circle. She clicks into it and enters the pin. Immediately, Sally and Evie appear in the tiny square at the bottom of the app. She adjusts the iPad slightly to allow a wider view of her daughter and neighbour's little girl and switches it to parent mode.

'Okay, Sally…' Ciara waves her hand towards her daughter's blank face to get her attention. Sally's favourite programme *Ninja Kids* drones on the TV. 'Hello? Earth to Sal?'

Sally glances up. She's sitting on the carpet, her legs folded pretzel-style, a hole in the knee of her once-white school tights, a Bluey blanket draped around her skinny shoulders.

'I'll be five minutes. Do not move, okay?'

'Sure, Mom.'

'Evie, love, I'm just popping out for a minute to the shops. I won't be long, okay?'

Evie, who lives a few doors down, nods robotically, her eyes never leaving the screen.

At the front door, Ciara hesitates. Glancing over her shoulder, she reconsiders. Maybe she could ask Aimee to call over for a few minutes and sit with the girls while she pops to the shops? But then again, her attractive, all-round-perfect Stepford neighbour already thought Ciara was as flaky as they come. Just because she worked long shifts and was usually chasing her tail when it came to make-from-scratch meals and science projects.

Ciara opens the front door and pokes her head out into the drizzly October night.

This is the sliding door moment that she will obsess over time and time again. What would have happened if only she'd decided to stay in, to kick off her shoes and settle for a cup of tea and beans on toast instead?

It's definitely too wet to take them out, she decides, picking up her keys from the hall table. Dragging the girls out into the car just wouldn't be fair on them. This way, she'll just race out, grab the essentials and be back in no time. Plus, she has the iParent app open. They can see her, and she can see them.

Ciara double checks her reusable bag is in her shoulder bag, and pulls the door closed behind her. It's gone six and pitch dark. She makes a run for the car, coat over her head and, once inside, throws her phone with the app still illuminated onto the passenger seat.

She shivers as she reverses her battered VW Golf quickly out onto the road. She can barely see past the rain, which is growing heavier by the second.

They'd only been renting in the small Dublin suburb of Kerryvale for six months – ever since Morgan had been let go from another job. Ciara feels a prickle of annoyance as she approaches the convenience store nestled within a row of shops beside a hairdresser, chipper, creche and dry cleaners. She has to circle the small car park twice before she finds a space, glancing nervously at her phone all the while. The girls are still on the floor, legs tangled together, blue light from the screen dancing across their faces. She glances at the clock. She's already been five minutes. Ciara presses the speaker button within the app.

'Good girls, just at the shops now. All okay?'

Sally gives her a thumb up. 'Chocolate milk, please, Mom,' she reminds her. 'Not that horrible protein one.'

Inside the small convenience shop, the queue is already four people deep. Ciara taps her foot impatiently. Her arms are now laden with sliced bread, low-fat milk, red wine and a frozen pizza.

The person in front of her moves excruciatingly slowly. They want a lottery ticket from the machine. Cash back, too. Then they can't find their card. The shop's internet connection is playing up.

Christ's sake.

She practises the breathing advice she saw recently on an Instagram reel about mindfulness. In for four, hold for four, out for four…

Eight minutes have passed since she's left the house.

Anxiety pools in Ciara's stomach as the card machine refuses to cooperate for another customer. She realises with a pang of guilt that she didn't put the battery back into the smoke alarm.

Come on, come on.

Ciara eventually unloads the items in her arms onto the countertop, then races apologetically to the fridge for the forgotten chocolate milk.

She throws in a Galaxy Swirl for herself. Nothing like having to testify at the medical council next week to trigger some eating of feelings.

Another glance at her app. Two little bodies, now on the couch.

The age of nine is still so young really, despite her daughter's talk of Taylor Swift and penchant for permanently crimped hair and saying 'literally' *literally* at the end of every sentence. Sally's recent ill health had added another layer of worry to Ciara's armful of worries. She hadn't been herself lately, constantly sick. The GP had said it was probably down to the recent virus outbreak at Sally's school, but they'd run blood tests anyway. It all emphasised how vulnerable her daughter still was. Ciara wonders for a moment if nine might be old enough to finally tell Sally the truth about her past. But, deep down, she knows there'll never be a good time to admit what really happened.

Goosebumps race along Ciara's arms. What was she thinking leaving two children alone? She shouldn't have left them.

Politely sidestepping small talk with a new neighbour, Ciara dashes to the car and tumbles the bag of groceries onto the passenger seat. Sweat gathers on the back of her neck despite the cold.

It's been eleven minutes since she left them.

She glances again at her mobile phone screen as she presses the ignition button of the car.

This time, her heart almost leaps out of her chest, the blood suddenly roars in her ears.

There's somebody in her kitchen.

There's somebody standing right behind her daughter.

Chapter 2

A shadowy figure hovers in the background of Ciara's house, standing in the kitchen behind the girls.

Ciara's stomach drops, then flips.

Her gut instinct is primal. Her finger claws at the screen, the distorted rainbow pixels chasing outwards at her touch.

Could it be Morgan? No, she doesn't recognise Morgan's short, solid shape. This person seems more willowy. Plus, Morgan's in London until Sunday. Her heart thumping wildly, Ciara makes a split-second decision: she drives up over the kerb, foot to the floor, avoiding the red snake of brake lights ahead of her. Ciara glances again at her phone as she revs her small car up the road, a long sound coming from low in her throat.

No, no, no.

The figure is moving from the open-plan kitchen towards the sofa. Ciara's whole body feels as if it's about to give way from the same, animalistic fear from all those years ago.

The girls sit unperturbed. They have no idea they are not alone in the house.

Ciara debates shouting something into her phone, but she doesn't want to scare the girls, or risk escalating the danger.

She doesn't want to make this any worse than it already seems.

Maybe there's a reasonable explanation why there's someone in her house.

Ciara hits a cone in the never-ending building works of the housing estate and swerves out of the way of another car that comes to a stop with a sudden jerk to avoid hitting her. It beeps angrily. The rain slices sideways in the illumination of her headlights. Ciara sweeps her blonde fringe out of her eyes as she peers through the windshield. She can see her house up ahead. She's taking great big gulps of air, willing the car to move faster. There's not even time to phone anyone.

Ciara launches the Golf into the small driveway and leaps out, leaving the engine running. She fumbles with the front door key, her shaking fingers sliding along the little monkey keyring Sally chose for her at their trip to the petting zoo last summer.

Ciara throws open the front door, the visceral need to close the distance between her and her child like a hole in her chest. 'Sally,' she screams, hysteria distorting her voice. *Please god, please god… just let her be safe.* 'Sally,' she yells again.

Her throat constricts with dread as the kitchen door slowly opens. 'Mom?'

Sally pokes her head past the door, looking puzzled by Ciara's frazzled demeanour. She pulls on the ends of one of her plaits. 'We were good, I promise. Did you get the chocolate milk?'

Ciara falls to her knees in the hallway and pulls her daughter towards her. She cradles Sally against her body, rocking the soft bones of her, stroking her hair. Sally is like her in so many ways – shy and timid, a people-pleaser. There's a fragility to her… but Ciara knows that's her own perception of her daughter, especially after the circumstances she was born into.

Ciara holds Sally at arm's length and crouches in front of her, her heart still beating wildly in her chest. Her daughter has had a growth spurt recently. She's tall for her age, with untameable blonde frizz around fine features. A spray of pale freckles sprinkle her nose.

'Did you see anyone here, Sal?' Ciara asks, trying to keep her voice light for Evie, who stands behind her friend, eyes round and frightened. Ciara's knees are trembling as she stands. She feels the edge of her voice about to fray into tears. 'Did anyone come into the house?'

Now Sally's eyes widen. She shakes her head vigorously.

'Nobody popped in to say hello?' Ciara repeats, hands moving quickly together, adrenaline making her twitchy.

Sally shakes her head again, then hesitates. 'I took some jellies from the drawer.'

'That's okay, sweetheart.' Ciara's heart swells amid the panic. 'If the two of you wait in the hall here like good girls, I'll get you another treat. I just want to check if there's any little mice in the house.' The girls smile at the game.

'Hello?' Ciara shouts into the mouth of her home, her voice strangled. She tries to sound courageous and fierce but feels anything but. She thinks again of Morgan away in London and uses the flare of anger at his absence to feel braver. She takes a step into the kitchen, honing her listening to hear past the TV noise.

She shouts again, turning on every light in the kitchen as she goes. *Light up the monsters*, her dad used to tell her when she was little. But as the former Detective Chief Superintendent overseeing organised and serious crime in Dublin, the great Jimmy Mooney had locked away monsters his whole life instead.

Ciara walks past the fridge with its hand-scrawled notes to order more toilet paper and crooked artwork from Sally stuck on with magnets. A white page adorned with Sally's baby handprints has fallen to one side, pinned in place by another magnet in the shape of Brighton Pier.

The page flutters suddenly, giving her a fright.

Ciara looks over her shoulder. *The fucking window.*

It is slightly ajar. *Is that how somebody got in?*

'You're not allowed to say fuck,' Evie pipes up, and Ciara realises she must have spoken aloud. Sally and Evie are peeking in at the door, looking shaken. Past them is the hallway and directly opposite is the living room. The lamp is on in there, casting a shadowy glow across the polished tile floor of the hallway.

'That's exactly right, Evie,' Ciara reassures her, knowing full well how many of those bad words Sally was unfortunately familiar with.

It's only as Ciara slowly opens the door of the living room that she realises she's clutching a kitchen knife in her hand. The one from the chopping board. She moves quietly. Ciara had a lot of practice at moving silently. When she was just eleven years old, she'd been woken by a strange sound in her childhood home, like something breaking. She'd peeled back her duvet and padded along the floorboards of the landing, listening carefully. Making her way to the top of the stairs, she'd heard the sound again. She'd knelt and peered down the stairs into the hallway.

Her father had been standing by the front door with a gun.

This was part of her father's job. To protect them from the associates of those he may have put away. He'd even had a security detail and a plan in case Ciara was ever kidnapped.

It had been hard to grow up in a household where danger always seemed to lurk: she'd never felt truly safe. It was why she was so adamant that she'd wanted to create a sanctuary for Sally.

But she's messed that up too.

Ciara's memories fade as she walks around the downstairs of her house. She's still wearing her raincoat. She reminds herself that she's an adult now and there is no lurking danger.

Right?

The more she creeps around her home, the more she starts doubting herself. The figure she saw was grainy, but it had been someone. *Hadn't it?*

Maybe she'd imagined it?

Trembling, Ciara puts her foot on the first step of the stairs and glances up. The landing light is off, but she was sure she'd left it on when she went out. Ciara's brain feels like it's playing tricks on her. It's scrambled with fear. She should probably call someone. That's what she'd shout at the screen if this was a horror movie, rather than continuing up the stairs alone.

But if she doesn't check now, she won't sleep. Ciara moves gingerly, taking one step at a time, one hand clutching the banister, the other the knife, wishing she'd done that self-defence course Aimee had been hounding her about a few weeks ago. Ciara's Converse trainers are silent against the old cream carpet as she inches up the stairs.

At the top of the stairs, Ciara hits the light switch. The amber-painted landing lights up. Three doors lead off it: two bedrooms and the family bathroom. She edges Sally's door open first. The light from the hallway casts a triangle across the unmade bed where Sally's bunny lies in one corner. Her daughter's nightie and dressing gown are draped on the chair beside it. Ciara takes a deep breath and flings open the wardrobe doors. Some of the hangers clang together with the force and it makes her jump.

Nothing but Sally's clothes and the dusty smell of mothballs from the previous renter.

There's nothing else. No trace of anyone.

Still quivering, Ciara's eyes move towards the bed, and the sheet that hangs down concealing what's beneath it.

She takes a breath and hunkers down. A chill runs the length of her spine as she suddenly whooshes the hem of the pink sheet upwards.

There's only the shadows of dusty old jigsaws and vacuum-packed summer clothes beneath it.

Ciara stands up again. Maybe her mind *was* playing tricks on her? Perhaps she was so afraid of the worst happening, her brain had conjured it all up.

In her own bedroom, she repeats the same process, beating herself up for being so stupid to have left the girls alone and the window open. But she'd definitely seen someone.

She's about to walk back downstairs to call her dad when she hears a noise.

Ciara freezes. Her hands are damp with sweat.

It's coming from the bathroom. Like somebody has dropped something.

Despite her fear, Ciara feels compelled to move towards the sound, pushing the door open gently.

Ciara briefly catches sight of herself in the bathroom mirror – blonde hair pulled back into a too-long ponytail. A shaggy fringe that needs cutting. A round face, pale and exhausted from what happened during her shift the previous week and the fear she's battling.

But there's no time to think of any of that now.

The bathroom shower curtain is closed.

Weird.

Ciara pauses, trying to listen for any sound at all. 'Is someone there?' she says, more desperately now. Trying to scare, but sounding pathetically soft. She suddenly hears the thump of the children's feet on the stairs and their approach gives her the jolt of bravery she needs. She whips the curtain quickly open, knife boldly brandished into thin air.

There's nobody there.

'Mom?'

'Coming, girls,' Ciara calls. She grips the sink as she lets the waves of adrenaline wash over her, her shoulders sagging, weak with fear.

The window is open up here too and the force of the weather must have knocked over the little plant pot she kept on the windowsill, as it's smashed into the bath, mud and tiny leaves covering the base of it.

Once she's checked behind every door and even the hot-press, it starts to become clear that there's nobody there. And after she's checked the garage and laundry room, her paranoia feels foolish.

She rubs a shaky hand over her face, completely drained.

'No sign of the little mousey,' Ciara declares to the girls, lifting a coat that has fallen to the ground off the bottom stairs' banister. She scoops her daughter towards her again. 'Silly Mummy.' She plants a kiss on her daughter's squirming head.

In the kitchen a few minutes later, Ciara throws the frozen pizza under the grill next to some garlic bread. She opens the wine, hoping it will quell the uneasy feeling she has about how the evening is unfolding.

The iPad is exactly where she'd left it.

Not for the first time, Ciara wishes they'd asked for curtains to be hung across the huge glass doors at the back. But the landlord of the Kerryvale house wasn't the easiest to deal with. In fact, he made her anxious a lot of the time with his lingering eyes and dirty fingernails. Another problem Morgan had left her to solve solo.

Maybe the movement she saw could have been from the glass flexing in the wind, Ciara muses. It had been unseasonably stormy all week.

Suddenly everything in the kitchen looks dangerous: the knives in the knife block, a lighter on the windowsill. Sally could easily have opened the cupboard with the bleach. Ciara brushes guilty tears away, her back to the girls, who are now making extravagant loom band bracelets at the kitchen island and discussing their school's upcoming hip-hop dance show.

Fifteen minutes later, they sit down together for dinner, but Ciara can't bring herself to eat. The smell of the cheap pepperoni turns her stomach. She nibbles the corner of some garlic bread and reaches for more wine.

Afterwards, she tries to distract herself, watching *The Real Housewives of New York* and eating her chocolate, attempting to ignore the niggling feeling in her stomach. Something tugs at the corner of her mind. She attempts to pinpoint what it is, but it escapes her. Was there something out of place perhaps? Ciara surveys the kitchen again, then double checks all the doors and windows are locked, telling herself she is safe.

And, more importantly, Sally is safe.

Ciara pours another large glass of red.

Outside, the storm gathers force.

Chapter 3

When Ciara tucks the girls into bed after dinner, there's still no reply from her message to her husband.

Bloody Morgan.

They'd had another fight that morning. It was as if it was almost a habit now to slide into the usual arguments over finances. Every conversation lately seemed to descend into low-level sniping and one-upmanship – a pointless friction that left her despairing.

There'd been a certain novelty about having Morgan at home all the time at first, once he'd been let go from his accountancy position. Ciara had been able to organise more playdates for Sally as he was around, and he could help her settle into another new school. They could save on childcare too, she'd pointed out, trying to ignore her frustration, but it hadn't been long before the novelty had worn off. Arriving home to dirty plates and a couch-rumpled husband while the laundry basket was still full and the laptop untouched started to sting.

Resentment simmered just below the surface of their relationship. Morgan seemed tired and more short-tempered than she'd ever seen him, even with Sally. They'd stopped being intimate. Ciara didn't like to think about her four-year marriage in terms of tit for tat, but sneaky thoughts of what her husband was actually bringing to their partnership had started to invade her mind. She'd seen a cruel streak to him that she'd never expected, and financially they were on their knees.

Still, the figure she saw on the screen is playing on her mind as she sits in front of the TV, and she knows she'll feel better after talking to Morgan about it.

Because what if someone *did* get in?

No, Ciara, she tells herself, feeling a little braver because of the wine. *Do not psyche yourself out like this. Not tonight.*

She pulls her dressing gown around herself more tightly and finishes her glass of red. She's only managed to complete a few lines of the statement for the medical council.

The incident that happened during her shift has been invading Ciara's dreams for days. The pleas from the poor, labouring mother as Ciara's colleague, consultant Dr Derry Cunningham, dawdled. His refusal to carry out a C-section more quickly had been a mistake; Ciara recognised that. She can't get that moment out of her head: the long, awful silence when the infant was finally pulled out. Tiny limbs, so ripe for life, unmoving against the mother's heaving chest. Then the howling from the husband as the mother grew weaker and weaker, haemorrhaging before they had time to help her.

Ciara knew her account of what had happened would form the basis of the entire case. And as difficult as it was to go against her colleagues and friends, she knew what she had to do. Her father Jimmy had raised her with integrity, even if it was painful in the long run.

Ciara closes her eyes and, as tears fall, she allows herself this release from her increasingly difficult few weeks. With too many spinning plates to manage, she feels as if she's just about making it through the days.

As she wipes her wet cheeks with a napkin, she wonders again why the hell Morgan hasn't called.

–

Ciara is a little unsteady on her feet as she checks once again that the doors are locked and taps the code for the alarm. On her way past Sally's room she pops her head in on the girls, who have finally settled down, then skips her skincare routine and collapses into bed after definitely too many glasses of wine.

Ciara has no idea how much time has passed when she awakes, but it's with a flinch of alarm.

The bedroom is pitch black. Something woke her. Did a door slam downstairs perhaps?

What time was it?

The tiles of the ensuite bathroom are ice-cold as she feels her way gingerly inside, not bothering to switch on a light. God, how she misses her old house in Rathmines, with the underfloor heating and big back garden with room for swings.

Ciara slides back into bed and stretches her legs, trying to regain some of the warmth from her sheets. Her head feels heavy and she knows she's going to suffer in the morning.

Suddenly, her leg brushes against something solid.

She instantly recoils, now aware of an uncomfortable energy to the room.

Something feels very wrong. Her brain tries to catch up with the shock of realisation.

There's someone in her bed.

There's someone lying next to her.

One of the girls must have climbed into her bed. Sally does that sometimes if she has nightmares, and curls her tiny body around hers, her head nestled into Ciara's chest like she did as a baby.

Ciara reaches her hand slowly across the duvet. It's damp. Perhaps Sally had an accident?

She hesitates. She knows Sally's shape off by heart. She can usually tell her daughter's form in a millisecond.

And even if it was Evie who had crept in after a nightmare, the solidness she senses is far too large.

Ciara slowly withdraws her hand in the dark, heart pounding.

This isn't one of the children.

She doesn't dare breathe. This is it. Someone must have been lingering in the house all evening. Hiding somewhere, under a bed or behind a door.

Waiting.

A surge of something wild triggers deep within her when she pictures her daughter sleeping in the next room.

Ciara leaps out of the bed, a scream lodged in the back of her throat, her heart thudding in her chest, fast and shallow. She staggers backwards, towards the door, towards the light switch, fumbling to find it. The room suddenly illuminates.

The first thing she sees when her eyes adjust is the blood. So much blood, covering almost every part of her previously white duvet. And all over her hands.

The second thing she sees is her husband.

Morgan is lying on his side of the bed, arms flung out, as if fast asleep.

But his eyes are open, staring unseeingly at the ceiling. And a kitchen knife has been rammed right into the middle of his chest.

Chapter 4

Their entire street has turned blue and red with emergency service lights.

Her teeth won't stop chattering. Ciara wraps both arms tightly around herself.

'Do you understand what we are telling you, Mrs Duffy?' One of the dozen or so Gardaí milling around inside the house asks her, his voice seeming to come from very far away.

Ciara turns her head away from the window with great effort. The officer has a round face, serious eyes, a navy Garda uniform. Ciara wonders absently if he'd been on duty all night or if he'd pulled on his uniform and turned up with the rest of the sirens after she'd called the emergency services an hour ago.

Ciara nods at the officer, but it's like nobody can hear her. She's been repeating over and over how there had been an intruder in her house. Now, her stunned senses are concentrated on the blue from the police cars outside, strobing across her skin, making everything seem like a dream sequence.

'This is now a crime scene,' someone informs her, and they'll need her clothes. She staggers from their front room, into the hallway, trying to ignore the chaos as she steps into the small bathroom under the stairs. Ciara removes her blood-soaked polka-dot pyjamas on autopilot. 'Don't forget the undergarments too,' a male voice calls in awkwardly. She hesitates and then slips off her nude knickers. Then she steps into the white crinkly paper suit they hand her, the material uncomfortable against her bare skin. Everyone keeps telling her it's all over now, like that was a good thing.

But even in the midst of the panic and grief, Ciara knows this will never be over. In fact, she knows it's only just begun.

'Can't you understand what I'm saying?' she finds herself yelling. 'There was someone in the house. Someone broke into my home.' But nobody seems to be listening.

Until the detective arrives.

–

The last hour had been a blur of blue lights, raised urgent voices and questions – so many questions.

After she'd seen Morgan lying there like that, Ciara had raced towards him immediately, instinctively. She'd wailed as she'd tried to pull the blade from his chest. It was a stupid thing to do really, wading into the scene of the crime like that, but Ciara had never been faced with something as awful as seeing her husband knifed in the chest. It was only after she'd lifted him up to sitting that it has sunk in that he was dead and she was covered in his blood. And worse, that there was a murderer in her house.

Sobbing, she'd dragged a petrified Sally from her bed along with Evie, and they'd huddled in the front garden waiting for help, scared the intruder was stalking them too, the girls crying in distress.

First there had been the ambulance, and a pair of green-suited paramedics asking urgently if they were hurt. Then they raced past them, making their way up the stairs until Ciara had warned them there could still be an intruder inside. Looking at one another, they'd hesitated, then backed quickly down the stairs. A moment later, three Garda patrol cars had pulled up. Radio calls, static and acronym orders being barked. The sound of heavy boots thumping up and down the stairs. Stamping all over her life.

Something unthinkable had happened. Something she knows that will change everything. It hits her again. The coppery smell, the sight of her husband's face, somehow bloated, the sticky black stain on his work shirt, blood seeping into a shamrock shape across his poor chest. How she'd had to abandon him, for the sake of her and the girls' safety.

But it was obvious to her, even then, even before the strangers in her home started using words like 'the deceased,' that her husband couldn't have been saved.

Her vision blurred with tears as Aimee from five doors down came and wrestled Evie out of Ciara's fierce embrace. 'Jesus Christ, what happened? Is everyone okay?' Aimee had demanded, her own maternal fear obviously kicking in.

'Evie's okay, Aimee. It's… Morgan. He—' Ciara had doubled over, completely overwhelmed. Aimee, satisfied her daughter was safe, had pulled her friend to face her. 'Oh, my God, Ciara,' she said, her hands clamped over her mouth. 'Poor Morgan,' she continued, clearly dazed. 'Poor you…'

Ciara continued to sob, more silently now, Sally wrapped around her like a limpet.

'I'll take the girls back with me,' Aimee said gently, squeezing Ciara's arm supportively. 'Can I call someone for you?' Evie had suddenly started crying hysterically behind her mother, shivering in her pyjamas with little red hearts, her hair a strawberry mess around her scrunched-up face.

Oh god, what a sleepover, thought Ciara, vaguely.

'Can you call my dad?' Ciara roused herself, reciting Jimmy's number. 'I just need…' She trailed off, concentrating instead on the puddle next to her, dimpling with rain. She realised she was soaked through, and she didn't have the faintest clue as to what she needed.

For this not to have happened.

For her husband to still be alive.

Aimee punched the numbers into her iPhone, but there was no answer from Jimmy.

Ciara noticed it was half past five in the morning.

'Mrs Duffy, can you come with me, please?' It was a young guard in uniform who had approached Ciara.

Aimee, in her dressing gown, put both hands on Ciara's shoulders, as if trying to keep her rooted in the moment, even though all Ciara wanted to do was float away up into the dark clouds overhead. 'Sally is safe with me,' she reassured. 'You just focus on what's happening here and I'll get her in, out of the cold.'

'Mom?'

'It's okay, darling.' Ciara fought tears. 'Aimee will take care of you until Grandad Jimmy comes. It's going to be okay.' She hugged her daughter tightly. Nobody would ever understand the connection that existed between them. She ran her fingers through Sally's fair hair, like she used to when she was tiny, noticing in horror that they were still crusted in Morgan's blood. Sally sobbed against her chest, her shoulders shaking.

'I don't want to go, Mom. Please let me stay with you. Please, Mom. Please don't make me go with her.'

There was no time to acknowledge the childish reluctance to be separated from her mother. No time for anything other than survival mode.

'You have to go, Sally,' Ciara implored. 'Aimee will look after you. And remember what I told you before. When you were scared to go to school. Even when you can't see me, I'm always in your heart.' She gently raised her daughter's head so she could see her face. 'Look at me,' Ciara said gently, her voice breaking with emotion. 'I'm always with you, Sally. You know that, right?'

'And Daddy?' Tears had swollen her daughter's eyes almost completely shut.

Ciara took a breath trying to comprehend the unbearable heartbreak of it all. 'Daddy's always in your heart too,' she reassured, biting her lip. 'I'm so sorry, baby.' She pulled Sally towards her tighter. 'I'm so sorry.'

She watched as Aimee held Sally and Evie's hands and they walked down the streetlight path towards number five, their shadows stretching long and eventually merging into one.

Suddenly, Sally was gone.

And that's when the detective had arrived.

–

Ciara is led into the kitchen by a Garda. She sits down at the table and a tall man introduces himself as Detective Inspector Clarke Casey. He's young, probably forty or so, slim with sandy hair, long legs and kind eyes. 'I believe you're Chief Jimmy Mooney's daughter,' he says, placing a cup of tea on the table in front of her. The movement makes her jump. He smells of the outside air and faintly of laundry detergent.

Ciara licks her dry lips and nods. She cups her hands around the hot mug, grateful for its warmth.

'He was my boss when I first started training,' Casey says.

She moves her head in acknowledgement, too exhausted and shocked to manage anything more energetic.

'First, I'd like to offer my sincere condolences for your loss,' Casey says. 'You work as a midwife…?'

She nods. 'At Trinity's. I've done so for the past few years.'

'And before that?'

Ciara glances up, thinking quickly. 'I was working abroad,' she says, stiffly. 'I was a private midwife, so I had a few different clients.'

Detective Casey scribbles something down on the notebook in his lap and she squeezes the mug tightly so it almost burns her hand.

'Do you think you can talk us through what happened here tonight, Mrs Duffy?'

She fixes her gaze rigidly on the kitchen sink. 'I saw someone in my house – a stranger.'

Casey nods.

She hesitates, her thoughts disjointed.

'Then I woke up in the night,' she begins. 'I'd heard a noise. A door slam downstairs, maybe? I thought it was Sally at first. I went to the bathroom and when I got back into bed, I felt… something.' Ciara shudders as she recalls the moment.

Detective Casey nods but doesn't say anything. He has an open face, straight teeth and a thin gold wedding band on his left hand.

'Earlier, though, I definitely saw someone—' Ciara continues, the words tumbling out. 'A person – here.' She gestures towards the sofa area in the open-plan kitchen. 'I saw them on the app when I ran out to the shops. It was about six-ish.'

Casey nods encouragingly. 'Tell me about this app.'

'It's called iParent. We use it at the hospital to keep a screen on the babies if we aren't in the nursery. We can watch them in real time on phones the odd time there's nobody there. I use it at home sometimes, if Sally is upstairs or if I'm working from home on admin. I put it on last night when I ran out to the shops.' She covers her mouth with a trembling hand. 'I was only gone a few minutes…' she insists. 'The shops are so close. You can almost see them from here.'

Casey glances up from his notebook, perhaps sensing her distress. 'I know this is really hard, Mrs Duffy, but it's important. Can you remember anything about this person that you saw on the screen? Build, race?'

'I don't think so,' Ciara shakes her head. 'It was dark, and the app doesn't record. Tallish, maybe? Sorry, it was so blurry. When I came back, I checked the entire house. There wasn't anyone here. I thought I'd imagined it. I checked everywhere just in case.' Her voice has gone up an octave as she relives the frenzied searching she'd performed just a few hours ago. She remembers scanning the kitchen, beating herself up for leaving Sally, but there was something else... It snags in her memory again. Something out of place.

The image of her husband's lifeless face comes at her without warning. The now blood-drenched French quilt his sister had bought them for their wedding bunched around his body. His blue lips. His wide, staring eyes.

'Oh god... Morgan...'

Ciara breaks off, fresh tears streaming down her face.

Casey hands her a tissue and pulls his chair closer to her. 'Take your time, Mrs Duffy.'

She can't get past the idea that she was lying in the dark as someone was tiptoeing around her house with a knife. How long were they waiting? Did they sneak up the stairs? Were they in the bedroom when she went to the bathroom? Would she have been killed too if she hadn't woken up? What about Sally?

She sobs into her hands.

'Do you think you'd recognise the person if you saw them again?' Casey's voice is soothing, a lyrical accent she can't place. Quite posh too. Maybe a private school upbringing, like her own.

Ciara shakes her head. 'It was just a shape on the screen,' she stammers, trying to think back.

'Could you describe this person's clothing?'

She thinks hard. 'I don't know exactly, but I have a sense that they were dressed quite formally. Like, not a tracksuit... work clothes, I think.'

'Colours? Details?'

'I'm sorry.' She bites her lip. 'It was just a shape.'

'And is there any chance that it was your husband you saw on the screen?'

Ciara shakes her head. Morgan had put on weight recently. The person she had seen had seemed to move more freely. Then again, she'd been wrong about someone hiding in her house. Suddenly, she's starting to doubt everything.

Casey pauses a moment and talks into his radio. Ciara tries to focus on what he's saying, but she's so very tired.

'You said your husband was away working in the UK,' he continues gently. 'Had he told you when he was due to return?'

'He was due back on Sunday,' Ciara says, using a scrunched-up tissue to pat her eyes dry. 'He hadn't answered my texts all day. He was over there for a work interview.'

'Do you remember what time you went to bed? Had you locked all the doors? So far, we haven't found any signs of forced entry.'

'I don't remember when I went to bed, probably about eleven,' she says, apologetically. 'I'd had some wine...' She'd already seen him glance discreetly over at the three empty bottles of wine set out on the ground next to the kitchen bin. 'That's a few weeks' worth over there,' she says quickly, shifting in her chair. 'The bathroom window was open when I got home from the shops but I closed it.' She's grasping desperately for anything that might help the police. A flip of guilt in the pit of her stomach. 'And I must have left the window open in the kitchen when I ran to the shops,' she admits. They both look over at the window. It was possible someone had climbed in, but unlikely. They were small, open-out windows. And surely the girls would have noticed.

'We are collecting whatever evidence we can get from your home, Mrs Duffy – the bedding, the bedroom, your own clothes... but we'll have to do a formal interview if you're feeling up to it. Would you mind if we brought you to the station where we can do the initial interview and get you into some calmer surroundings?' Detective Inspector Casey gestures at the forensic team milling around the hallway.

Uneasiness creeps over her like a dark cloud. She's watched enough Netflix true crime documentaries to know how this goes. She'd be heavily scrutinised. A wife covered in her husband's blood, talking about a mysterious intruder. It never ended well.

Ciara pushes her fringe out of her eyes. She thinks of Sally sitting in Aimee's house, a few doors down, traumatised and needing her as much as Ciara needed her daughter. They'd rarely been separated. And never overnight. A visceral pang radiates through her.

'What about my daughter...?' she manages, an icy shiver running through her whole body. 'She's only nine... and she's been really unwell lately.'

'Your daughter will be well taken care of, Mrs Duffy. She's safe now with your neighbour, I believe. Do you have family close by?'

'Can you get my father to come. I… we need him.,' she says, simply.

Casey nods, standing up. She notices he has a slight limp as he rights himself, stretching out his long limbs. 'Of course. And, just one more question, Mrs Duffy—?'

She looks up at him, forcing her eyelids to stay open. This is exhaustion like she's never felt before in her life.

'Can you think of any reason why someone might want to target your family?'

Ciara grips the edge of the kitchen table.

She thinks about the sanctuary she'd tried so hard to build for them and how that had all been destroyed overnight.

She shakes her head, and despite the very real trauma of what's happened here, she's amazed how easily the lie slips out.

'I've absolutely no idea,' she says, carefully.

Clarke Casey looks at her intently, his gaze unwavering. 'Are you absolutely sure, Mrs Duffy?'

Ciara's knuckles whiten against the grain of the pine. 'I'm positive,' she lies to the detective.

Chapter 5

'There was no intruder, was there, Mrs Duffy?'

DI Ruth Greyson taps an accusing finger on the table of the inter-view room, eyes blinking rapidly like a hawk's, challenging Ciara. She has clean, half-moon nails and a gold watch on her right wrist just visible beneath her sleeve.

This was the good cop, bad cop act if ever Ciara had seen it.

Detective Clarke Casey's counterpart at Sandymount Garda station is short and has that sort of ageless appearance that means she could be anywhere between forty and sixty. She's wearing a dark bulky suit, as if she's trying to hide her wiry frame. A thick sweep of eyeliner adds to her severity.

Ciara clamps her lips shut and hugs her sides, rocking back and forth. The walls seem to move and close in until there is only Greyson and her voice, accusing Ciara of the unimaginable.

Ciara's solicitor, David Keane – hastily organised by her father – sits next to her in the small room redolent with the lingering smell of cigarettes. An unsmiling man with a thick beard and glasses, he had explained to her that she was there voluntarily to give the police information and she could leave at any time. But, he warned, they could arrest her and detain her for up to twenty-four hours if they felt they had sufficient evidence.

That was when her legs had buckled beneath her – when she realised just how high the stakes were.

'There was someone there,' she insists, as she has done for the past three hours of questioning. 'I saw them on the screen of my app.'

Ciara pictures her father slumped outside in the hallway having waited for her all night, desperate to shake whatever tree he could to help his only daughter in a system where he usually reigned supreme. Jimmy Mooney didn't do well with being stone-walled, especially in a police setting.

Ciara realises she is beyond stretched to her limits. She just wants to lie her head down on the table and let everything disappear. She just needs to get back to her child, to crawl into bed and pretend this was all some kind of nightmare.

'And yet,' Detective Greyson says, dropping her voice low, 'there's no proof of this mystery man, or woman, to be found anywhere at all.'

Tears flow down Ciara's cheeks which she brushes quickly away. They'd been through this time and time again. 'And, in fact, the murder weapon is your own kitchen knife.'

Ciara shudders as the picture of the knife is once again flashed under her nose – the very same one she'd held walking around the house with, searching for whoever had broken in. Of course her fingerprints would be on it. She'd also tried to wrench it out of her husband's body. But someone else's fingerprints *had* to be on it. Or their DNA. Her solicitor had explained to her than the DNA tests had been ordered and would be back later that day.

There's a split second of hesitation and then Greyson continues: 'How do you explain the cuts on your hands?' she demands.

Ciara turns her hands over in her lap – tiny cuts from when she nicked herself picking up the broken bathroom plant pot. 'After I saw the intruder, earlier that evening, I searched the house to find them,' she tries to explain yet again. 'In the bathroom, a plant pot had been knocked over. I cut myself while cleaning it up.'

Greyson raises an eyebrow. She opens a plastic wallet on her lap and pulls out pages of a document. 'Mrs Duffy, given there was no forced entry, and as we are awaiting DNA results, we have applied for a warrant for both your phone and laptop as well as any other devices in your home.' She slides the piece of paper across the table but it means nothing to Ciara.

David picks it up and examines it. The clock on the wall ticks loudly.

'A team is going through your house right now, so we would advise it's best not to return there. We would also ask that you keep yourself available for further questions over the coming days.'

Ciara flinches, picturing her and Morgan's soft beige bedroom being analysed by a team of forensics. The most intimate of spaces; so telling about a person – from the glass of water by the bed, to the types of books she reads. She imagines it cordoned off with police tape, being photographed, every item tagged and scrutinised. She pictures her trainers thrown by the side of the bed, the shoelaces hanging out of them like little tails. The heat of violation creeps up her neck as Greyson continues to implicate her in Morgan's death.

'Can I please leave? I have to see my daughter,' Ciara asks again, suddenly finding all of this just too much to bear.

Her solicitor goes to end the interview but Greyson motions that she has one more question.

'Did you love your husband, Mrs Duffy?'

Ciara starts to speak. 'I—of course I do,' she stammers, indignant. But how do you begin to unravel the complexities of what goes on between a husband and a wife behind closed doors? The coexistence of love, and yes, sometimes hatred. Morgan was… difficult. She hated to admit it, but he'd kept her down. It had been small things at first: a dismissal of her work, a cruel jibe about her weight gain, a muttered insult under his breath when she couldn't figure out the Wi-Fi code when they'd first moved house. Recently, the dynamic between them had shifted. What had begun as a whisper of superiority and disrespect had grown into something much louder between them over the past few weeks. Until it had become rotten.

Morgan was belligerent at times. Frequently domineering. But she hadn't killed him.

'And were there ever any extra-marital affairs?'

That question catches her off guard. Ciara feels unmoored from everything, untethered, as if she might float away from everything and everybody and simply disappear like smoke. She looks at David Keane for help. Her solicitor had said that strategically she could choose not to answer a question, but that it might also go against her if they ever ended up in court.

She traces the jagged pink blur of the deepest cut on her hand. 'Absolutely not. My husband and I love… loved… one another very much.'

After the interview ends, Greyson rises from her chair and rubs the base of her spine. Outside in the hallway, Ciara falls into her father's arms, glad of the cool sweep of air after the stuffiness of the interview room.

Jimmy Mooney is in his seventies now, but her father is still the toughest man she knows. He rubs her back as she sobs into his chest in the narrow corridor of the police station, his blue-veined hands patting her shoulder gently.

The corridor is deathly quiet, their footsteps muted by the blue-grey carpet. 'Come on, love, let's get you home,' he whispers gruffly, pushing his dark-rimmed glasses to the top of his head and glaring at Greyson, who nods curtly at the former Detective Chief Superintendent as she passes.

Outside, it's mayhem.

It's already daylight and dozens of camera crews and journalists have turned up, now waiting to get footage of the daughter of such a high-profile member of the police force being questioned over what seems to be a grisly domestic murder in a Dublin suburb.

Ciara allows her father to shield her with his jacket as she's wrestled towards a waiting car, head down, trying not to lose her footing. So many questions are shouted at her that she can barely think straight, but the word 'murder' stands out.

It hits her like a bullet.

Do they really think her capable of something like this?

'Let me take you home with me, love,' Jimmy says, pulling his daughter towards him as they sit in the back of the car, but Ciara shakes her head.

'I need to get to Sally, Dad. I'll just stay with Aimee tonight.'

'Marcus, take us to Kerryvale,' her dad says to the driver, who catches Ciara's eye in the rearview mirror and nods respectfully in silent greeting. Jimmy may have retired, but he has an army of local security personnel who he'd worked with all his career and who continued to protect him from the risks that came from putting away some of the most dangerous criminals in Ireland. 'Listen, Ciara, they'll want you to go back in to speak to you again once they get the DNA results, and go through all the devices. I'll come with you, of course. But I want you to try and get some sleep today. To try and just be with Sally and...' His words seem to get stuck in his throat, and that's when Ciara understands that her dad knows all too well that without proof someone else was in her house, things don't look good for her. 'And... just rest,' he finishes.

Father and daughter ride the rest of the way to Kerryvale hand in hand, Ciara's head resting on her dad's shoulder, like she used to when she was tired after a long day at school.

She draws comfort from the familiar smell of his tweed jacket. All her life he's protected her from harm, but as she dozes next to him she knows how hard it will be for Jimmy to feel this helpless when it comes to his only child. She feels the weight of worry emanating from his shoulders and squeezes his bony hand. 'Thanks for being there, Dad,' she whispers.

'I can't tell you everything will be all right, Birdy.' He squeezes back, using her childhood nickname. 'I wish I could.' His voice breaks slightly. 'But I'm telling you that I'll be with you, no matter what. I'll make sure you and Sally are okay, I promise.'

Ciara wipes her eyes with her sleeve. 'I'm sorry,' she says gruffly.

'It's okay,' her dad tells her. 'I've never gone through what you are experiencing right now, but I've be in a room with enough people who have and I think I understand it. You feel as if you've got a stamp across your forehead that says you killed somebody.'

'Yes,' says Ciara, nodding. 'Exactly that. It makes me feel desperate to make them believe that I didn't kill Morgan. And the killer is still out there. Who knows what they might do next.'

'But you didn't kill him. And *you* know that,' says Jimmy.

'Yes, but nobody else seems to see it that way. Did you hear those shouts outside the station?'

'Everyone will know, given time,' reassures Jimmy, the lines around his eyes seeming even deeper against the early morning shadows. 'Until then, you may just have to carry that stamp around, Birdy. I know it's hard, but when we get whoever did it, it will be gone forever.' He pulls her into a hug and she draws strength from his embrace.

At Aimee's house, the driver pulls up cautiously, making sure there are no journalists lingering. A tiredness envelops Ciara as she allows her father to lead her to the door. Her neighbour opens it, clad in expensive yoga pants and a matching hoodie. Still perfectly groomed despite the circumstances of the past few hours.

In fairness, Aimee can't do enough to look after Ciara. She insists to Jimmy that Ciara can stay with her as long as she needs. To be near Sally's school, she explains, but they all know there's no way Ciara is going back to her own house. A longer-term solution is needed.

'Do you want anything?' Aimee asks, fussing over Ciara after Jimmy leaves. 'Tea, coffee… vodka?'

Ciara gives her a wry smile. 'No thanks,' she says, sagging against the doorframe.

'Do you want to talk about anything? Everything?' Aimee tilts her head to one side, lying an arm on Ciara's right shoulder. Aimee is a good five years younger than Ciara, and although Ciara isn't keen on her gossipy side, they'd formed a friendship of sorts, mainly because the girls were friends – or perhaps because they'd bonded over Aimee's admission that she was struggling with fertility issues. But Ciara is still wary of her.

'I don't think so,' she replies, trying not to let intrusive thoughts of Morgan's body lying in the bed flash back into her mind. 'Okay if I have a shower?'

She is completely wiped out as she drags herself upstairs to find Sally. She's still in her nightie, playing with slime in Evie's room.

'Mom!' her daughter cries, jumping into her arms when she sees Ciara.

They cling to one another.

–

'Come and snuggle with me, sweetie. I'm so tired.' Ciara breathes into her daughter's hair after a quick shower, knowing by Sally's pale face her daughter is exhausted too. They climb into Evie's bed, wrapped together, mother and daughter, face to face. As Sally tells her about what she and Evie have been up to, Ciara tries once more to stop the flashbacks of images from the night before.

The blood all over her hands.

The smell of copper that still filled her nostrils.

The life completely leeched from her husband's face.

She tries to be in the moment. To stop worrying about the dark circles under Sally's eyes that have been getting progressively worse. To stop worrying that the person who killed her husband will come back to hunt her and Sally down next.

But the last thing Ciara worries about before she falls into a dreamless daytime sleep is how much the police are going to start digging down into every detail of her life.

And just how much they are going to uncover.

Chapter 6

'You said yesterday that you and your husband were having financial struggles,' Greyson probes.

Ciara feels paper-thin, having expended all her energy on mothering Sally as much as she could these past few days. She'd barely eaten a thing, nauseous every time she thought about Morgan. It didn't feel real. Now she's back at Sandymount Garda station with her grim-faced solicitor.

Though they are vastly different sizes, she's borrowed clothes from Aimee – a long skirt and knit jumper – and the elastic from the band of the skirt digs into her waist.

Aimee has been trying her best to help, but even she still can't hide her horror and sorrow over everything that is happening in their neighbourhood. Her phone had been hopping all day with alerts from the neighbourhood WhatsApp.

Ciara tried to ignore the commotion outside her own house as her dad came to pick her up for this second interview earlier today, but as she drove past her home, she could see people in white suits bringing bags out of her front door, news vans parked on her flowerbeds and people everywhere. It seemed so incongruous, all of it: the police tape against the green of the lawns, the police cars and crime vans, the people going about their day – some in uniform, others in white coveralls. The camera people with their heavy gear and the reporters with their heavily made-up faces, their curiosity and their lack of respect. *Vultures*, she thinks to herself, ducking down as her dad's driver shepherds her out of the street and safely past the rubber-necking neighbours. Most of those people gathered don't care about her, she knows. They were simply there to pick at her bones.

'Yes, we had money problems. Morgan had lost his job and we were struggling.' Ciara responds truthfully to Greyson.

'Is that why you were you searching divorce lawyers online?' Greyson locks eyes with Ciara. 'Doesn't sound like love's young dream to me...'

The silence begins to build in her ears.

'No marriage is perfect,' Ciara attempts weakly. But it sounds powerless even to her. Lately, she'd considered a different type of life – especially when Morgan started getting harder to deal with. It didn't mean she'd wanted to end her marriage. But she'd have been a fool not to have tried to understand what a break-up might mean for her and Sally. She had been information-gathering when she looked up divorce online. But saying that out loud to Greyson sounded fickle. Worse, it sounded *suspicious*.

–

Ciara and her father had talked endlessly why Morgan might have been murdered. Perhaps Morgan's murder had been a punishment – a warning of sorts. Could it have been connected to Ciara's father's job?

However, both Ciara and Jimmy knew there were other possibilities too, but how could they raise those without drawing attention to those dark corners of her life that needed to remain hidden?

What they both agreed on was that the kind of violence involved in Morgan's death came from someone familiar with causing harm.

Ciara knew she needed to give the police alternative, plausible scenarios for motive, because right then they seemed frighteningly fixated on her.

She points this out to DI Greyson: 'In the hospital where I work, there was a baby born a few weeks before Morgan was killed,' she explains, swallowing nervously. 'It was deprived of oxygen. A mistake, but he... the baby died.' She pauses. 'And so did the mother.'

There's an uncomfortable silence in the room.

'The father,' Ciara continues, 'blames the medical team. He threatened us. There were witnesses. He was a scary kind of guy.'

Greyson raises an arched eyebrow. 'You think a disgruntled parent came into your home somehow, without breaking a window or forcing a lock, or tripping the alarm, hid all night, and then stabbed your husband, who was supposed to be away for work, to death… all while you slept?'

'Jesus Christ. He wasn't disgruntled, he was grieving,' Ciara shoots back, suddenly disgusted with this woman's lack of respect. 'His baby and wife died. On our fucking watch.' The solicitor puts a hand on Ciara's arm in warning, but she shakes it off. 'People would do anything for their children,' she continues. She looks from Detective Inspector Greyson to her solicitor. 'It's not right, is all I'm saying. Anything that affects your kid. It does something to a person. It's another level of desperation.' She runs a hand over her face shakily, remembering the depths of pain in that father's eyes. 'This guy was desperate.'

She tries to calm herself down. Another thought strikes her. 'Some people at the hospital were adamant that I shouldn't write my statement for the medical council about that incident,' she points out. 'The deadline to submit one is this week. It would have been the third infant mortality in three months, which would have triggered a wider hospital investigation. Someone on the staff there might have wanted to silence me.'

A vein in Greyson's temple throbs against the tautness of her skin. Ciara can make out the dry lines that break up the skin of her lips as she waits for the woman to acknowledge there is a possibility of a different reason for why Morgan was stabbed.

'I'll follow up on what you've said, Mrs Duffy. But let me ask you something else: if that were the case, then why weren't you targeted?' Greyson inquires.

'Well, I haven't been able to do the statement… so maybe it worked?' Ciara ventures, but she knows it sounds far-fetched, even to her.

She considers telling them about the lighter that she'd noticed on the windowsill after she got back from the shops the night Morgan was murdered. It had been niggling at her non-stop that evening. Then, while locking up, she'd remembered its appearance on the windowsill. Neither she nor Morgan smokes, and she has a pretty box of extra-long matches a friend had given her a few months back which she used for her candles. Instinctively, she'd swiped the lighter into her handbag before DI Clarke Casey had accompanied her to the station. It was bright red with the lettering 'The Red Lion' written on it. She'd never heard of the place.

She and her dad had Googled it and found it was a bar located in Howth – the farthest tip of Dublin's north side. Somewhere they'd never have frequented. Jimmy had promised he'd look into it for her. He had contacts in most places around Dublin. He also wanted to be one step ahead of any investigation which is why he decided to keep it on another channel he could control.

'Were you able to find out why Morgan was even home that night?' Ciara asks softly. The exhaustion over the past few days has been relentless. She just wants to get back to Sally, to curl up with her daughter tucked next to her and let the world go on without her.

Detective Inspector Greyson shakes her head, her eyes like glass, cold and watchful. 'He took the Aer Lingus lunchtime flight back from Heathrow at 1:55 p.m. on Friday, and he's seen on CCTV entering your street at around midnight. But we don't know where he went for those few hours in between. All we know for sure is that he was stabbed where he lay. And yet, you didn't hear a single thing.' Greyson's voice drips with scepticism.

Once again, grief hits Ciara like someone has punched her in the stomach. Morgan had come home to her that evening. She'd been wondering if he'd encountered the intruder in the house, and maybe fought to protect her and Sally? Or had he come to bed and then been killed as he slept, as oblivious as Ciara was about someone lying in wait.

'I'd had a bit of wine...' she stutters, still horrified at the idea of a murderer potentially standing over her that night as they stabbed her husband to death. Had they considered killing her too?

'But if Morgan came back on the lunchtime flight, that would have meant he departed for London first thing Friday morning but then turned straight back around when he landed to fly back to Dublin,' Ciara points out. 'It doesn't make any sense.' She runs her hand through her unwashed hair that now lay in straggly strands down her back. Her stomach growls.

'There's something else that doesn't make much sense,' Greyson continues. 'We saw the texts from you to your husband that morning, telling him how unhappy you were with him. How you—' Greyson checks her notes '—wished he would "just fuck off and die".' There's no trace of empathy in her voice. She glares right into Ciara's eyes.

Ciara squirms. She remembers the text exchange, right after Morgan left that morning to get the taxi to the airport, slamming the front door because she'd dared stand up to him for once. It was an impulsive, frantically typed message through frustrated tears, designed to hurt him, not be cited back to her by police after his violent death.

'Maybe he arrived in London, but felt awful about how bad things were going in the marriage,' Greyson suggests. 'He came home early to discuss it and the argument continued... then turned considerably more violent...' The detective pauses. 'You'd had a bit to drink, and once he was asleep, you felt a bit braver... went upstairs with the knife...'

'No.' Ciara shakes her head adamantly. 'No. It wasn't that.' She swallows. 'I'll admit that the past few weeks have been rocky...' She tenses at the memory of their argument. 'Financially, we were stretched to our limit, which put a lot of pressure on our relationship, but I'd never hurt Morgan. Plus, as I keep telling you, I saw someone in the house.' The frustration is obvious in her tone.

'Maybe you were so drunk you don't remember what happened with Morgan,' Greyson challenges. 'I'd had a few glasses of wine,' Ciara admits. 'Probably too many – but I set the alarm, I made sure the doors were locked. I checked on the girls... I wasn't *that* bad.'

Greyson let Ciara's words hang in the air.

'Not that bad,' she repeats, nodding slowly. 'Even though there were two little girls in the house at the time.'

Ciara shakes her head, knowing anything she said could be used against her and twisted into something uglier. She digs her nails into her palms. This women really knew how to get under her skin. Maybe that was a tactic.

Ciara glances up and notices the cameras in the corner of the room – small black cubes with a red dot that seem to bore into her. She feels like an animal at the zoo. Caged, scrutinised... *judged.*

'With Morgan's death, you will now come into a healthy amount of money,' Greyson challenges, 'given an unusually high life-assurance policy. That will no doubt solve a few of those money worries you've mentioned.'

It was Morgan who had insisted on them increasing their payments on the policy after they realised they were unlikely to get on the property ladder any time soon. The idea had been that should anything happen to them, Sally would still be well taken care of as they didn't have the security of an asset, like a home, to cushion her. But what

Greyson was implying was disgusting – suggesting that Ciara could put a price on her husband's life.

'People have killed for less,' Greyson adds unnecessarily, and Keane has a word with the detective about Ciara being there voluntarily, and willing to help the investigation but not at any cost, so Greyson changes tack.

She pulls out a sheaf of papers and taps the pen in her hand against the page. 'DNA analysis shows that there was no evidence of anyone else in the house except you and your family the night of Morgan Duffy's murder. Your DNA is also on the murder weapon.' Greyson looks up at her.

Ciara has had moments over the past two days where she feels as if she's falling through a gap in the universe. An overwhelming incredulity that this is happening to her. How could her life be distorted so dramatically over such a tiny space of time? She should be in St Trinity's doing heel-prick tests on newborns or helping a mother bathe their baby for the first time. Tears rise up behind her eyes.

Nothing has changed.

Yet everything has changed.

'I didn't do this,' she insists, her voice cracking with raw emotion. 'It wasn't me.'

Why won't anyone believe me?

'What about the company who fired him?' Ciara suddenly suggests, grasping at any alternative to what this women is suggesting. 'He'd been so distracted by that job. Maybe there was someone in his work that had it in for him. Maybe that was the stranger who broke in?'

'Mrs Duffy.' Greyson sighs, her voice changing tone. She sounds impatient. 'We have texts and emails suggesting things were extremely strained between you and Mr Duffy in the weeks leading up to his death. There was a huge argument ahead of your husband's death. Financial debts that his death will now presumably help plug. There is also no evidence of a break-in, or any trace of this stranger you keep mentioning. No video footage, no recordings, no forced entry. No sightings.'

'The window—' Ciara attempts, but Greyson cuts her off.

'The paramedics have also pointed out that you delayed them from entering the house, precious moments that might have saved your husband's life had you allowed them access. You told them not to go inside.'

Ciara glares at the detective inspector. 'I thought there was an intruder in the house. I was trying to keep them safe.' She throws her hands up in the air. 'He was already dead!'

'So you are a doctor now?'

'I'm a midwife,' she retorts, taken aback at the lack of respect this detective is affording her. 'And yes, I've been there when they call time of death.'

An uncomfortable silence sits between them, a clunky energy that didn't seem to be getting either of them anywhere.

It felt to Ciara that everyone had already decided she was guilty. That stamp across her forehead was still there, flashing in neon. The problem was that if the police didn't find out who did this, she knew she'd be blamed, and Sally wouldn't have her mother to keep her safe anymore. Maybe that had been the intention all along. Maybe someone had deliberately framed her to render *Sally* more vulnerable.

Ciara's brain hurts trying to come up with reasons for why.

Could they still be in danger now?

She tries to think what kind of person would do this, but her mind stalls. She doesn't know *anyone* who could do such a thing. But maybe she didn't know her husband as much as she thought she did. Morgan was raised in a rural area. He had a difficult upbringing. She thinks of his shaggy brown hair, his brown eyes and crinkly smile. He'd never complained about his childhood, but his sister Courtney had once confided in Ciara about some of the challenges they had faced being raised by tough parents. Morgan had never wanted to talk about it but maybe Ciara should have pushed him to get therapy. Maybe she should have done something, reached out to him, when he had started lashing out at her recently. Maybe she should have been more understanding about his inability to keep a job.

Morgan wouldn't have been considered classically good looking, but Ciara knew he'd say she was no stunner either. Morgan was a simple guy. He'd made her laugh, but the chip on his shoulder over the difference in the worlds in which they'd grown up seemed to get heavier and heavier throughout their marriage. In a recent fight he'd berated her for being spoiled, for demanding too much from him because she'd always gotten what she'd wanted.

The truth is that she'd only ever wanted love and respect, and maybe for her husband to earn a consistent living.

Greyson's chilling words snap her out of her thoughts. 'Witnesses heard you tell your daughter that you were "sorry" that night. What were you apologising for?'

'For fuck's sake.' Ciara buries her face in her hands in frustration. 'I was telling my nine-year-old that I was sorry her father was dead. This is completely ridiculous. Can we go?' She glances over at David, the solicitor, who smiles thinly at her. He'd warned her not to say a thing at this stage of the investigation. His worry was palpable.

'But Morgan wasn't her father, was he?' Greyson shoots back.

Ciara freezes from where she'd been starting to rise from her chair. She glares at the other woman, hot anger coursing through her veins. The way Greyson had spat it out like that.

'No. Morgan wasn't Sally's biological father,' she says slowly. 'That's no secret. But he loved Sally like his own daughter. And she loved him too.' Ciara's voice wobbles with emotion, thinking of her daughter's tear-streaked face the other night.

'Mrs Duffy, why didn't you tell us that your first husband died in extremely suspicious circumstances?'

The room spins. Even Ciara's solicitor seems to sit forward suddenly, elbows finding the table. 'And that you were a person of interest in his death.'

Ciara slumps in her chair as if she's been struck. That's the problem with weaving a web in the guise of a safety net: it tangles every which way.

She opens her mouth and closes it again. Here it is, the door swinging open from the past into the present, bringing this detective straight through it.

Greyson draws her next words out, slowly and carefully, so there's no doubt about what she's saying. 'Ciara Edith Duffy, you are under arrest for the murder of your husband Morgan Paul Duffy...'

The words seem to echo around the room.

'No,' Ciara immediately shouts, banging her hands flat on the table between them. 'You can't do this... I didn't do this.' She swallows desperately, searching for something, anything, that will prevent what is happening to her. She takes a slug of water, hoping it will stop her tears. 'My daughter—' she tries to say, but there are no words that can fix this.

She'd been to a water park as a child and had snuck onto an adult slide, where a trapdoor had released beneath her feet and for a few short seconds she had fallen through the air, straight down, before hitting the pool with a slap. This is exactly the same feeling – freefalling, not knowing where or if she'd land.

'You can't do this,' she repeats, her entire body shaking.

But Greyson is standing up, closing her folder with a snap as if this is just some casual business meeting, rather than a moment that has just turned Ciara's life upside down and inside out.

'Get that other guy back,' Ciara begs. 'What's his name… Casey,' she pleads. 'Clarke Casey.'

A uniformed Garda steps forward and helps Ciara to her feet. She brings a shaking hand to her mouth as he begins to read out her rights.

'Jesus fucking Christ,' is all she manages through the thick emotions that overwhelm her. 'This can't be happening.'

Someone is messing with the future she and Sally have planned.

Someone has just ripped from her everything she holds dear.

Someone has framed her for her husband's murder.

Through her tears and shock as she's led away, Ciara has one clear thought that she clings to like a lifeline.

That no matter what happens, she'll find out who's done this to her.

And she'll make them pay.

Chapter 7

The things nobody ever tells you about prison: it's not at all like the movies.

Ciara had always imagined prisons as distant, abstract things – grainy shots on the evening news, or whispered about in scandals that happened to other people. But here she was, Logan Prison towering over her like a blunt force.

The first thing she noticed was the smell: damp concrete, mingled with disinfectant that failed to mask something a little more primal – a sharp, sour tang that told her this place would leave its mark whether she liked it or not.

Inside, the air seemed different – heavier, making it harder to breathe. Or maybe it was the panic attacks that had returned, each one worse than the next. Funny how she'd taken in her stride dealing with some of the sickest babies at the hospital, yet a year into her marriage to Morgan, her panic attacks had started.

The clamour of voices ricocheted off the walls, a relentless din, the backdrop to her new life. It wasn't chaos, exactly, it was something more controlled, something more terrifying: a system she didn't understand yet, but instinctively knew she'd have to learn fast.

The guards didn't meet her eyes as they processed her, their gloved hands cold and efficient as they rifled through her belongings. She'd heard them laughing with each other earlier, and the sound had been surprisingly soft, almost friendly. Now, they were stone-faced, their indifference louder than anything they could have said.

Everything around her was stripped down, entirely functional. The walls, a pale green that might have been calming in a hospital like St Trinity's where she'd worked, here felt cold and institutional. The floor tiles were dull and dirty, marked with years of scuffs and stains.

She was assessed by the prison psychologist. 'Do you have the urge to harm yourself?' the woman asked, her eyes flicking down to the clipboard in her hands. Ciara shook her head. As grim and shocking as being in this situation was, her priority was to prove she hadn't killed Morgan and get out to see Sally.

Led to her cell, she discovered it was no bigger than the bathroom at home in Kerryvale. The bed looked like it might collapse under her weight, the blanket thin and scratchy. Her cellmate, a woman who introduced herself as Paula, had barely looked up when Ciara entered. 'Hiya,' she'd grunted, her voice flat, before turning her back on her.

Ciara nodded, too stunned to speak. It didn't feel real. *Nothing does.* She climbed into bed, shoes and all.

She cried all night, quietly.

–

As the days passed, Ciara saw that Logan wasn't just a prison: it was a world that had its own rules, its own language, its own sense of justice. And she was an outsider, which showed.

The prison was meticulously organised. Four blocks, all named after trees, radiated out from a single yard. Netting stretched above it like a grim canopy, preventing drugs from being thrown in or dropped by drones. Each block had a kitchenette and about twelve rooms, most shared by two or three women. It wasn't overcrowded, exactly, but it felt suffocating all the same.

Ciara had a feeling that the longer she stayed, the more the place would sink into her skin and seep into her bones. She would have to fight to hold onto the pieces of herself that still felt familiar. The battle would also be with her own mind.

But even that felt like that might be a losing battle. Because the truth was, the longer she stayed at Logan, the less certain she felt about who she really was. There was just too much time to think about how she ended up in a place like this.

A few weeks after her imprisonment at Logan, Ciara had received a letter from St Trinity's. After she had read it, she let the paper fall from her fingertips and lay on her bed for the rest of the day. It felt as if she'd been hit across the head. She replayed the letter over and over in her head '...in the interests of the hospital and patients... the board of management... felt we had no choice... suspension without pay.'

She shouldn't have been so naive as to think her life would be waiting for her when she got out of there. There was no going back now. Not to anything that resembled her old life. That grief was, in a way, just as hard to process, like the death of who she had been.

Meals were delivered on a tray at first as she was being observed – silent offerings of limp sandwiches and lukewarm tea. The guard, who never bothered to look at her, always swept the tray away afterwards like clockwork. It wasn't until Ciara had been fully processed – a word that stripped her of humanity – that she was told she could eat with the others in one of the small kitchenettes. Only because she was on remand awaiting trial, they said. A privilege, although it didn't feel like one at all.

The kitchenettes weren't much: a few battered appliances, a communal table scarred with scratched initials and slurs. But it was there that Ciara first met some of the other women. Many were young, some heartbreakingly so, all with their stories scrawled across their faces. Ciara avoided eye contact, kept her head low and didn't say much. *I don't belong here*, she kept telling herself. But then again, maybe none of them did.

She remembers what Jimmy had always told her growing up: *Stay sharp. Read the room. Adapt.* It was ironic, really, that she'd ended up being among those her father may have helped put away or who were relatives or friends of some he'd arrested or questioned in his past. Her dad had never hidden from Ciara the danger of what he did, not with the security codes at the house changing every few weeks, or the two plainclothes officers stationed discreetly outside her school in bad times. But Jimmy had been a realist. He hadn't shielded Ciara from the world. He'd prepared her for it. She just hadn't imagined she'd need to use those lessons somewhere like Logan.

It was possible that the whispers, the looks and the slow, deliberate jostling from some of the women were about being the daughter of a cop. But that wasn't all she feared.

What shocked Ciara most in those early days was how broken so many of the women were. Addictions, untreated mental illnesses, the kinds of wounds you couldn't see but that bled all the same. It made some of them unpredictable and volatile. And it made Ciara jumpy. A half-raised voice, a slammed door, the sudden, sharp scrape of a chair across the floor; all of it made her muscles tense and her heart race.

The medical floor was the worst. Women locked in for their own safety screamed throughout the day and deep into the night. They raved about conspiracy theories or invisible enemies, emitting strings of curses and – worst of all – desperate, raw pleas for help.

How can you get used to heart-breaking screams of, 'Please… why won't somebody help me?'

Ciara would lie in her narrow bed beneath her cellmate fists clenched against the impulse to scream along with them. She felt it rising in her throat sometimes, the urge to give in, to howl out everything she'd lost. But she couldn't. She knew they were watching, waiting to decide where to put her. Good behaviour was the only currency she had.

Her mind kept circling back to Sally. That was the real terror. Worse than the women shouting in the medical unit. Worse than Paula, her cellmate, who, when she wasn't silent for days on end, spoke constantly a stream of gossip and unwanted advice, as if she'd never spoken to another human before. For Ciara, not even the thought of someone punishing her for being a cop's kid was as bad as being separated from her child. Her everyday horror was the thought of Sally growing up without her. It was the fear that this place might actually be her home for more than a decade, that Sally's life would unfold somewhere without her there to see it.

And then there was the press. She could picture the headlines in bold block letters around the time she was arrested: "Murdering Midwife Awaiting Trial in Logan Prison." She'd been the villain in their story from day one. They didn't care about what really happened; they just wanted a narrative, and Ciara fit perfectly into the one they'd already written in their heads. Imagine a middle-aged suburban midwife – a *mother* – as a cold-blooded murderer. The sensationalism of it all had shocked her, but thrilled them. Overnight, she was thrown into the role of some kind of caricature 'killer nurse.'

And now, with all the digging going on into her life; the main thing was that nobody must find out the truth about Sally. Ciara has spent a lifetime trying to keep that part of her life under lock and key.

–

Each morning begins with a rattle: trays banging against doors, guards shouting names, the screech of metal on metal. Even when the Oak block is quiet, the noise from the other wings seeps through.

Every day, she lies in the cell that they call a room, wondering if the pale light making its way through the thin curtain outside is dawn or dusk. She barely cares anymore. Every day, Ciara has to fight against crushing despair. She has lost everything. Morgan is dead. The hospital has suspended her indefinitely. Sally is alone out there.

She spends most of her days now lying there in this exact position in her bed. Blaming herself. Pining for Sally. Plotting vengeance that she has no energy to undertake.

Eyes closed, she wills the day not to begin. But somehow it always does.

Life as she has known it is over. And Ciara is increasingly unsure if she is going to be able to survive the nightmare that has replaced it, her thoughts growing more and more agitated the longer she is in Logan.

Maybe the person who killed Morgan was a drifter passing through, or someone out on parole? A complete stranger and nothing to do with her at all? But the alternative is possibly even more disturbing.

What if the killer wasn't a stranger at all?

What if it was someone she actually knew?

Chapter 8

'Mom?'

Ciara fights the urge to scoop her daughter up and run. Sally sits opposite her at the visiting room table and scrutinises her mother's dramatically altered appearance.

'You look different.'

These days, almost two months since she'd been arrested, Ciara wears her hair in a long, scraggy plait, the lengthening grey roots matching her increasingly grey complexion. She sits slumped in her chair, feeling like the most hollow version of herself. Her skin, when she looked in the mirror, was almost translucent under the fluorescent lights, and the dark shadows under her eyes emphasise how gaunt her face has become in just a few short weeks. It's almost funny to remember how, back in her old life, she'd never left the house without makeup, organised for Botox every six months and taken her HRT religiously.

Here, everything feels sluggish. Depression has settled over her like a weight she can't lift. Even for Sally's sake. Imagine believing that those fanciful things – lotions and potions could help... *this*?

'I know. I look a bit different, sweetie. I'm sorry.'

'When are you coming home?'

The visiting room is clean, but it's not enough to mask the sadness in the air. The walls are off-white, and empty save for a few faded cartoons – princesses with oversized smiles and animals hopping around with an abandon that makes Ciara want to scream. There is little joy to be taken from the few broken toys that lie stacked in one corner. Who could stomach a sea of mothers stifling endless tears sitting to one side of snotty toddlers who wail and try to cling to them? Shrieks of 'Mama' and 'cuddle' – words to tear the skin from their mother's bones.

Ciara's chest tightens at the innocence of her daughter's question. 'Soon, sweetheart. Soon I hope.' Her voice cracks slightly.

Sally's small hands are clutching a crumpled drawing. Her shoulders are hunched, as if she's trying to shrink into herself. Her clothes hang off her far too loosely and her face is almost as pale as Ciara's. She's significantly thinner than she was when Ciara last saw her; her cheekbones far too sharp for someone so young.

Silence stretches between them. A single fluorescent light buzzes slightly somewhere nearby. Chair legs scrape along the floor, children whine and jostle to sit on laps. The room smells of cheap coffee and wet coats. Utterly suffocating.

'Evie says only bad people go to prison,' Sally suddenly whispers, staring down at the drawing in her hands. A single tear lands, a heart-breaking wet smudge soaking a corner of it, splotching the pink dress of the carefully drawn 'Mommy' in the picture. 'Does that mean you're bad?' Sally glances up at her with pain-filled eyes.

Ciara flinches. She can tell her daughter has been thinking a lot about this question. The answer she gives feels... important.

She wants nothing more than to pull Sally close to her and tell her daughter that everything will be all right, even though she knows it may not be true.

Ciara takes a deep breath and lets it out slowly. Her fingers press into the table, trying to ground herself. Her voice is steady when she speaks, but only just. 'No, darling. It's... well, I'm sure Grandad explained to you, there's been a big mistake. The police think I did something bad, but I didn't.'

Her heart hurts at having to explain this, but she swallows that pain down, forcing the words out. 'Remember when I thought you'd hit Evie on purpose with the hockey stick that time, but then you explained that it was another boy in your class—? Well, it's like that.'

Sally thinks about this for a moment before nodding, her face earnest. 'But what do they think you did, Mom?' she continues, her hands still clenched tight around that piece of paper.

Ciara blinks. She can't trust herself to talk. As Sally waits for her answer, her small face is full of something too hard for Ciara describe – something too grown up. She has the feeling again that whatever she says will hold a lot of weight for Sally, for a long time.

'Sometimes things happen that we can't understand,' Ciara says softly. 'Now, I just... I need to fix it.'

'But you're not bad, Mom. Why don't you just tell them you didn't do anything wrong? Why don't you just tell them you didn't do the bad thing?'

The question hangs in the air, simple and full of hurt. Ciara looks at her confused little girl and feels the burden of everything. The helplessness, the injustice, the prison walls that seem to be closing in around them both.

I'm trying to. I'm trying so hard.

'You're right,' Ciara says quietly. 'I'm not bad, Sally. I'm good, like you.'

'Then why are you still here? I don't understand.' Sally looks around, frustrated. 'Just tell them...' Her voice gets louder.

'I don't understand either,' Ciara says, wiping her nail-bitten hand across her face. She feels that pain again, in her chest. A tightness, almost like a burning sensation; almost as if she were being strangled from the inside. She tries to slow her breathing, one of her panic attacks threatening to return. She tries to cover it up with a cough and takes a moment to let her breathing to return to normal.

'I don't understand either,' she repeats. 'But you have to trust me, Sal. I'm going to get out and I'm going to come home.'

'I miss you. I miss Daddy.' Sally's voice is trembling, tears in her eyes. 'I want you to come home *now*.'

'I miss Daddy too, but...' Ciara fails to find the words that will provide the comfort her daughter needs.

'I don't like it. I want you to come home. I just want things to be normal,' Sally weeps.

Ciara reaches her hand across the table, her fingers curling into her daughter's. 'I know, darling, I know. I want that too.' She closes her eyes and pictures the before times. The good times with her little family. Before Morgan had been so brutally killed. Before her life had imploded.

'This is for you, Mommy. Because you missed my birthday. Remember?'

Ciara's heart closes over. It had been the worst day of prison life so far, that she hadn't been able to be with her daughter on her tenth birthday.

Sally tries to smile, her cheeks wet with tears. She places the drawing down on the table carefully, like it's something fragile – and she looks up.

Ciara holds back tears. It's a picture of her, Morgan, Sally and Jimmy around a table with a birthday cake and candles. There are floating unicorns and colourful bunting and Sally has added glitter to everyone's head, like crowns. She's stuck on pieces of wool for hair and even cut out material for their clothes. Ciara is decked out in a bright pink gown while Morgan is smart in a tuxedo.

'I love it,' she whispers.

'Mom, can I give you a hug?' Sally suddenly asks, her lower lip wobbling.

The words hit Ciara like a brick. She inhales sharply. She shakes her head slowly, tears pricking the corners of her eyes. 'I wish I could, sweetie. I really do. But they won't let me.' She glances towards the prison guard a few feet away from them, who avoids meeting her gaze. Ciara knows their priority is not allowing drugs to be smuggled into the prison, which happened often through cuddles.

'But I just want to hug you.' Her small voice cracks. 'I'll be fast, I promise.'

Ciara's heart aches. She can't move. Instead, she has to sit there and watch her daughter crumple right before her eyes, the effort to hold it together too much for her tiny body. 'I know. I know you do,' Ciara replies, her voice tight, an anger rising up in her along with the devastation. *Who the fuck is responsible for all of this?* Who had torn her life so badly apart that her ten-year-old was begging for a hug and she couldn't give her that necessary comfort?

'And I want to as well, so badly, Sally. Why don't we hug with our hands instead,' she suggests, longing to feel the softness of her daughter's cheek next to her own. She places her hand across the table and Sally grips it tightly, her fingers trembling. But despite the touch, they still feel so far apart.

'I love you, Mommy.' Her daughter's eyes glisten with tears, trying to be brave.

'I love you, Sally. Always.'

'Can you come home soon to me?'

In the corner of the room Ciara sees the guard gesture that it's the end of visiting hours. It's almost time to say goodbye. Ciara clutches

Sally's small hand in her own, never wanting to let it go. 'I promise I'll come home soon.'

Sally's face brightens with hope. 'Pinkie promise?' she says, hooking her smallest finger around Ciara's tightly. She swallows a sob.

'Pinkie promise.'

They move their fingers up and down like a handshake – Sally's face solemn, Ciara biting her lip.

A long beat passes and neither of them move until the guard finally tells them time is up.

Chapter 9

'Yo, Nurse?' Paula uses the nickname that has inevitably stuck for Ciara when everyone learnt she was a midwife.

Ciara kicks off the sheets which have tangled around her ankles. She doesn't need to check the time on the clock on the locker beside her, as it's always the same time in the evening when her cellmate starts talking.

She could try to close her eyes and go back to sleep, but even her dreams don't bring her any comfort. Late at night in her prison bunk, Ciara sometimes asks herself the questions she thinks they'll ask her in court. It is a routine of sorts. She answers them in different ways, but the answer is always the same.

I'm innocent.

From her perch on the top bunk, Paula's voice comes again. It seems to Ciara that her cellmate has watched every TV show, listened to every podcast and has an opinion or conspiracy theory about everything. Her questions range from the mundane to the extremely irritating. 'What's the scariest sound you've ever heard?' she asks now, hanging her pixie-shaved head upside down to see her cellmate.

A month into Ciara's remand, and it seems that Paula has warmed to her newest cellmate.

This place, Ciara thinks, with a sigh. Sleep is her only escape from the spiral of worry she's been sucked into since her dad's last visit. She can think of nothing else except Sally.

'Go on,' Paula cajoles. 'What's the scariest sound you've heard?' Paula's childlike enthusiasm in the face of their grim surroundings both irks Ciara and endears her to her, depending on Ciara's mood.

She smooths her fringe back out of her eyes and turns over, thinking. Ciara remembers asking her own father a similar question, back when he took her hunting as a little girl to Wicklow with some friends.

It was a silly game she'd played at school. 'Being in a dark cabin alone and hearing a toilet flush upstairs,' one girl had ventured. 'Hearing someone breathing behind you when you are in the car alone,' another squealed.

'Shhh,' her dad had hissed, when Ciara had brought up the game. And, just at that moment, a huge stag had stepped into sight as they'd crouched behind a fallen tree. Her father had carefully manoeuvred behind her, his arms coming around her fourteen-year-old frame, his lips moving in her ear. 'One more step and squeeze the trigger,' he'd breathed.

And Ciara had held her own breath, transfixed by the majestic creature, thinking that in that moment, the scariest sound of all would have been the crack of the gun between her fingers. The power she wielded was so foreign to her.

For years it had been just her and her always assertive Detective Chief Superintendent father, and she knew her role was appeaser and diplomat. To ask questions, but ones that weren't too challenging. To be curious but never sassy. Ciara loved her dad, but the truth was that Jimmy had always scared her a little with his ability to face life with such vigour.

'Shoot, Ciara!' he'd commanded that day back when she was young, urging her to squeeze the trigger, but fourteen-year-old Ciara couldn't bring herself to move a muscle that would result in the destruction of this beautiful creature in the most brutal of ways. 'Do it now, Birdy,' Jimmy had hissed again, but Ciara had lowered the gun shakily. Even her father's wrath was more welcome than slaying this poor creature in the name of sport.

Years later, as a grown woman, when she'd needed rescuing herself, Ciara remembered her father reprimanding her for being 'too soft.' She'd wanted to tell him that he'd made her that way; that his endless pursuit of dirt and death had made Ciara run towards a career where she got to be there for the first breath of so many new lives. She'd chosen the good. The most gentle life. Or so she'd thought.

Now, stuck in a prison cell, Ciara was starting to realise that being a good girl had never gotten her anywhere at all.

She'd also learnt one other thing: that the most frightening sound in the world is never just one single noise.

Over the past few weeks, it had been so many. It had been the ambulance crew's muttered, 'I'm so sorry,' as they'd stood over her husband's body. It had been a judge remanding her into custody to face trial for Morgan's murder. It had been the words 'bail denied' and the reading out of her mortifying Google searches and having her text messages leaked to the papers, every exchange between her and Morgan catalogued and analysed. It was the despair at night of the women ripped from their children over crimes they committed while trying to survive in the unsurvivable environment they'd been born into, through sheer chance.

It had been Sally's desperate cries during the first visiting day.

Until Morgan's murder, Ciara hadn't appreciated how privileged she was and what it might be like to lose it all in an instant. Having spent her whole life being presumed worthy because of her position in society; a midwife, a mother, a school volunteer, a taxpayer. But the moment her husband had died, and she had been arrested, the police, the media, even friends, had turned on her. Here at Logan, she had been stripped of respect, amongst everything else. Even little things, like deciding when to eat, the lack of phone calls, the lack of a phone, of taking pictures... even of tiny freedoms like grocery shopping or driving or jumping into the sea on a cold morning with a friend. Every day at Logan, Ciara opened her eyes onto a day without dignity or freedom, and she hadn't even been found guilty.

Yet.

The longer she stayed in Logan, the angrier Ciara seemed to feel about the inequalities she saw every day. What she had realised was that most of the women in there had never really had a chance. Most were born into poverty, crime accepted as a way of life for some. And the tiered system that existed in the outside world had only stretched that gap further. She'd known this, of course, but she hadn't lived it first-hand. She hadn't seen the red-raw desperation of other women's journeys through the same system she'd glided through because of her education, her birthplace, her family circumstances.

She hadn't known that she'd been born into a speedboat in life's great regatta.

–

A sharp rap at the door makes Ciara start. She flinches, still not used to the frequent and any-hour-of-the-day interruptions.

The prison guard opens the privacy flap to her room. Dark eyes peer through. 'Visitor, Duffy.'

In the evening? That's weird, she thinks.

David, Ciara's solicitor, isn't due until the following day and external visitors are usually on the weekend. *Maybe he has an update?*

'Who's the visitor?' she asks nervously, sitting upright and scrambling to pull on her trainers. Her heart rate is suddenly high.

The routine at Logan is one thing that Ciara has warmed to. In the outside world, she thrived on order; on lists and Excel spreadsheets and organising files into neat piles with carefully written multicoloured tabs stuck into pages. At the hospital she had been the queen of charts – her tidy handwriting recording every tiny detail. *Foetal heart rate 140 bpm at 10.15, 136 bpm at 10.45, steady rhythm noted.*

At work, Ciara was always calm, taking her role at this most precious moment of her patient's lives extremely seriously. She'd prided herself on ensuring every patient interaction was respectful and informative. This attention to detail was exactly why she'd understood the extent of the emergency when she'd urged Dr Derry to perform a c-section on the mother who eventually died.

But, lately, she's started to think that maybe it isn't order she craves, but the process of fixing things and restoring order. A desire she now desperately feels about her own life.

'I'm not a mind-reader, love.' A sardonic laugh from the prison guard as he escorts her out into the brightly lit hallway.

'But is everything okay?' Ciara insists, concern in her voice. She knows Officer Jackson and he's always been kind – he'll tell her if he knows anything.

He shrugs uncomfortably.

Ciara walks next to the guard down the green corridors, trying not to inhale the pervading smell of disinfectant and soup. She keeps her eyes down as they pass through a common area where women sit sprawled on a couch and at a table. A few of them are playing cards. Here at Logan, she's had to learn a new language – not just to fit in with the others, but also the complex legal terms and confusing prison service acronyms. But above all else, she's learnt to stay in her own lane, not draw attention to herself, not to be baited into the conflict that was all too common around here. In here even looking at some of the women can start a fight. *Not looking at them too*, she thinks, remembering how even keeping her head down resulted in her being tripped as she walked into the common room the other night.

The past few days she's been consumed with thoughts of Sally, especially after Jimmy's harrowing words ten days before telling her that Sally was being admitted to hospital. 'She just can't shake this bloody virus,' he'd explained, trying to mask the concern in his voice. 'She's constantly exhausted.' More blood tests had been ordered. 'She's probably just pining for her mum,' he'd said kindly, looking much older somehow under the pale lights, as Ciara dug her nails into the thin skin on her wrist, drawing blood, feeling so horribly guilty she wasn't there. She'd heard the shake in her father's voice and known it was serious.

It's a long time to be running tests without answers, she thinks to herself now, as she carries on through the stairwell behind Officer Jackson, praying this visit has nothing to do with Sally.

The few times Sal has been to visit Ciara at Logan has been torturous for them both. Ciara can't bear the visitors' room anymore, heaving as it always was with pent-up emotion so damaging you could almost feel their devastating effect on these tenuous family bonds – a grenade bouncing right before it explodes. Ciara's despair had kicked up even more once she realised that that the visitors' room might just be the place from where she would watch Sally grow from a child into a young woman. The thought was too much. It was all too much.

Since that first visit, Sally usually sat opposite her, eyes down as Ciara spins endless Styrofoam cups of tea in her hands, asking meaningless questions about school and life. Everything greeted by silence from her daughter. Then Jimmy's whispered assurances that he'd keep her safe and he was trying his best to figure all of this out for her. 'I told you I'd get you out of here, Birdy,' he'd say, but even his words feel hollow as more and more evidence is gathered against her. They'd even tried to weaponise her menopausal symptoms, trying to insinuate her irritability and short-temper were precursors to violence, when she tried to reply honestly about her mood in the time leading up to the murder. Then it was wine-shaming her, insisting that she had been drunk with children in the house instead of seeing it as her having had a tough week and overdoing it.

That's when she had realised that nothing she was saying was helping, and it was better for Jimmy and her solicitor to try and drum up some possible element of doubt for her case.

Just as being good hadn't helped her in life, now being honest – *in the parts where she can be honest* – wasn't serving her.

No comment.

No comment.

No comment.

She sighs now, entering yet another endless labyrinthine corridor, remembering the last visiting time with Sal. How do you not gather your child and press them to your heart when you haven't seen them in weeks? How do you not crave the warm outline of their small bodies, when you've missed countless bedtime stories or important milestones, or cut knees or hugs. So many lost hugs. How do you not want to rain endless kisses down on their salty-freckled cheeks? How do you reconcile that... that *lack*?

How do you ever make up for it?

Logan is a four-hour drive from Dublin, on the farthest tip of the west of Ireland. An impossible place, a nightmare.

And now likely her home for the next fifteen years.

Her solicitor, David, had made no bones about it. It wasn't looking good for Ciara. Her intruder theory seemed implausible without proof. The judge would be more lenient if she'd just admit guilt. David had listed all the possible defences they could mount, including being intoxicated; or stressed over the upcoming testimony against her colleague Dr Derry at the hospital; that the loss of that mother and baby on her shift at St Trinity's hospital might have triggered some kind of trauma shock; or maybe Morgan had provoked her? Had he hurt her? Had he been violent towards her?

No, no, no, no.

Ciara could not, would not, admit killing Morgan when she absolutely hadn't. Strange behaviour wasn't grounds to murder someone and though Morgan had been very much acting out of character in the weeks before his death, that defence wasn't going to be enough to exonerate her or plant doubt. She needed *actual* evidence.

Her dad was working on her case too, using all the policing resources at his disposal. He'd told her on the phone only yesterday that he finally had a lead about the pub from the lighter found in her kitchen that night. He described his own private incident desk set up in his office at home. She'd almost smiled when he said that, picturing red string pulled from list to list, a wall of notes, a picture of Morgan at the centre of a web of possibilities, his loyal band of security personnel in the scrum alongside him. The tireless and unique dedication reserved for parents who wanted to help their child.

Maybe her dad had come tonight to tell her something in person?

Ciara allows herself feel a frisson of hope. They just had to create one shred of reasonable doubt, after all. One tiny shred.

'In here.' Officer Jackson stops just short of the visitors' centre and indicates another room instead. Alarm bells start in Ciara's head as Jackson holds the door open for her.

When she sees who is waiting inside, she feels all the blood drain from her face.

It's the prison chaplain.

Ciara had lost faith in anything resembling religion the day she'd buried her mother when she was just seven years old. For weeks back then, while her mother was sick, she had done what all her father's friends had told her to do – to pray for her mother to get better. She remembers taking her little red chair into their landscaped garden, clasping her hands together and screwing her eyes shut, whispering Hail Marys. She'd prayed with all her might, her pudding bowl blonde bob hanging into her eyes as she whispered to God for her poor mother to improve, reciting every prayer she'd ever known, until she had a headache. Ciara must have been there for hours, eyes pinched shut, lips moving silently as night fell and until a family friend noticed her outside. Even to her seven-year-old mind, the betrayal when her beloved mother died the next day never really left her.

Ciara's now rooted to the spot, an icy chill running up and down her spine.

Behind her, Jackson closes the door gently.

The room is deathly silent as the priest clasps and unclasps his hands, avoiding her eyes. It's a small, windowless room and he takes up too much space.

All she can think about is what Jimmy said about Sally being admitted to hospital.

She struggles to catch her breath. Life couldn't be that cruel. Surely it couldn't be?

Waves of regret pound in her head. She should have demanded her daughter get seen by a doctor sooner, when she first seemed unwell.

Weeks ago. Ciara should have done more. She worked in a hospital, for goodness' sake. What had she been thinking...?

I should have done more.

'Come and sit down please, Mrs Duffy,' the chaplain encourages gently, gesturing towards an empty chair opposite him. He still doesn't meet her eyes. The only items on the small table next to the chairs are a glass of water and a box of tissues. A lone sheet pokes out if it like a white flame. It was so horribly predictable, so heartbreakingly clinical. On the wall past his head, a half-hearted picture of a beach hangs in a slightly crooked frame. Ciara trains her eyes on the beachscape, wishing she could dive in and swim away, right into those waves.

'No,' she says, folding her arms. 'I don't want to sit.' She doesn't want to hear what this small, sweaty man has to say to her. She doesn't want his feigned concern. His *prayers*. Whatever he has to say won't be any good. It won't help. Tears spill from Ciara's eyes at the pain of life's continuous blows.

Not Sally. Please not her. Not after everything they'd been through together.

'I'm so very sorry to have to tell you this...' the priest begins, his voice low and practised.

Ciara falls to her knees, hands over her ears, eyes screwed shut.

Lying on a beach. The sun warm on her skin, Sally collecting shells.

'Please no, please, don't...' she begs him, rocking. 'Please stop.' If she doesn't hear his words, it won't be real.

A cry of pain and loss comes from somewhere within the room. It's only later she realises it came from her.

Through the small, muffled space between Ciara's cupped hands placed over her ears, through the dark of her makeshift cave and the ocean-like rush-shush of blood in her ears, Ciara can hardly believe what comes out of his mouth next.

It's the scariest sound yet.

'It's your father,' the chaplain reveals, with hushed compassion. 'I'm so sorry to tell you that he was found dead just a few hours ago.'

Chapter 10

The day after Jimmy Mooney is found slumped in the driver seat of his car, a gunshot wound to his stomach, is the day Ciara decides to escape from Logan.

The thought hangs around her like fog she can't get away from.

Perhaps it's a naive sentiment borne out of the sheer heartbreak and horror she'd felt as she was led back to her room, howling uncontrollably. But the more Ciara swirls the idea of trying to escape from Logan around in her head, the more she realises she has to do something. She has to at least *try*.

She can't stay locked up in Logan for another year, or longer, waiting for a trial that will most likely condemn her to life in prison anyway. Especially if nobody in the outside world is trying to uncover what really happened that night, and who the fuck had decided to murder her husband.

She tries to forget what the chaplain had said to her about Jimmy's death, and thinks instead about the stark choices facing her. But she feels hollowed out, spooked by what has happened.

Waves of grief crash over Ciara again and again as she paces the yard in her scratchy grey tracksuit and white trainers, still swallowing in shock, having not slept at all. She pictures her larger-than-life father with his booming laugh and no-nonsense personality. Jimmy couldn't be dead. He just couldn't. Who could have done this? The same person who killed Morgan? Or someone connected to her father's dangerous career?

Some people are built to survive and Ciara likes to think she is like that – able to take whatever life throws at her. But she's taken some seriously heavy hits over the past few weeks and her father's death feels like it has knocked her down so hard that she'll never get up.

Her overriding thought: *This is all my fault.*

Ciara wipes away fresh tears, trying to shake the feeling that what she'd set in motion had been the root cause of everything. If she is convicted she dreads to think what might happen to Sally.

Though she is relieved beyond words that Sally is okay, the thought that it *could* have been Sally has jolted her into a new kind of desperation. She paces, feeling like a lioness in a cage. An exhausted, grieving, angry lioness separated from their child.

Jimmy Mooney had been her champion, and the only other person who knew how high the stakes were with his granddaughter. He'd also played a huge part in keeping them safe, using his work contacts and discreet computer programmes to make sure Ciara's story never got out. Not even Morgan had known the truth, accepting at face value that Ciara simply had a child from a previous relationship. *Of course, that will all be revealed now too*, she thinks, with another lurch of dread.

A tiny snippet of a memory creeps into Ciara's mind: the day in the fairground in Brighton when Sally was just six months old. The huge teddy bear Ciara had won for her dwarfing her little frame as she was wheeled along the pier as Ciara bought candyfloss. Alex, her darling first husband, Alex, smiling alongside her.

'Duffy?'

Ciara snaps out of her thoughts.

'Heard about your da. I'm sorry.' Paula has approached her and now hands her a slightly crooked cigarette – prison love language.

Ciara shrugs her thanks and accepts the cigarette. She hasn't smoked since she was a teenager, but it feels appropriate somehow to start up again in here. Especially now. Everyone in this place has tragedy running through their veins. It's the common backdrop to most of their lives. But Ciara appreciates Paula's small gesture of solidarity at this particularly painful time.

They walk in silence for a bit, the hit of nicotine making Ciara nauseous, the idea of escaping consuming her.

'So what happened?' Paula asks, as she exhales twin streams of smoke into the chilly December air. Ciara hadn't been able to speak about it during the night as she'd been crying so much.

Ciara shivers and puts the filter to her lips. 'He was found yesterday in his car parked down some alleyway, miles from his house,' she says, and tries to inhale but coughs. Her eyes water but she welcomes the sting.

The most Officer Jackson has said to Ciara so far is that her father been shot and that an investigation would get underway into Jimmy's death. He added quietly that they couldn't rule out suicide as the gun had been his own, and found next to him.

'As if he'd do that to himself,' Ciara exclaims.

'They are all fuckin' idiots.' Paula spits onto the hard, scrubby ground. The globule of saliva sits on the surface of the impenetrable dirt next to some half-hearted weeds.

Ciara had been told by the governor on her intake meeting that she could always request protection – due to her father's former position – so she wasn't in with the general population. She's glad now that she refused it. Being alone with her thoughts after losing her family so abruptly would have isolated her further.

'Has anyone ever tried to get out of here?' Ciara turns to Paula, risking a question that could land her in hot water.

Paula might be a talker, but she was also extremely knowledgeable about the ways things were done in Logan. She'd been in long enough to be considered an expert.

Ciara stubs out her cigarette on the side of a bin.

'Are you fucking joking? There's no way out of Logan. Look around, Nurse,' Paula replies, waving her hand around her head.

Ciara sighs, surveying the high smooth walls and barred service doors.

Her only reference – all the prison break movies she'd ever seen – involved excavating tunnels or scaling walls. She is a slightly overweight, perimenopausal hospital worker with bunions. There'd be no digging holes or shimmying through vents. But there *must* be a way. There must be a smarter solution. Ciara has an overwhelming sensation that she cannot let all of this just happen to her. At her job, among the staff at St Trinity's, she was the safe one.

Reliable.

Predictable.

But that was before.

Now she's a mother torn apart from her child.

Now, she has nothing left to lose.

Ciara pulls herself up to perch on the table part of one of six brightly painted picnic tables in the bleak concrete yard, resting her feet on the

61

bench. Paula leans against the concrete wall facing her. One leg bent, foot flat against it, her head tilted as she regards Ciara.

'You're not fuckin' serious, though, are you?' Paula says, raising an overplucked eyebrow.

'I'm just trying to figure out my next move,' Ciara says honestly. 'I can't do *nothing*.'

For a long moment Paula stares at Ciara, her expression a mix of shock and cynicism. Then she shakes her head in disbelief and lights another cigarette. 'You're a mad bitch, aren't ya,' she decides.

'I have to find out who killed Morgan. And my kid is sick. Like, really sick.' Ciara pictures Sally alone at the hospital – her mother, father and grandfather all whipped away from her in the space of just a few months. Alone.

Vulnerable.

Panic rises up. Literally every second counts at the moment. Jimmy had been appointed as Sally's guardian at Ciara's request. Who would make Sally's medical decisions for her now? Not Morgan's bloody sister Courtney, the antivaxxer who refuses to even sign up for WhatsApp. She couldn't be considered Sally's guardian formally, but there really was no one else, family-wise, that Ciara could call on.

Paula makes a sympathetic noise. 'We're all desperate to get out of here.' She shrugs. 'But the thing is, everyone has something we need to get out for. I guess it's just a matter of how badly you want it. Plus, think about what happens if you do get out – which is pretty impossible, by the way. You'll be hunted down. Punished. What will you do, walk to fuckin' Dublin? Hitch?' Paula flicks a long trail of ash onto the ground. 'It'll go against your sentence, Nurse. No library privileges no more, no phone calls. 'Cause they will catch you. And chances of you finding something the police missed is unlikely. That only happens in TV shows. You'll have no money, no car, no ID...'

Ciara watches the dead leaves chase one other around the yard in the wind. It's much colder now. Christmas is on the horizon. Everything there is just so goddamn bleak. Her bottom is freezing and damp from the bench and Paula's assessment of her predicament has left her even colder.

'Maybe they'd let me visit Sally in hospital?' she ventures.

Paula shakes her head violently from side to side. 'No way. Every Tom, Dick and Harry say their kid is sick to try and get out for a day. Automatic no.'

'Yeah, but I'm on remand. I haven't been found guilty, or even been sentenced.' Ciara pulls at a hangnail. Paula has been convicted and sentenced. Something hovers in the air between them. A line in the sand that still separates them. The you and the me.

Paula blows out her cheeks, seemingly considering Ciara's point.

'It would also make you look guiltier,' she says.

On one side of the yard, two woman are arguing loudly with one of the officers. A string of sharp curse words bounce easily off the concrete walls of the small exercise area. Standard daily background noises on a good day at Logan Prison. On the high, spiked walls of the yard, a few seagulls look condescendingly down at them.

'Honestly? I'd say you've a better chance if you had a medical emergency yourself,' Paula finally decides. 'They can't administer injections or even treat major illnesses here at the prison – triage and pills only. Everything else has to be referred over to the hospital. Make like you're in bits, like, half-dead, then go there, make a run for it. But I'm warning ya, it's not possible.'

Ciara feels a fizzle of something for the first time in weeks – a spark of hope. Her dad always said nothing was impossible – maybe she'd just have to channel that positivity. Along, perhaps, with her naivety…

'Yeah, but I still need to get to Dublin. Plus, I'm not sure I can fake a stroke.'

'What about your da's funeral?' Paula says suddenly, eyes widening. 'You would be allowed compassionate leave for a death in the family. They'd have less control over those surroundings, less guards, less *protocol*.' She sneers at the word. 'Then fuck off back to finding out who killed your Morgan.'

Ciara exhales deeply, considering.

Of course, it made sense that she could request to attend Jimmy's funeral. With the shock of hearing the news, she hadn't even thought about being allowed to go to say her goodbyes. She'd just presumed it was another freedom that had been removed, like everything else. It astonishes her how quickly she'd become institutionalised. Ciara keeps having to remind herself that she hasn't been found guilty, even if she's being treated as if she had.

–

After a chat with David Keane when he visits the next day, they submit a form 7A request to attend Jimmy Mooney's funeral service at Blackrock Church in Dublin. As his next of kin and only local living relative, it is much more likely to go in her favour.

But as the parole officer explains, when he gets back to her the next morning, there's still the public to consider. And though she's not yet gone to trial, the preceding judge hadn't granted bail because of the possibility of flight risk and public safety. They can't ignore that aspect, the letter said. Those risks still stood.

Ciara holds her breath as she reads the decision.

> Permission is granted to leave under licence for a short visit to Finnegan's Funeral Home in Monkstown, Dublin, where former Detective Chief Superintendent James Mooney is reposing, for the inmate to pay their respects before the establishment is open to the general public. There is too much high-profile media coverage of both Mr James Mooney and Mrs Ciara Duffy to allow a compassionate funeral attendance at this time.

Ciara's stomach flips at the thought of both her father's funeral and the possibility of escaping. She has no idea what to expect, or even if she will succeed, but what she does have is a vendetta. That had to count for something.

Someone had murdered her husband. And they had separated her from Sally. And now her father was dead too. She intends to make them pay for messing with her family.

Paula continues to whisper advice to her during dinner the next evening, a new pep in her cellmate's step – a vicarious adventure a welcome distraction in a place like this. Ciara is unlikely to be hand-cuffed on this type of expedition, Paula points out. 'They don't use electronic tagging systems anymore in Ireland, either,' she advised. 'They'll probably have two guards with you, at least one female guard,' she explains, as they shovel stringy chicken curry into their mouths, eyes down, side by side.

Later, huddled in the doorway outside as it rains, Paula hands her another cigarette. Her face illuminates orange in the dark as she lights it. She exhales, her eyes narrowing against the sting of the smoke. 'So, what's the actual plan, Nurse? You see, I heard this thing on a podcast once… and it might work.'

In bed that night, Ciara can't sleep a wink, weighed down with a new kind of anxiety. Could she *actually* do this? She's no hardened criminal.

But maybe all she needs is guts.

She thinks of her dad, of his voice in her ear urging her to squeeze that damn trigger.

'You can do this, Birdy,' she imagines he'd say – another jolt of grief.

Ciara glances at the time. She has just a few hours left to decide.

Jimmy's words when she was first taken to prison float into her head like a mantra: *Adapt to survive. You do what you have to do, girlie.*

Besides, even if she doesn't succeed in finding Morgan's and Jimmy's killer or killers, she can always grab Sally and run away to start a new life.

After all, it's what she did ten years ago. And she won't hesitate to do it again.

Chapter 11

Ciara Duffy smooths down the skirt Jimmy had brought for her for a previous court appearance, now far too big on her increasingly gaunt frame, and runs a hand through her stringy hair. In the mirror on the wall next to the picture Sally drew of them, the woman reflected back at her looks haunted – her eyes hollowed out with dark circles, her face blotchy from crying. The digital clock on her bedside table flicks to 5:03 a.m. as the cell door opens. Her shoulders tense at the thoughts of everything that lies ahead.

Today they'll bury her father, without her.

Ciara is led from her cell, her heart in her mouth at the enormity of it all. It's a Tuesday morning and the world is waking up but all Ciara wants to do is crawl back into bed and pretend this is just a nightmare.

At Logan, there isn't any silence, even when the rest of the world sleeps. The corridor is filled with its usual cacophony of desperate sounds. In one room she passes, she sees cleaning staff wearing surgical masks sponging off the navy waterproof mattresses in the cell that is usually reserved for late-night admissions. Five to one room until you've been processed. Or detoxed. A pained voice screams distressing obscenities that appear to barely register with the prison guard she follows. *The psychiatrist has their work cut out for them today*, Ciara thinks grimly to herself. The main door to the outside is unlocked and relocked – no modern automatic door locks here just yet.

Outside Logan, the dead air of morning presses down. Ciara wishes she'd just taken the bloody Valium the prison doctor had prescribed for her, but she needs to be clear-headed. She needed every tool in her arsenal to be as sharp as possible to get through today. At least knowing it was in her pocket was enough.

Ciara zips up the black puffer jacket that Jimmy had brought her a few weeks ago along with the skirt and other few items of clothing, and

66

follows Jackson towards an unmarked car. A female officer joins them – Officer Katie Forde, a short woman in her thirties who is wary and watchful. 'All okay?' she directs towards Ciara, who nods quickly.

There is a hint of friendliness, no more. While they are tasked with supervising Ciara, Jackson and Forde aren't obliged to necessarily chase her down in the case of an escape. Paula had explained this to her as Ciara's entire body clenched in fear even at the thought of absconding. 'Prison guards are able to use legitimate ways to detain you, but if there was an escape, they'd have to call the actual police,' she'd revealed. Then again, Ciara wasn't entirely sure Paula knew as much as she made out. But when she questioned the accuracy of some of Paula's wilder musings, her cellmate got snippy with her. It was easier to nod and try to take everything with a pinch of salt.

The thoughts of what she's tasked with makes Ciara's head spin, but she tries to focus on the fact that she just needs some time. She needs to go through all of Morgan's documents that Jimmy had taken back to his house in Donnybrook. After Morgan had died and they'd had to leave the rental house, Morgan's sister Courtney had helped Jimmy move a lot of the documents to his house. She just hopes Courtney hadn't taken anything important back to her small house in the Dublin mountains.

Thinking about all this brings another thought to Ciara's mind – one that has been going around and around her head for some time now: there was something about the way that Morgan had talked about losing his job that had immediately raised Ciara's suspicions *weeks* before he died. It had all been very abrupt. That's when his behaviour started to change – there had definitely been something he wasn't telling her. In the lead-up to Morgan's death, he'd been leaving the house at bizarre times, staying out late, talking in hushed tones on the phone when he thought she didn't notice. Then the London trip had come completely out of the blue, just a few weeks after a similar trip.

Jackson pumps the breaks on a roundabout that signals they are nearing Dublin, and the movement jerks Ciara back to the present.

They are approaching the city. Her hometown. She tries to stop her hands shaking as she gazes out of the window. A ceiling of white clouds hang low above the city. She pats her pocket where she has folded one of Sally's drawings and her most treasured belongings – a worn photo of her, Alex and Sally.

The officers chat as Ciara drinks in everything around her. Early morning life: a woman in a hijab pushing a double buggy, a man on an electric scooter zipping past, a broken-down bus with neon triangle warning signs set up in front of it next to the huge spire that marks Dublin city centre. Overflowing bins being emptied into a rubbish truck outside a department store, commuters in suits and runners with white earbuds jammed into their ears hurry past. She absorbs all of it, as if hungry for life as she once knew it. Cranes swing across the sky, a teenager on a bike breaks the lights and gets irritable honks in return. Oh, how she'd love to be an anonymous morning jogger with nothing to worry about except how far to run.

Nobody ever appreciates freedom until it's taken away.

Ciara tenses as they pass the city centre hospital where she worked as a midwife. An image of her colleague, Dr Derry, floats into her mind. A jolt travels through her as she thinks of the consultant obstetrician at St Trinity's. She'd told him she was compelled to tell the truth when the baby on their watch had died, despite his pinched face and worried eyes when they spoke about it. But then everything happened with Morgan and she'd never had the chance to write her testimony to the medical council in the end.

Derry had actually sent a few letters of support to her at Logan, but Ciara had known better than to respond to them. She'd appreciated the gesture all the same, especially as nobody wanted to be caught up on the wrong side of this particularly grisly scandal. But she had become used to keeping everyone at arm's length over the years, afraid to get too close in case she tripped herself up about her past.

When Ciara didn't respond, the letters had slowly become less frequent, the correspondence from Dr Derry eventually petering out until the only things she received from the post drop were the usual postcard from her dad, and pictures from Sally. She received heart-breaking drawings of herself, Ciara and Morgan standing under giant rainbows, on islands with a single palm tree, Ciara on one side holding Sally's hand, Morgan on the other. All with huge smiles on their faces.

Morgan.

Ciara closes her eyes, suddenly grief-stricken. Her husband had been hard work and yes, Ciara didn't consider theirs the best marriage in the world, specifically after he'd lost his job, but she'd loved him. In her own way. She just didn't understand the person he'd turned into in the weeks before he was murdered.

As the navy Kia they're travelling in makes its way past the city and out towards the suburbs, Ciara's stomach tightens. The idea of seeing her father's body makes her feel weak. Poor Jimmy had fought so hard to get her out of Logan. She thinks of his hopeful eyes, his reassuring squeezes of her hand, the 'don't let the bastards get you down' mentality. But she knows that she is alone now and no matter what happens next, she has to at least *try* to salvage her and Sally's lives.

A wave of nausea overpowers her and she presses her forehead against the window, overcome with doubts about what she's about to attempt. After hours of Paula's endless relaying of prison-break podcast ideas, Ciara has been left more confused than ever. The only good gem she'd gleaned was to keep her eye open for opportunities to make a break for it. A bathroom window, a feigned illness, any type of kerfuffle that threw the officers out of their usual surveillance mode would allow her to seize the moment. Especially in unfamiliar surroundings, according to Paula. But Ciara was going in to this funeral home as blind as her captors were to what circumstances lay ahead.

She closes her eyes and tries to steady herself.

When she opens them again, the funeral home looms in front of her.

Ciara spots the empty hearse outside first. It's like a punch to the stomach. She knows that it's waiting there to take her father's coffin to the funeral service that she wasn't permitted to attend. The finality of that one last journey is immediately sobering. Everything else falls away except that car, and the thoughts of what lay beyond those double doors. For a moment she thinks she might not be able to get out of the car, so overwhelmed she is by her rush of emotions.

Jimmy Mooney's passing would undoubtedly attract a crush of politicians, of prominent solicitors and Irish personalities later that day. Her dad was high-profile himself, gaining a reputation with the media over the course of his career in policing for being a straight shooter – someone who wanted to clean up the city and wasn't afraid to be tough about it. He'd established new and often controversial measures to disrupt the gangland groups that had been a scourge on some inner city neighbourhoods.

The news that Ciara was being allowed to leave Logan had already ruffled feathers. Her solicitor, David Keane, had explained on the phone that it was all over the news. Morgan's sister had even called the prison authorities, trying to block Ciara leaving Logan at all. The media specifically hadn't been informed for logistical reasons of her temporary release, but like everything else in her upcoming trial, she knew leaks weren't just possible, they were highly likely.

Ciara concentrates of taking big gulps of air as she's helped out of the car by Forde. Finnegan's funeral directors is located along a row of six or so shops set back off the main road. There's enough parking for about fifteen cars in front of the shops. Traffic cones painted a melancholic black have reserved at least four of the spaces directly outside Finnegan's, presumably for others coming to pay their respects later that morning, when the funeral home opened.

Ciara trails her fingers along the shiny black of the hearse as she's led towards the funeral home. Walking next to two uniformed officers attracts attention from school-run mums and teenagers hanging around outside the newsagents, vaping bubble-gum scented clouds into the air. She keeps her eyes cast down. Even escaping doesn't trump her main priority this morning – saying goodbye to her dad.

Inside, overly floral and sickly-sweet scents of plug-in air freshener overpower. Flickering cream candles are dotted around the reception area, which has a light green carpet and four comfortable chairs set to one side around a low coffee table with leaflets and a jug of water with a wedge of lemon floating on the top. The viewing room has double doors, currently closed. Ciara remembers her aunt reposing here, a few years back. A sombre affair before burial on a freezing cold Saturday morning.

A bearded man in a black suit and tie approaches the small party. 'I'd like to offer my sincere condolences, Mrs Duffy,' he says respectfully, bowing his head slightly, so she catches a glimpse of a thinning patch of hair. 'I'm Marshall Finnegan. We've been looking after your dad during this very sad time for you and your family.'

'Thank you,' Ciara responds softly, taken back by his kind words. It's been a while since she's been treated with such respect.

The officers stand slightly awkwardly behind her.

'Would you like to come through?' Finnegan invites, gesturing his right hand towards the double doors.

Ciara remains rooted to the spot. Her legs won't move. Her body doesn't want to see what's on the other side of that door. She smooths back her long blonde hair, which she's worn loose today, with a headband in an attempt to conceal the greys.

'I'm sorry,' she says simply. It's the female officer, Forde, who steps in and puts her hand gently on Ciara's arm. 'I'm not sure I can…' Ciara whispers, her mouth dry. She's never felt so alone, so unsupported in her life.

The officers must sense it too. 'You'll be glad you did,' Forde reassures her. 'We'll be right outside here. Take your time.' Ciara nods in acknowledgment. 'I lost my dad a year ago,' Forde continues simply. 'I'm so sorry for your loss, but I promise you will be so glad you saw him and got to say goodbye.'

Goodbye. How could she bear to never see her father's face again?

Everything seems to move in slow motion as Ciara follows Marshall Finnegan, her eyes firmly planted on his shoulders as he opens the doors slowly and steps to one side.

Ciara closes her eyes. Composes herself. Tries to remember her father's booming voice, the backdrop to her entire life. Jimmy Mooney didn't suffer fools gladly. His impatience, his urgency, his temper were all famous with anyone who'd worked with him, yet Ciara had known his other side – the sometimes tender moments of compassion with his only child.

The doors click softly closed behind her. Then it's just them. She opens her eyes slowly.

She exhales.

Her father is lying in a bamboo casket with white silk lining, his pale face slack and empty. He's wearing his full Garda uniform and there's a set of rosary beads strung between his folded grey hands.

Oh god, his hands.

Ciara stifles a sob and takes a tentative step closer. 'Oh, Dad,' she whispers, tears spilling down her cheeks when she's beside him. She reaches out to touch him but hesitates. She can't bring herself to connect with what she knows will be nothing like the usual warmth of his skin.

It's hard to imagine that those same hands had thrown her into the air as a little girl. They had spun her in circles, his muscles surely aching as she'd squealed in delight. They had clutched her hands tightly on her first day of school, clapped madly at her graduation, stroked her cheek the morning after Morgan's murder. These hands had been pressed flat against the police car window the day she'd been arrested as police took her away. He'd been her everything. And now, probably because of her, those same hands were deathly still, his wickedly smart mind no longer turning.

She places a hand to her mouth. Because of her, he is dead.

Ciara paces up and down next to Jimmy's coffin, devastation keeping her moving, sobs shaking her shoulders as she absorbs the implications of her father's murder. Steepling her hands over her mouth and nose, she drops into the seat next to where he lies, trying to steady her breath.

'Dad,' she whispers. 'I know you are here somewhere.'

She cries harder hearing her own foolish voice disperse into the quiet of the room. But this is the only chance she has to be this close to her father, even if it's just his body. She'd always thought that proximity didn't really matter when it came to having a connection to the dead. That's why she hadn't visited her mother's grave very often, figuring talking to her mother's energy was something she could do just about anywhere. But now, next to the body of her father, she understands that being here with him isn't about her, it's about him. About respecting the body that had carried him through life, given her life, saved lives…

Though diminished now, Ciara can't take her eyes of his features. She's spent her whole life monitoring those eyebrows, deciphering his demeanour which could change like the seasons. Though she'd cut her feet walking on the sharp eggshells he'd trailed, more recently, her father's face had seemed softer, less angular, and she knew it was because of his concern for her.

She notices his Mooney nose is still held proudly, even in death.

'I'm sorry, Dad,' she says, brushing fresh tears from her cheeks. 'For not being a better daughter. I'm sorry for involving you with everything with Sally. For all the stress I've caused. For this…'

She stands and gently braves touching his forehead. It's as cool as she expected, but she feels compelled to process that this is the last time she'll ever touch her father's face. A twinge of sudden anger twists her grief. 'I needed you,' she tells him, accusingly. 'I needed you. And Sally needed you. And you needed us,' she hisses. 'What are we supposed to do now? You always had to go to every bloody edge, didn't you? I told you not to do anything that would get you in trouble and look at you now...'

An empty laugh at the absurdity of admonishing a dead man.

Then, in a smaller voice: 'You were all I had left, Dad. How am I going to keep Sally safe now?' She draws a breath. 'What am I supposed to do now?'

There's a soft tap on the door.

Ciara jumps, embarrassed, and brushes her tears away with the back of her hands.

'Just a few more minutes, please,' she calls, in a strangled voice. Then, speaking quietly to her father: 'I'm not sure how long we've got here, but I need to find my way back to Sally, Dad. I'm going to find out what happened. You didn't deserve this either.'

She stares at him, wondering why everyone she loves ends up leaving her. Her mother, her darling Alex, Morgan and now Jimmy.

'How did we get here?' she sighs to Jimmy Mooney's closed eyes, her thoughts moving too fast in competing directions. 'How do we get back?' she murmurs.

She reaches out and strokes his cheek with the back of her knuckle – just like he'd done to her so many times. Tears fall onto his suit but she doesn't wipe them away. 'I love you, Dad,' she whispers. 'I know we didn't tell one another often, but I do. I love you so much.'

She straightens his lapel and runs a hand over his navy uniform, removing imaginary fluff. Jimmy would want to look perfect for the stream of visitors that would no doubt come to pay their respects later that day. 'Go be with Mum now,' she says softly. 'I'll be okay.'

Ciara bites her lip. She's never felt so alone in the world, yet seeing her dad has brought her a new kind of peace – a resolve that she is his daughter and that means she is brave. She lets a hand linger on his frame. 'I'll be okay, Dad,' she repeats, trying to gather herself. 'Sleep tight.' She takes a step backwards, feeling a hole in her chest similar to the one she imagines lies beneath the stiff material of his uniform when he doesn't respond like he used to with, 'Don't let the bed bugs bite, Birdy.'

–

Dragging her logical mind forward with considerable effort, Ciara glances around the room. It was time to get pragmatic, because if she doesn't do this now, she'll be back in the patrol car, driving back to Logan, away from Sally, away from finding the truth. She has to be brave.

Bristling with purpose, she looks around the small room. Perhaps, Ciara thinks, she should have paid better attention to the exterior of the funeral home.

There are no windows in this room, but a small door to the right next to a huge floral display and a condolence book catches her eye. She darts over and opens the door quietly. It's a small room with a lot of shelving. Piles of brochures sit on the shelves, boxes of candles and some spare chairs piled up to one side. On the opposite side is a mountain of cushions, folded white sheets and bottles of spring water. Ciara's heart hammers in her chest. She takes one last long look at her father, then she quickly moves to the back of the storage room, where there's another opening. She pushes through that second door. It opens.

She finds herself in the back hallway of the funeral home. To one side is a small outdoor courtyard, where they sometimes perform masses for those not having traditional funeral services in a church. She glances over her shoulder as she tries the handle to the glass doors.

It's locked. She gives it another soft jiggle, trying not to make any noise, but it's firm.

Damn it.

Hurrying further down the corridor, her mouth sticky dry, Ciara opens a door into a space marked 'Private.' She shivers as the temperature drops. There are two empty silver gurneys in the middle of the room and to one side, a tray of medical tools and some tubing. It's likely the embalming room, she thinks in horror. To another side she sees the area they must store the bodies. An overpowering chemical smell catches in the back of her throat.

Oh god.

Outside, she hears voices approach. There's no way out of this room. It's now or never. But there's nowhere else to go. She turns in a circle, her hands on her head, her body covered in sweat. *Think, think.*

The voices grow closer, and Ciara holds her breath. The only other door in this room is into the cold storage area. She finds herself contemplating darting into it for a brief second before shaking her head.

That's too much, even for her.

She moves towards the door and listens, her body pressed against the wooden frame. The voices don't sound frantic. It doesn't sound like Forde or Jackson. The chattering staff pass the room and Ciara releases a breath.

She opens the door and peers out. She can barely hear past the hammering of her own heart. There's no way they'd let her have this long with her dad. Any second now she knows they'll come barrelling through those doors looking for her.

She moves swiftly down the corridor, cautiously opening various doors. One is a box room, another a bathroom...

'Duffy,' a sharp voice calls out.

Ciara freezes, hand on the door handle.

Forde is standing at the end of the corridor, hands on her hips. 'You weren't allowed to leave that room,' she barks angrily.

Ciara can see the stress written all over her face. After all, keeping Ciara in her custody is her responsibility. Her job would be on the line if Ciara fled on her watch.

Ciara slowly turns to face her.

They are still ten yards apart. Ciara knows she could turn and run if she wanted, but what then? She'd probably run straight into Jackson's arms if she races to the front door. There's no way she'd come out of this well if she tried to charge Katie Forde.

Her entire body quivers with adrenaline.

Forde takes a step towards her. 'Duffy,' she says again, in a warning voice. Forde's neck is splotchy-red in places. She obviously feared the worst when she looked into the room and didn't see her prisoner.

Ciara sighs. She feels her body sag. Blinking back tears, she feels defeated, overly emotional, completely spent. *What was I thinking? If it were this easy, there'd be people escaping every day of the week.* She feels foolish again.

'I was just using the bathroom,' she stammers.

Forde reaches her and grabs her arm roughly. 'You know you can't go anywhere without our permission.' She glances at Ciara's face and her own softens at the sight of the tears. 'I'm sorry, Duffy. It's just we can't have you wandering all over the place.'

Ciara nods mutely. She allows herself to be led back down the corridor and out through another door, into the reception.

Jackson is standing at the front door, as she suspected.

He nods briefly at Forde. A relieved look passes between them.

Suddenly, Ciara is being led out of the front door and over to the Kia. Away from her daughter.

Ten steps and she'll be confined once more, whisked back to Logan. Back to Paula's I-told-ya-so face, back to wearing her coat all day, every day just to feel one added layer of protection around her. Back to feeling paper-thin and panicked twenty-four seven.

There are a lot more people milling about now outside the funeral home then when they'd arrived. Ciara spots a TV Today van across the street. A cluck of reporters, heads bent together comparing notes perhaps, huddle to one side.

Eight steps.

She can smell Forde's perfume as the three of them hurry towards the car: a gingery, lemony smell she'd enjoyed in the car on the four-hour journey here.

The journalists suddenly spot them. Someone shouts Ciara's name, and the sound is like the crack of a starting gun. People rush toward her.

She turns her head, and a bright light blinds her temporarily.

Flash.

Jackson moves quickly towards the first photographer as Ciara instinctively shields her face. Of course, she should have realised this would make headlines. Nobody has laid eyes on her for weeks. Now her famous father has been found dead.

Flash.

Four steps until they reach the car. Forde's grip tightens.

Ciara notices beads of sweat on Forde's forehead as the media scrum swells, swarming them. A microphone is pushed into Ciara's face, and impertinent questions shouted as Jackson battles to move the growing crowd from between them and the car.

Ciara remembers Paula's words about a kerfuffle. She glances frantically around but Forde has strong fingers around her upper arm, the other clamped around her waist, guiding her forward.

Flash.

Flash.

Flash.

Just two steps left.

Jackson angrily demands people move back immediately.

Officer Forde shoves Ciara in through the back door of the Kia and quickly slams it, turning to manage the journalists. Jackson climbs into the driver's seat.

Disappointment courses through her veins. No, something bigger than that. Something a lot more destructive.

'Fuck's sake,' Jackson mutters, shoving the keys into the ignition roughly. Ciara can see how thrown they are by the number of media outlets who've turned up. The prison guards seem unprepared.

Her knees, under her skirt, are trembling.

'Come on, come on,' Jackson whispers to himself, as Forde remains outside the car, swamped by photographers pressing their lenses up against the window. The officer tries to peel back a few photographers so she can get into the passenger seat. Someone elbows her roughly, trying to get a shot of Ciara inside the car. She hears Forde's indignant yell.

'Jesus Christ,' Jackson curses, opening the door against at least four more photographers on his side and shouting at them to back off, NOW. He jumps out to help Forde.

The keys remain in the ignition.

Ciara hears the blood rush in her ears. Everything seems to move in slow motion as ideas click into place in her mind's eye. Thinking about it is one thing – actually taking action is another thing entirely.

Ciara takes a deep breath. She makes a split-second decision. The first in a row of falling dominos. One that, deep down, she knows will have irreversible consequences. She doesn't even have time to think properly about what she's doing. She hears Jimmy's words in her ears, like when he brought her hunting. 'Do it now, Birdy.'

Ciara leans forward between the two front seats, and presses her index finger against the button for the central locking system.

It clicks closed with horrifying satisfaction.

Jackson and Forde both immediately spin around, shock registering on their faces. She knows there's no going back now. She catches Forde's eye.

Jackson and Forde turn their backs on the journalists and start to pull at the door handles aggressively.

'No.' Forde shakes her head violently, rapping on the window. 'Do not do this, Duffy. Do not do this.'

Ciara clambers awkwardly into the front seat, trying to gulp in breaths of air. Her skirt gets caught on the lever for the handbrake but she yanks it free. Once sitting in the driver's seat, she presses the start button. The engine jumps to life. The dials swim before her eyes.

Oh god, oh god. What has she done?

'Duffy!' Jackson shouts, his face so close to the glass it almost touches it. 'Open this door immediately.' He jabs a finger towards the lock. 'Open it now,' he commands, the whites of his eyes large behind the window pane.

Forde bangs on the bonnet violently with the palm of her hand. 'Ciara. Don't do this.'

Jackson is pounding so hard on the glass next to her head that it feels as if the window will break.

And a strange calmness descends on Ciara. It's as if she's watching the scene unfold from behind a screen. She observes impassively as the woman in her mind-movie jerks the car into first gear, swallowing in fear, her eyes wide with shock. This woman is wearing an ill-fitting skirt and quilted coat. Her long hair is wild and unkempt, her mouth clamped in a straight line. Her gaze is fixed on the crowd around her.

The woman hesitates for a fraction of a second before she slams her foot down hard onto the accelerator and the car lurches forward, revving wildly. The scene jumps and Ciara is back inside her own body. She narrowly misses hitting a man in a grey suit clutching a microphone. He rolls heavily to the grass verge as Ciara winces, her eyes screwed almost completely shut.

'Holy shit,' she yells, as the car mounts the kerb, slamming heavily over it and bumping down the other side. She swerves past a parked white van with the words 'O'Hanlon's Painting and Decorating' written in red on the side, bashing off its wing mirror with her urgent need to get as far away from there as possible.

The last thing Ciara sees in the rear-view mirror is both officers speaking frantically into phones, surrounded by a sea of media hyenas snarling and snapping, ravenous for the scoop that's just unfolded right before their eyes.

Pinpricks of rain dot along the windshield, trying to race the wipers which have been activated onto their fastest setting. Their frantic repeated swipe-scrape movement adds to the chaos. Ciara realises she's screaming.

She grips the steering wheel tighter, trying to find her way through the chaos she's just created.

But also just holding on for dear life.

Chapter 12

Ciara's breath comes in short, sharp bursts as she manoeuvres the car at speed along the motorway northbound. Her hands tremble as she uses the indicator to switch lanes, her brain whirring with the enormity of what she's just done.

A sudden surge of euphoria bubbles up as she presses her foot further to the floor. There's nobody behind her. She opens the window and lets the wind buffet her long hair. Freedom, even short-lived, is so enticingly sweet. For the first time in months, Ciara feels a tug of rare happiness, one that spreads slowly throughout her body, lapping at her insides, whispering promises about things working out.

She's done it.

Fucking hell, she's actually done it.

She shouts, slamming the palm of her hand on the steering wheel suddenly, almost smiling, thinking of Paula's face at being given the news. She might even get to watch it on the TV tonight.

But it's short-lived. Ciara glances at the petrol gauge. She's still rusty for not having driven in weeks. It's below a quarter of a tank.

She knows she needs to get off the roads, to get somewhere to think, to regroup and figure out the next steps. Because if Morgan's murder isn't related to her and Sally's past, then Ciara has to find out what was going on in Morgan's life that might make him a target for someone. And she needs to know if Jimmy's death was connected to all of this.

She passes a familiar sign. A family petting zoo. A sign with a colourful parrot and bubble writing with 'Court Bay Animals' written in large writing. She remembers going there with Aimee and the kids last summer when they'd first moved to Kerryvale. It's where she'd got her little monkey key ring. Ciara remembers Sally begging her for a pet rabbit for months afterwards.

It's close to where Aimee's mobile home is located. This is the first part of the very loose plan she'd come up with late last night as she stayed awake, trying to think of one. Off-season, the caravan park would be empty. *Hopefully.*

Ciara takes the next exit. There's no way Aimee and her husband, Tony, would be down at the mobile home park this time of the year. The mobile home is next to the ocean, in an isolated spot on Dublin's northside. It has just one small supermarket and an indoor leisure centre, a godsend on rainy summer afternoons. She figured it would be the perfect place to lie low for a night or two while she decided what to do next.

Ciara also knows she has to get rid of the Kia. There'll be roadblocks, she figures, a sudden jolt bringing her even further down from the earlier burst of joy, especially when it appears on the news. People would be nervous about a perceived killer on the loose.

Another quick glance over her shoulder as she takes the road towards Battenstown. Traffic is heavy coming up to lunchtime as she drives through Brennanmore, and she keeps her head down as she passes a small police station on the corner, her heart racing as the cars snake back waiting for the lights, trapping her. By the time she hits Ballyowen twenty minutes later, the fuel light is glaring orange. She turns on the radio and is just pulling into the archway of the trailer park, Lennon's Hill, when she hears the main news headlines.

'*The forty-five-year-old widow of Dublin accountant Morgan Duffy, who was remanded in Logan Correctional Facility for his murder, escaped police custody early today. Midwife Ciara Duffy was granted temporary compassionate leave to pay her respects to her father, James Mooney, who formerly headed up Dublin's Organised and Serious Crime Unit, when she absconded in Monkstown, Co Dublin at lunchtime today. She was last seen wearing a dark skirt, trainers and a black North Face jacket when she…*'

Ciara shuts it off. An eerie calm descends. She's surprised herself over the last few months, coping with things she'd never thought she could. This is just an extension of that, she tells herself dispassionately.

Her earlier adrenaline rush has plummeted. She hasn't eaten anything yet today and barely slept last night. A weariness overpowers her as the tyres of the Kia crunch slowly towards the car park of the holiday park. There's a new barrier across the gate, erected since she'd been there with Aimee the August before last. That was going to be a problem.

Ciara glances over her shoulder and reverses slowly, praying that there's no security guard on duty at the caravan park. She finds a small inlet amongst the trees farther up the road where someone has stored a large sailboat on a trailer, presumably for the winter.

She pulls the navy Kia in on the other side as close to the trees as she can, next to the verge, which is lined with yellow-tipped heather. Then, glancing around the car, she searches for anything worth taking. A bottle of water half-drunk sitting in the central cup holder in between the arm rests. She runs her fingers down the side pockets – lozenges and two biros, an empty chocolate bar wrapper. She pops one of the blackberry sweets into her mouth, relishing the sugar hit. She takes a crowbar from the boot, tucks it under her jacket, unsure why exactly, and with her hood up, starts to make her way on foot cautiously towards the area the mobile homes are located.

It's freezing cold but clear, the sun offering some respite from the chilly breeze. *At least it's stopped raining.* Ciara scrambles through the weeds and grass until she reaches a fence.

It's only once she's over and on the other side of it that her heart starts thumping with the realisation of what she's done. Ciara crouches on the ground, putting her face in her hands. She's shaking. There is so much to do and so much to keep in her head, but she has to be strong for what's coming next.

Ciara feels a pang for her old life, for the uncomplicated monotony of dropping Sally at the school gate and heading to her job at the hospital on the bus. She'd loved her job, tending to the babies, so pinkly new in the world, unblemished by life's inevitable grind. She loved caring for the love-dazed mothers who existed for those few days with her in a haze of pain and joy. Ciara got to see people at their most vulnerable, and helping them through that was a privilege. She misses that more than anything. She thinks of the cards that adorn the cork board wall of her station at St Trinity's – all the thank-yous, all the updated pictures of the much-loved babies. Sometimes, if she'd had a bad day at work, Ciara would nip into the nursery, with a dozen or so babies lying kicking their tiny legs in the cots, or sleeping peacefully. She'd sit and absorb their endless possibilities, as if the babies' innocent energy could somehow absolve her from what she'd done. More than anything, Ciara wishes she could have bottled that feeling, to be able to smear it all over her now, like a protective balm, to ward off the evil that seemed to follow her lately.

She thinks back to that night in her house when Morgan died. A horrible vision of blood flowing to the floor in streams. Morgan's open eyes fixed on the ceiling. There was no part of her that was prepared for what she'd seen that night. That trauma had enveloped her over the past few weeks in prison, isolating her. But nobody on the outside could ever understand how it feels to be that alone, and what that does to a person.

The low rush of a car in the distance makes her leap into some nearby greenery. Ciara watches as it glides past, a silver flash against the weak sunshine. She sees the entrance to Lennon's Hill up ahead. She scoots past the barrier, holding her breath, but there's nobody in the small security box next to it. It's so seasonal around here that there'd be hardly anyone braving the December coast today. But you never know.

Ciara glances over her shoulder as she jogs down the path marked with small speed bumps and 'Caution: children at play' signs. Her legs are freezing, the long formal skirt flapping as she runs, her chest wheezing. She imagines how ridiculous she looks, and for a second almost laughs at the absurdity of the fact that she's broken out of prison and is on the run from the police. *She*, who can't even finish a Bodypump class without practically puking. The stint at Logan had left her a few stone lighter, but she's still extremely unfit. She pulls the coat tighter around herself and continues to jog ahead. To her right is a tarmac tennis court with some straggly weeds struggling through some cracks. To her left is the playground Sally and Evie had played in. Back last summer, they'd thrown their bikes to one side and whooped, hanging upside-down on the monkey bars, their hair sweeping the ground as they'd slowly swayed. This vision of Sally hits Ciara like a tonne of bricks. Her little nose, the rosebud lips, that cheeky grin. What she'd give to be next to her, to be able to hold her. The reality is that she has no idea if Sally is with Morgan's sister, Courtney, or if she's still in hospital.

Ciara, realises, with a jolt, that she is now a mother who doesn't know where her child is. The guilt overwhelms, but it's also sobering. She just has to use this feeling to drive herself on – to make this all worth something.

Be brave, Birdy.

Ahead of her in the distance, the sea is a foaming beast, slamming into the sand, then retreating for another turn. There are two mobile homes next to one another in the field of about twelve or so, and she thinks one of them is the one that belongs to Aimee and Tony.

Ciara walks casually to the first, just in case anyone is watching her, and swings open the gate to the decking area that surrounds it as confidently as she can. You can tell many of the units are uninhabited by the covered BBQs and waterproof outdoor furniture shields. It's spectacularly bleak and totally at odds with the seaside vibe they'd experienced in summer here. The decking is mossy in places, and she almost slips in her haste, but steadies herself against the rough outer wall of the mobile home.

A quick peer into one of the small windows sees a kitchen cum living room with three bodyboards propped in one corner and folded football goals stored next to folded deck chairs. A small yellow gas tank sits next to the glass doors. Aimee and James only have Evie, so Ciara doubts that this mobile home is theirs. *The problem is that all of these bloody houses look the same from the outside.* Life replicated over and over – the perfectly samey shells trying to contain everyone's messy lives from oozing out into a spectacle.

Ciara hastily walks over the wooden decking and closes the small hip-height gate behind her. There's still no movement from any of the other units. She unclenches her teeth, trying to relax, but she's aware that she can't be out in the open for much longer.

The other mobile home she suspects is Aimee's is father down the hill, towards the sea. It's a little less well-kept. The deck is unpainted and some of the roofing slightly rusted, but these places still cost a small fortune.

The interior of the place seems a lot more familiar as she cups her hands against the glass and peers in. The small dining table is also in the same position as Ciara remembers it and the framed poster on the wall looks familiar. Shivering violently now, she slides her hand under the BBQ cover and inches the grill open. This is where Aimee had put the key when they'd gone out to the beach. Tony had been due to also travel down that particular afternoon, so she'd left the spare key for him in case they weren't back in time for his arrival.

'Please,' Ciara says aloud, through her chattering teeth. 'Please let something go my way...'

Her fingers grasp something solid. She eases it out, grimacing at the angle of her arm and the freezing air against her bare ankles.

She exhales as she pulls out the small key. All she can think about is crawling onto the sofa and steadying her heartbeat for a few minutes. Warming up. To centre herself so she can think. To eat something.

To pee.

The key is stiff in the lock and Ciara says a silent prayer of thanks as the door finally opens. Inside, there is a musty, damp smell of disuse and old wetsuits, but Ciara is jubilant as she quickly locks the door behind her. She quickly pulls down the cheap blinds and finds the bathroom, still trying to steady her breath after a turbulent few hours.

Every bone in her body aches as she begins searching through the cupboards. She finds a tin of beans in date, but the gas hasn't been connected. She doesn't dare to try and faff about with hooking it up, so she eats them cold from the can, her body craving sustenance. Then she drains the water bottle and lies on the sofa, shivering under a slightly damp blanket she found in one of the bedrooms, trying to warm up. She plans to take just a few moments to rest her eyes.

Everything floats above her, a montage of all the stress and pain of the past few months. It's as if she hadn't come up for air until now. Morgan's strangely shaped face as he lay, mouth open in their bed; Sally bawling outside the police station; David's summation that things weren't looking good; her father's excitement over a lead he said he'd had; the look on the officers' faces when she'd driven off. It all coalesces into a confused ball of fear and disappointment that weighs on her chest, pushing her down as she takes shallow breaths, her eyes so very heavy. There's too much to absorb. She pulls the blanket tighter around her. Her eyes droop closed, delivering her into a deeper darkness than any she's ever known.

Ciara jolts awake.

It's almost dark outside. Instant panic floods through her. Her head is aching. It's as if she's been hit by a truck, every muscle sore from the tension she's been holding all day. She stretches, listening, still disorientated as the horrible reality of what she'd done comes back to her. All bravado slips into another realm. The mobile home is shadowy in the dark with only the small park lights on outside casting any light. Ciara guesses it's around four p.m. She's been asleep for hours.

Prison sounds rage in her head, phantom clangs she doesn't know how to remove.

She massages her eyes with her hands, suddenly chilly.

Now what?

Exhaustion has brought doubt about her mission. Her brain feels too fuzzy to come up with a plan. It's as if she's suspended in treacle, every movement slow and clumsy. Her thoughts weigh her down. Ciara feels her way into the bathroom and risks turning on the small light above the mirror as there's no window in this small area. She splashes freezing cold water on her face, gasping with every icy splash. She stares at herself in the mirror – the face of a stranger. Her skin is dull and saggy and has lost whatever youth it once held.

Dark circles bring out the navy in her bloodshot eyes. Her hair, once coloured in honey highlights, is mousy blonde with an inch of grey at the roots. The frown marks she used to treat with Botox every six months have deepened, making her look a lot older than her forty-five years.

She looks as she is… stripped of everything and everyone she loves.

Alex Knight was the only one who'd ever really truly known her. Known who she really was, deep down. Ciara pictures her first husband and bites her lip, hard. She cannot let herself think of him, of the fleeting paradise that he, Ciara and Sally had shared for those very short years. It will be her undoing. She swallows back the grief.

The sting of the cold water has turned her cheeks bright red, but Ciara sees another change in her face, a new glint in her eyes that hasn't been there before today. An edge she didn't know she'd had.

Maybe, she thinks slowly, you aren't born a certain way – maybe life and circumstance shapes you into something new entirely. Anger and resentment simmers as she picks up the nail scissors that lie on the sink next to the toothbrush holder.

Such a tiny thing that could do so much damage with one small action.

She presses it against the soft folds of her neck, picturing Morgan's blood as he lay in their bed.

She traces the blade gently across her skin, feather-soft. A slow beading of red appears, but she's barely pressing on it. Another feeling descends, a surge of something she's never felt before. A strange sense that she has the power to reshape her destiny. She can't remain inside a prison forever. Not physically. Not metaphorically.

She has to go and find her daughter.

Ciara grabs a fistful of her hair in her left hand, and with one deft movement, she cuts. She watches, mesmerised, as her blonde hair falls, thick, soft clumps landing into the ceramic sink.

Chapter 13

It's the baby pram in the corner of the back bedroom of the mobile home that gives Ciara the idea.

Aimee's sister, who has a young child, uses the mobile home from time to time. It's a carriage-like pram with a deep hood, more suitable for infants rather than older babies who like to sit up.

Ciara knows that she needs to somehow get food and hair dye and find out about buses in the area. Time isn't on her side either. She knows the longer she's missing, the more resources the Gardaí will throw at finding her, and the more frenzied the media will get.

The police will be looking for an older woman with long hair, not a new mother with short, dyed hair. After chopping her hair into a short shapeless halo around her head, Ciara finds some scrap paper in a drawer and grabs one of the Biros she took from the Kia. She sketches out a rough list of possible next steps.

The first is the most obvious: she needs to find Sally and find out how her daughter's health is. She writes *Sally* beside a large number one. And then, what if all of this had something to do with running away with Sally as a baby? If that's the case, it might be time for Ciara to let the authorities in on some of it. She remembers Detective Clarke Casey's gentle manner and sincere words. Maybe she needs to get some information to him? That way she could ensure Sally is kept safe too. But it will be a huge risk to expose herself like that. She writes *Clarke Casey* next to *Sally*.

The second scenario is that Morgan himself was mixed up in something. As an accountant for a property firm, Ciara believed that Morgan had been fired for fiddling the accounts. He'd actually started telling her one evening about being involved in property deals that weren't above board, but at the time Ciara had her own stuff going on and she hadn't paid too much attention.

There were also the late-night phone calls and mysterious trips away for days at a time to consider too. Ciara writes *Morgan? Work?* and underlines it twice beside the number two. She has to get to those boxes that contain his files. That means heading to her father's house.

Ciara gets a pang thinking of the family home she grew up in. Kinloch was located on one of the city's most prestigious avenues, a manor home next to embassies with huge iron gates and red brickwork and white wooden gables. What would become of her childhood home now that Jimmy was dead? Ciara also writes *Courtney* beneath Morgan's name.

Courtney Duffy is convinced that Ciara is guilty of her brother's murder, but what did she know about Morgan's work that perhaps Ciara didn't? Perhaps it was time to pay her a visit.

Lastly, she writes number three: *St Trinity's deaths*. She knows her statement about what happened to that poor newborn and its mother who died would have led to possible suspensions at the hospital; specifically for Dr Derry, who had been hoping for a promotion. Could there be some reason someone had wanted to stop Ciara writing that statement? It had worked, after all.

It had been Ciara who had paged Dr Derry when the baby was delivering breech, and as senior obstetrician on duty it had been up to Dr Derry to have instigated a C-section earlier. She and Dr Derry had grown close in the lead-up to Morgan's death, and was why her testimony against him would have been so difficult. The fact were that while Derry was an amazing doctor, he had seemed distracted the day baby Archie and his mother had died.

These are all the same questions Ciara's been grappling with since Morgan's murder, but at least now she has a chance to look for evidence. She swaps her uncomfortable prison trainers for a pair of Aimee's old Nikes, pulls on a blue beany hat and is about to manoeuvre the pram out onto the mossy deck when she considers adding a fourth lead to her list. The landlord at Kerryvale – George. A creepy landlord who used any excuse to call in, usually when Morgan's car wasn't in the driveway. She used to joke with Morgan that George was the perfect fit for a psycho killer – a single, overweight loner in his fifties, who still lived with his mother ten doors up from them in the estate.

He'd buzzed the doorbell one evening and asked, stacks of invoices in his hand, if Morgan might help with him with some accountancy queries he had. Morgan had had a quick chat with him on the doorstep, Ciara hanging back in the kitchen, surprised Morgan hadn't asked him in. She'd heard the door click closed just a few moments later.

'What did George want this time?' she'd asked lightly, stir-frying some prawns as Morgan came into the kitchen.

'Just some clients who owe him money,' he'd answered, swiping a steaming piece of focaccia from where it was cooling on the rack.

'Can you help him?' she'd asked.

'Nah, can't be giving up my time without charging.'

'Yeah, but he's not exactly just anyone. He's our landlord and some-times it's good to be nice.' She'd swatted his hand away from the cooker.

Morgan sighed and Ciara sensed an argument brewing. 'Are you telling me how to do my job now?'

Stomach-twisting tension.

'No, I just wanted to...'

'I said no, okay? Give me a break.'

Ciara had felt it – the abrupt change in his mood. 'And if he keeps coming around with excuses to call in just to ogle at you, I'm going to have to have words with him.'

Ciara had closed her eyes, wondering why everything had to be so conflict-based. 'I'm sure he'll find someone else,' she soothed her husband. 'It's just that he sounded so... desperate.'

'Jesus, give it up, Ciara.' Morgan's eyes had darkened, and she'd changed the subject, not wanting Sally to think they were fighting again.

Thinking about it now, Ciara realises that George had been a bit off with her since then. She draws a biro box around *George Gainsborough* but then, after a moment, puts a line through it. The landlord was a bit strange but highly unlikely to be a killer.

Outside, it's fully dark. The evening is sharp, the cold almost painful against her skin. There are a few spotty drops of rain in the air again, that float around under the streetlamps. The weather feels like it's worsening somehow, like a warning sign she shouldn't be out in it.

There's just one car a few doors down with a light on in the mobile home.

As far as anyone knows, she might just be Aimee's sister, or just another exhausted mother trying to get her baby to sleep. Ciara has pulled the cover of the pram right up to the top and bulked it out with blankets. She pulls the door closed behind her, her breath making small clouds of fog ahead of her. The path ahead is dark save for a few small outdoor lights that glow pale white as she tries to stay in the shadows.

Ciara glances around nervously. The caravan park is mostly silent, except for the crashing waves a few hundred yards to her right. She makes her way back up the winding road, pushing the buggy over the speedbumps, remembering the walks she used to take around Brighton when Sally was this small. She hadn't a fancy travel system like this for her back then, just a cheapo buggy you could easily extend backwards so she was comfortable while sleeping. Ciara fondly remembers those long walks up and down Brighton Pier with her first husband, Alex, whenever he could snatch moments away from his demanding job.

–

A car is coming towards her.

Ciara holds her breath. It dips its headlights as she comes into view and slows down. She swallows. The shop, an Aldi, is just another five minutes' walk away. She remembers how Aimee had taken them there for pretzels and ice pops to make up a beach picnic. Ciara tries to keep her head turned away from the road. The car slows to a crawl as it passes her and it would be weird of her not to acknowledge it. She raises a hand to salute her thanks and sees a curious face turned towards hers as the dark car continues.

Ciara walks faster. She just needs to get food and survey the area for some kind of transport plan. On the main road, she jogs quickly along, hoping to avoid as many cars as possible. This area is usually jammed in summer, with cars parked haphazardly on grass verges, families spilling out of them with huge picnic baskets and sporting inflatable rings and buckets and spades. An ice cream van is usually stationed halfway between the supermarket and the mobile home park. There's no sign of it this evening.

The neon sign for Aldi finally in sight, Ciara hurries towards it, breathing heavily, vowing to work on her health and fitness someday soon when she finds herself on the other side of this... whatever *this* might be. The friendly yellow glow from the sliding double doors of the supermarket both frightens and entices Ciara. She takes a breath and pushes her pram full of blankets past the security guard on the door, pretending to fuss in her bag. Sweat trickles down her spine. Her throat feels like she's swallowed sandpaper. Once again, Ciara is astonished at her own audacity. She's never shoplifted anything in her life – even a bottle of soy sauce Sally had picked up as a toddler at a supermarket had been returned with an apology when she'd spotted it in her hand after a shopping trip.

Right now, she has exactly €1.65 to her name. Most of it scraped from the back of the couch at Aimee's mobile home. The rest she'd found at the bottom of one of the coat pockets in the closet.

Ciara makes a beeline for the bakery counter, the smell making her mouth water. Her fake baby is behaving as she reaches for a warm bread roll. A dark-haired woman with a long green cardigan and painted nails passes her with a basket casually hanging from her elbow. She smiles at Ciara, who attempts a smile back. A memory comes out of nowhere – an older lady in a coffee shop peering into the pram to see Sally as a baby and Ciara's joy when the woman told her she looked like her. It had been the first time anyone had said that.

It had also been the last time.

'Aww, how old?' The woman has stopped beside the pram.

Ciara's insides turn to mush and she gapes at the woman, who is indicating the pram. The woman leans forward, her dark hair falling over her shoulders as she moves.

Ciara jerks the pram backwards. 'Sorry, he's just fallen asleep,' she lies, the words slipping out frighteningly easily. 'He's just eight weeks. Not a sleeper.'

The woman is unfazed. She has nice, crinkly eyes, electric blue nails. 'Mine just turned fourteen.' She smiles. 'He was the same. It absolutely flies by. Enjoy every moment. You know what they say – long days, short years.'

Ciara nods politely and the woman moves on towards the fruit and veg aisle. Tears spring to Ciara's eyes. The lying, pretending someone else's baby is hers, the fact that she's missed so many of Sally's moments already… it all catches up on her. She blinks, lost in the swirling fog of the past, before it all went wrong.

She reaches for a bread roll through a blur of tears but she composes herself and calms her breathing as she moves towards the toiletries section to browse the hair dye. Bright red, jet black… what does she dare choose? *What the hell does it even matter?* The ridiculousness of the situation comes at her then and she shakes her head at the rollercoasters of emotions that she's experiencing, feeling almost manic at this stage. Ciara reaches for a box called 'Ebony Dark' and, as she balances a single banana on the flat pram cover next to the baguette, she slips the hair dye into the base of the pram where it falls, concealed beneath another chunky blanket. A handful of protein bars are hidden there too. Ciara's heart races as she approaches the tills. A young girl with a messy bun on the top of her head is in front of her in the queue as the lanky teen on the till slides her items through so quickly, it's as if he has something to prove. Out of the corner of her eye, Ciara sees the evening papers stacked tidily next to one side. Her stomach drops. There's a picture of her on the front cover. She's emerging from the funeral home, one arm braced against the flash. She looks ghostlike, her eyes wide, her mouth twisted into a grimace, her blonde hair almost white against her dark jacket. They've deliberately chosen the image that makes her look the most unhinged.

Ciara swallows at the tabloid headline, trying to keep her head down. *On the run*, it shouts. *Dublin midwife accused of butchering husband in marital bed escapes police custody.*

Butchering? Oh god.

Ciara's fingers shake as she lines up her two meagre items on the conveyor belt, her head bent low as if tending to her invisible baby. The teenager barely acknowledges her. She jigs her foot as she waits. Then hands over her pathetic coins and turns to leave, tucking the bread into the bottom of the buggy, quickly peeling and taking a bite of the banana in a bid to conceal her face further as she hurries out of the shop.

Every cell in her body is tense as she walks past the security guard, praying the hair dye doesn't have a magnetic safety strip on it. She ignores him as she walks briskly past, concentrating on not hyperventilating.

'Excuse me.'

He's calling her. Oh, my God, he's trying to her attention. Ciara keeps walking, her legs like jelly. The half-eaten banana dangles in her right hand, slimy skin flopping along the sides of her fingers as she pushes the buggy with her left.

Just act casual.

'Excuse me, miss?' He's behind her now, staring at her intently.

Ciara keeps her eyes down. Her mind stays as calm and frozen as the ground outside, but her body is rebelling: her stomach twists, a panicked high jolt. If she looked down at her torso, she is sure she'd see it moving, coiling in fear under her bulky coat.

'You dropped something.' The security guard points. He has high cheekbones and dark, soulful eyes.

Ciara sees the box of hair dye on the ground a few paces behind. She bends and picks it up with shaking hands. 'Thank you. I just…'

'Me missus is the same.' He smiles. 'Never remembers the bags.'

Ciara face-palms with exaggeration. 'Head like a sieve,' she jokes back. Her throat is now painfully dry, every cell in her body screaming to get out of there.

She puts the hair dye into the pram basket and forces herself to walk ultra-slowly out into the car park, trying to ignore the burn of the man's gaze behind her.

Suddenly, she freezes.

She hears the unmistakable scream of police sirens in the distance.

She glances back. The security guard has come out from the doorway, craning his neck towards the road, puzzled. He glances over at her and shrugs as if to say 'Beats me…'

Ciara swallows. She thinks of anything she has left back at the mobile home – her hastily scribbled plan and other things she cannot leave behind. She knows exactly who they are coming for. Then she does the only thing she can do.

She runs.

Chapter 14

The pram is the worst fucking idea she's ever had.

It bounces uselessly ahead of her, too lightweight for the momentum of her sprint as Ciara races along the roadway towards the turn for the mobile home park. The police must have located the car. Or maybe someone in the shop recognised her. She thinks of her notes on the table back at Aimee's cabin, as well as the picture of her, Sally and Alex she was allowed to carry with her from Logan, so old and worn that it is frayed at the edges. A blanket falls out of the bottom of the pram with the force of the speedbump. She's nearly there. The sirens are getting louder. She doesn't have long.

Ciara grabs the blanket and throws it back into the pram. Her lungs are screaming for air as she darts past the tennis court and lugs the buggy up the three wooden steps of the mobile home. Her heart is in her throat as she slides the lock across the small gate, then the door behind her, locking it, then shoving the pram into the galley kitchen. Trying to quell the shaking in her hands, she makes sure the blinds are pulled down in every room and grabs her notes and photo off the table and stuffs them into the backpack. The sirens are almost deafening now as she replaces the cushions on the sofa, removing any traces of herself, grateful she binned the clumps of her hair and old prison trainers on her way to the supermarket. She frantically looks for somewhere to hide. Ciara spins around, her brain refusing to focus. She paces a moment, unable to gather her thoughts, but then she remembers watching Aimee take things out of a built-in seating area in the kitchen with storage beneath. She lifts it up now. It's a tight squeeze, but she'll just about fit.

She folds herself into the dark space under the bench, next to deflated arm bands, outdoor seat cushions and a pump for an inflatable toy. She tries not to think about the spiders and other insects that thrive in the dark as she wedges her legs in at an awkward angle. Ciara is about to close the lid down on top of herself when she spots the key still sitting in the inside lock of the front door.

It is a dead giveaway.

Fuck, fuck, fuck.

Ciara clambers out again, breathless with fear and panic, scraping her back painfully against the hinges as she levers herself out. Red and blue lights ricochet off every surface now. She grabs the key. She's darting back towards her hiding place when she spots bouncing white beams of flashlights outside the window. There are boots on the deck.

The voices are louder, but she can't give up now. She eases herself quickly back into the storage space, holding her breath as she lowers the foam-covered storage seat on top of herself.

Through a crack in her hiding space, she sees a sliver of light as it streams into the mobile home from the kitchen window, slowly sweeping the room from a small gap in the blind.

Ciara sees the outlines of officers making shapes behind the white blinds against the light from outside. She jumps as the police try the door handle. A pair of shadowy hands cup the window into the living room, still obscured by the blinds but the light finds a way in, around a slit of uncovered window at the side, tracking the sofa, the carpet, the lino hallway. Ciara holds her breath. The smell of cheap rubber from the inflatables and mildew from whatever blankets were stored in there overpowers. The voices are behind her now, at the dining area window. She can hear the officers' words clearly. They are checking every mobile home for possible break-ins. No way she'd ditch the car and then hang around, another guesses. No sign of forced entry here. It's empty, a voice says. More thuds of boots and then the gate clicks closed.

Ciara exhales.

But she doesn't dare move.

For a long time, she sits there, her nose squashed up against the scratchy plywood surroundings. The waves, beyond the windows, churn methodically in and out, in and out. There's a certainty to the swirly pattern of the sea that she finds oddly comforting. As she sits, she plays over the events that had led her to this place, to this moment. If she's being honest with herself, she's been walking towards the edge she's on for ten years now. Ever since the day Sally came into her life. It was Morgan's death that had been the last step that eventually toppled her over the inevitable clifftop.

But if all this was because of Sally, would she have changed anything? In and out, the sea answers back. In and out.

Every way Ciara looks at it, she knows she'd have done the same thing a million times over. She'd do it again, she thinks recklessly, as she trembles in the small space, her limbs painfully cramped. She'd had no choice. Nobody takes risks with things so precious to them.

But she's not convinced Morgan was murdered because of Sally. It has to be something more. A hot, stabbing pain forms in her right foot, but she breathes through it.

After what feels like an hour, Ciara considers coming out, but instead finds herself reflecting on what her life used to be like – the smallness of it all. She realises that she's always felt like she was short-changing those around her with her lack of time. Late for Sally at pick-up, she'd feel the eyes of the other mothers on her – those who didn't work, those who hung about grabbing coffees and croissants that cost about five euro from the bakery near the school, those who wore fancy yoga pants and who wouldn't dare be seen to venture down the avenue where Ciara lived in her small rental house on the wrong side of Kerryvale. She'd spent so much time admonishing herself over worrying about Sally while she was at work, she found herself constantly behind, constantly rushing and racing, trying to spin every plate in the world until they'd smashed into a horrible heap on the ground and then went on to make front page news. She'd had no time for Morgan, no time for her own self-care, no time for her friends who she'd exchange memes with, trying to arrange a coffee with them because they needed a catch-up, knowing she'd probably have to cancel.

Looking back, she realises that she had it all, and it had been peeled away one layer at a time: losing Morgan, losing her reputation, her daughter, her father, her dignity... And for what? The things she'd had, that she'd worked hard for, she hadn't prioritised or enjoyed. She'd been sleepwalking through her life, worrying about money and blaming Morgan for not being more financially responsible. If she could magic herself back in time, she'd shake her exhausted shoulders and tell her frazzled self to slow down, to remember how important these plates had been to obtain in the first place: her degree in midwifery, how she'd fought to get Sally, her promise to Alex. These were worth stopping everything for.

Why had she taken it for granted? Where along the way had she lost herself?

The desperate need to use the bathroom finally forces Ciara out from the storage box, wincing as she straightens her legs. It's freezing inside the cottage, the damp smell so strong now she feels like the spores catch in the back of her throat when she tries to breath to slow down her heart rate.

Ciara slowly opens the lid and climbs out gingerly, listening. Outside is silent, save for the whispering ocean.

She crouches in the kitchen for another few minutes, just in case police are still outside, her shoulders up around her ears. Then, tiptoeing into the bathroom, she relieves herself without flushing.

With only the mirror light on, she massages the inky purple dye quickly through her hair and enjoys the slight burn as it transforms Ciara completely from blonde to dark, her eyes red-rimmed and almost black against the dim surroundings. Then she rinses her head under the tap after the allotted time, not daring to risk the whirr of the shower. A rough towel dry to finish. It stands on end, a startled black baby chick.

Staring at her reflection, Ciara realises she looks surprisingly like her mother. Elfin and fierce. Even in the lead up to her mother's untimely death, Emma Mooney never took any of Jimmy's guff when she was alive. His need to bluster and bark his way through life intensified after his wife died and Ciara had learned to keep the peace. But her mother had been the softest person she'd known; kind and careful with Ciara's sensitive heart.

Ciara closes her eyes for a moment remembering her mother. When she looks at herself in the mirror again, she has bags under her eyes the colour of bruises. She's aged years in the past few weeks, easily.

She's too tired to even eat one of the protein bars stashed at the bottom of the stupid buggy. Her head is pounding, her vision swims. She slips the Valium into her mouth and swallows, barely enough energy to climb under the duvet in Aimee's room, every muscle aching.

She dreams fitfully about Alex Knight, the love of her life. The only person to ever love her without looking for something in return.

The one who helped her steal Sally away from her real parents.

Chapter 15

Ten years ago, Ciara's life had taken a turn she never could have anticipated.

It was a freezing cold night in Brighton when Sally came into the world. Ciara had been employed by sixty-five-year-old Emmet Berg, in the weeks before the birth of his grandchild, and to stay on for a spell afterwards. A towering figure with the stoicism of someone who had long learned to command respect, he explained to Ciara that she was being employed to help his daughter Angela and her husband, Roger, whom he referred to as 'that good-for-nothing waster.' Angela was wayward, he'd said, pacing the plush carpets in the luxury townhouse overlooking the sea at Brighton, his mouth pressed into a thin line.

It never bothered Ciara, the circumstances surrounding any child's birth – the politics, the nuanced relationships between family members, their socioeconomic status. She'd learnt to tune it out. It was all about the baby. And when the baby had arrived, she'd been a dream, snuggling into her mother's chest, despite Angela's hesitation, sleeping soundly in her little bassinette, her tiny eyelids fluttering as she dreamt.

Alex had agreed, when Ciara had taken the baby out for walks on the nearby pier and met up with him, that she was a particularly gorgeous baby.

Ciara had always been the one to cradle life in her hands. She'd spent countless nights delivering babies into the world, wiping sweat from their mothers' brows, and reassuring nervous fathers pacing in hallways. But there was something different about Sally.

From the start, their bond was unshakable.

Now, in the mobile home, Ciara's dreams are filled with Sally. In one, Ciara is running through a dense forest, the trees closing in around her like prison bars. She can hear Sally calling for her, her voice weak and plaintive. 'Mommy, where are you?'

'I'm coming, baby,' she shouts, but the forest is too thick and the trees drag her farther from the voice she so desperately needs to reach. Branches claw at her skin, tearing at her clothes, but she doesn't stop. She can't stop.

Then she sees her – Sally in a hospital gown. Ciara runs to her in this dream, her arms outstretched. 'I'm here, my love. I'm here.'

Sally places her small hand out towards her, her eyes filled with tears. 'Don't leave me, Mommy,' she whispers.

'Never,' Ciara sobs. 'I'll never leave you.'

Ciara reaches out, her fingers brushing Sally's, but the moment their hands meet, the ground gives way.

Her and Sally's bond has always been her anchor. Ciara remembers the nights she'd stayed up with Sally, rocking her through fevers, singing lullabies until her cries subsided. She remembers the feel of Sally's tiny arms wrapping around her neck, the way she'd say, 'You're my favourite mummy,' and Ciara would laugh and tickle her child saying, 'I'm your only mummy' as a sadness blew through her. She was always far too aware of the falsehood in that childish statement.

Ciara tosses and turns, in that twilight space between dreams and nightmares. Who knew what lay ahead. Love was her driving force. And Ciara couldn't stop. She wouldn't stop. She had to reach Sally.

Because she knew, she just *knew* in her bones, that Sally needed her.

Just how badly, she never could have possibly imagined.

Chapter 16

Ciara's eyes snap wide open in shock and terror.

She's being shaken awake. Strong hands grip her shoulders.

Her dreams disperse around her in a million sparks, like fireflies disappearing into a summer's night.

The mobile home is flooded with the pale light of morning. It's ice cold. There's a face close to hers, shouting her name. Her head aches.

'Jesus Christ,' she gasps, her fist raised.

Her own voice seems to come from far away as Ciara tries to reorientate herself. The previous day comes at her with an overwhelming intensity, her stark reality slamming her as hard as the person is shaking her.

'Ciara, what the fuck?'

'Aimee?'

Ciara raises her hands to shield herself.

'You scared the shit out of me,' Aimee hisses, her fear lacing her words.

Ciara pulls herself slowly to sitting, glancing towards the doorway behind Aimee. Are there others? Have they found her?

Aimee blinks twice. 'I can't believe you are actually here. Oh, my God. People are...'

'People are what?' Ciara stares at her friend, frightened, her eyes bone-dry and scratchy.

'...looking for you.' Aimee looks frightened suddenly, two red spots appearing on her cheeks. 'Why are you here?'

Ciara closes her eyes for a moment, feeling wobbly, trying to figure out what comes next.

Outside, the clouds scud past. Aimee continues to stare at her.

'Your hair...' Aimee touches her hand slowly to her own head, an absurd red bandana tied around her perfect golden bob.

Her neighbour is wearing a yellow T-shirt and denim dungarees that give her the look of a children's TV presenter. She's the sort of woman that lived as perfect a life as she possibly could. She ran five kilometres every morning to stay fit, and Ciara would be lying if she didn't experience a twinge of jealousy whenever she met Aimee for a walk or a coffee, always feeling slightly unkempt next to her immaculate neighbour. At first, like Sally, Morgan hadn't warmed to Aimee, calling her the neighbourhood busybody, do-gooder or the estate gossip. But Aimee had been nothing if not persistent with the new arrivals to Kerryvale, and even Morgan had eventually enjoyed Aimee's company, often helping her with some gardening bits when her husband Tony was away working. Evie and Sally also got on like a house on fire from day one, and though Ciara always had her usual guard up when it came to letting people into her life, she'd found herself looking forward to her evenings with Aimee. They'd spent time out at the wine bar or the cinema or even just drinking tea in the garden after the hip-hop classes their daughters went to. Ciara recognised Aimee's insecurities ran deep, and that the illusion of perfection was extremely important for her. Ciara liked to think that Aimee enjoyed her irreverent sense of humour and stories from the hospital. Was she her best friend? Absolutely not. But then again, at this stage of her life, she might be her only friend.

However, the two women in the mobile home now – one surrounded by a puddle of sheets and one perched at the edge of the bed – are far from the friends who joked about the school's panto last year.

'I know… A lot has changed,' Ciara says simply, waiting a beat, trying to decide if she can trust that steady gaze, that perfectly shaped brow.

'I'm sorry,' she says, eventually, looking searchingly at Aimee. 'I need you to take me to Dublin, Aimee. I need to get to Sally.'

'Fucking hell, Ciara.' Aimee shoots to her feet. 'No way.' She takes a step back, rubs a hand over her eyes. 'I saw on the news last night that Lennon's Hill was being searched by Gardaí, so I came down to check everything was okay. I can't believe you broke in here…' Ciara had never seen her this flustered. 'I'll get in trouble for you even being here. If Tony found out…'

Tony was an accountant like Morgan. Aimee's husband was polite if a little distant, never seeming particularly interested in Ciara, or indeed his wife, for that matter. Aimee had once tried to talk about their unravelling connection, but even after a few glasses of wine, she'd clammed up and stopped herself saying too much about her own marriage.

Aimee places both her hands on her head. Ciara can feel the tension radiating off her. 'I think you should leave, Ciara. Do you hear me?'

'I can't, Aimee. Where am I supposed to go?'

The atmosphere crackles between them.

What happens now?

Ciara knows the only way she can get out of there is with the help of this woman standing in front of her. Her so-called friend. Aimee doesn't know it yet, but she's going to be Ciara's angel – her glimmer of light in the dark.

'Aimee.' Ciara's voice breaks. 'My dad died… he was killed.' Ciara searches Aimee's eyes. 'Murdered.' She tries to steady her voice as she says it aloud, fresh realisation hitting. 'You are my friend and I need your help right now to try and prove I didn't have anything to do with Morgan's murder.'

Aimee continues to pace. She's shaking her head, her hands to her face.

'You know that, right?' Ciara continues, speaking slowly, slapping her hand onto the soft duvet with each word. 'You know I didn't kill Morgan, Aimee?'

'Tony is going to fucking kill me,' Aimee says, her shoulders sagging. She glares at Ciara for a moment before continuing. 'You need to get out of here now, Ciara. I can't be found with you. You are all over the news.'

'Aimee, you believe me, right?'

Silence stretches between them.

Aimee eventually speaks. 'I can't talk about this with you, Ciara. Morgan… Morgan was a friend too. To us, I mean.'

We were hardly going out double dating. Ciara raises an eyebrow. 'Yes, but you don't think I had anything to do with his death, right?'

Aimee stops in her tracks midway from between the bed and the door of the ensuite bathroom.

Ciara sees her considering her answer. 'I don't know,' Aimee eventually stammers, and Ciara suddenly sees that it isn't anger in her neighbour's eyes, but fear.

Of her.

She doesn't have time for this crap.

'You are going to take me to Dublin, Aimee, at least to my dad's house, and if you get stopped, you will tell them that I made you take me, okay?'

'I can't,' her neighbour whispers. 'I've Evie in the car.'

Ciara glares at her. 'What, you think I'll *harm* her? Oh, my God, Aimee... seriously?'

'She was in the house when Morgan was murdered,' Aimee splutters, her voice choking with emotion. 'She could have been killed, Ciara...' Aimee pulls at her neck nervously with her hands.

'And this intruder you say you saw...'

'I *did* see him,' Ciara snaps.

She knew it had been all over the news – what Ciara has claimed happened: the intruder theory written about in double-page spreads, analysed... mocked. Features with a black silhouette of a person, a mystery mark in a diagram as the media click-baited frenzied readers with elaborate theories and maps of her home. The speculation had been sickening. Everyone had an opinion and most eventually came to rest blame on her – The Wife. The cold-blooded nurse.

'You said you saw this intruder on the camera. But what possessed you to leave them alone?' There's a note of anger in Aimee's voice now. 'And you still let the girls sleep there... knowing that...'

Bad mother, Ciara hears. Bad wife. Bad nurse. Bad daughter.

'What were you *thinking*?'

But Ciara doesn't have time for this now. She doesn't have time to pander to Aimee's horror. She has a bellyful of her own.

'Aimee, if you don't take me to Dublin, I'm going to hurt Evie.'

The words come out of nowhere. Out of desperation.

Aimee's eyes widen. She grips the bedpost, her knuckles white.

Ciara holds her gaze. Keeping her voice calm and firm as she speaks. 'You are going to drive me to my dad's house on Abbey Road in Dublin and never tell anyone about this interaction, do you understand?'

Aimee swallows, then eventually nods, taking a step backwards, fear written all over her face. And shock.

'And if you get stopped on the way, you are going to lie and then keep going, got it?'

Ciara climbs out of the bed, still fully clothed, and ignores how Aimee has now pressed herself against the thin wall of the small bedroom.

'And then you will take me to my daughter at the hospital.'

The colour drains from Aimee's face but, lips parted slightly, she nods again.

Their power dynamic has shifted. Into what, Ciara has no idea. She'd never hurt Evie. She wishes Aimee knew that too. But she's the fugitive. The burden is on her to prove she's sane. Even if she has to go a little mad to prove that first.

Five minutes later, she shoves her notes, photos and a crowbar she finds in the wardrobe, into a backpack. Then spikey-haired Ciara follows Aimee out to her neighbour's BMW. There are a few people around the campsite, and one waves at Aimee, who waves stiffly back.

Ciara climbs quickly into the back seat next to Evie, who is perched on her booster seat. She's wearing black leggings and a sparkly top with a bright pink butterfly.

'Hi, Evie.'

'Hiya, Ciara.' Evie glances at her mother, who catches her daughter's eye in the rearview mirror.

'I thought you were in jail,' Evie continues, with the blatant innocence only children can manage. 'Mummy said you'd be there for a long time.'

Ciara shoots Aimee a look but Aimee stares straight ahead as she starts the car.

'I'm just visiting a few people and your mum's giving me a lift,' Ciara replies. She arranges the blanket she'd also brought from the trailer over her body and the backpack. 'It's a surprise, though, so we can't tell anyone.'

'Mummy says I'm not allowed secrets,' the child shoots back.

'This isn't a secret, and your mummy is right here in the car with you. She doesn't want to give away the surprise either.'

Evie seems to accept this and goes back to playing with her Nintendo Switch. But then as they turn onto the main road, she pipes up again. 'Are you surprising Sally because she's sick?'

Ciara flinches.

'Yes, darling, I am,' she says in a small voice.

'Do you think she'll die?' Evie asks suddenly. 'Because she's my best friend and Laura is only my second best friend so I need Sally to come back and play with me.'

Ciara's heart feels as if it's breaking.

'So she can't die.'

'She can't,' Ciara agrees, trying to ignore the sting of tears behind her eyes.

'Yeah, but she's already been off school for a long time.'

'Evie,' Aimee admonishes in a sharp voice.

'It's okay, Evie,' Ciara explains. 'Sally will be fine and she'll be back playing with you in no time. But right now we have to play a game so I can go and surprise her and make sure her doctors are doing everything they can for her, okay?'

'Okay.' Evie nods, satisfied.

Ciara pulls the blanket over her head and the world goes dark.

She has to trust that Aimee will do the right thing and get her to Jimmy's house so she can search for information about Morgan. But Sally is in her head the whole hour-long drive to Abbey Road. Ciara wishes Sally could be sitting tucked into Ciara's hip, safe in her arms on their way back to start a new life in Dublin.

In prison, there were days where loss was everywhere: in her clothes hanging on the hooks behind the door, the inoffensive pictures stuck on one side of the room, a shout from the corridor that reminded Ciara of something from before. She had been soaked in regret and nostalgia that everything triggered.

For at least an hour, curled under that blanket, hearing only the soft sighs from Aimee and the tinny music from Evie's Nintendo game, Ciara allows the terror to slowly ebb away as she remembers dancing with her Alex to a jazz band on the pier in Brighton. Sally tucked up in the pram. Ciara's breath slows as she smiles from her material igloo. She's peaceful for the first time in so long as she moves towards her child in her imagination.

A buzz from the vibration of a phone drags her back to Aimee's car. Before she can say anything Aimee answers. Tony's voice fills the car.

'All okay?' His voice is deep, with a flat, south Dublin edge.

Ciara sits up and catches Aimee's eye in the mirror. She frowns at her. Aimee rubs a palm along her jawline. They are on the main road towards the city. Ciara's dad's house is only a few minutes away.

'Yes, just on the way back now. Nothing was disturbed.'

Tony sighs. 'This is the last thing we bloody need.'

Aimee glances at Ciara nervously.

Ciara shakes her head slowly. Don't say a word, she mouths.

'What's wrong?' Tony asks.

'Nothing.'

'Aimee, you need to tell the police what's going on. It's a bloody murder investigation. What if Ciara turns up out of the blue now, asking questions?'

'Evie, pop on your headphones, please, for a moment,' Aimee calls to her daughter, who dutifully pulls on a red and white headphones that straddle her head.

'Tony,' Aimee drops her voice. Ciara can hear the edge to her tone. She's never seen Aimee upset or angry or anything really. It wasn't part of her I've-got-everything-under-control persona. 'We shouldn't talk about this in front of Evie,' she hisses. 'Plus the signal isn't great,' she lies, as her eyes dart to meet Ciara's. 'I understand you are upset.'

Tony scoffs. 'Upset? My *darling* wife betrayed me in the worst possible way. But, more than that, I can't believe you are continuing to hold back information from the police, Aimee. Accept it. You are involved in this whole shitshow whether you like it or not.'

Aimee's had enough. She slides the phone to red. She stares ahead as they make the turn towards the sign for the river Liffey. Evie hums away to whatever cartoon she's now watching on her iPad, oblivious to the tension in the car. Aimee's phone starts to vibrate insistently.

'Are you going to tell me what's going on?' Ciara glares at her friend. Aimee fixes those dark eyes on Ciara. She shrugs.

'What have you not told the police, Aimee?'

Aimee doesn't answer. She shifts in her seat.

'Aimee,' Ciara challenges, siting forward, fingers gripping the leather headrest that sits between them. 'Talk to me.'

'I'm scared of you,' Aimee mumbles, and Ciara hears the threat of tears in her voice. 'Okay? I'm petrified of you, Ciara.'

'Listen to me, Aimee,' Ciara says, in what she hopes is a soothing, reasonable manner. 'I never would have hurt Evie. I didn't do any of this. How often do you have a crime of passion with one single fatal stab wound? The police say I was hopping mad, furious, but what kind

107

of frenzied attack goes that way? Morgan was killed by someone who planned it, who knew what they were doing.'

She closes her eyes, the horror of Morgan's final moments still raw. His face, drained of his usual watchfulness, seemed almost alien to her. Otherworldly. It's a wound of her own she knows won't ever heal.

Ciara shakes her head to dispel the image, suddenly unable to bear having to constantly explain that she hadn't taken her husband's life.

'Now,' she continues after a depth breath. 'Tell me, what Tony was talking about?' She's afraid to believe what she thinks it might mean.

Aimee chances an awkward glance over at her. Her usually peachy skin is a blotchy red. She doesn't answer. Ciara waits, and watches as the swans float down the canal as Aimee navigates the approach to the city centre. Traffic grows sluggish. The majestic birds are only visible in between the reeds here and there, snowy white necks elegantly bobbing into the water sporadically. Ciara takes in the stillness of the trees framing the waterway; nature next to the cityscape. A woman, dark and slight, hangs out her washing. Next, a sign for a service station. Then a man wheeling a bike along the cycle path, a leather satchel in the front basket.

Normality is so jarring against what's happening inside her head.

But it's about to grow increasingly complicated.

Because finally Aimee speaks: 'Morgan was helping Tony with some work, Ciara.'

Ciara nods, watching Aimee intently in the rearview mirror.

'It was an investment he wanted help with. He was spending a lot of time going through all the paperwork in our house.' She meets her friend's eyes in the mirror. 'Things got a bit... messy. Tony was spending more time away working, and well, Morgan ended up helping me with it. Things got a bit... confusing.' Aimee shakes her head, looks away for a moment, as if struggling to get the words out.

Ciara's knuckles are white against the car's headrest. 'What the fuck are you trying to tell me, Aimee?'

Aimee's eyes dart back to hers and sighs. 'There's something you should probably know.'

Chapter 17

Aimee's next words are like a punch in the stomach.

Even after so many sleepless nights in prison, lying awake staring into the dark and constructing a thousand scenarios what might have happened, it never occurred to Ciara that it might be her friend who would be the one holding something back about what happened that night.

An affair with Morgan.

'Stop the fucking car.'

Aimee starts to cry. Evie is still oblivious, glued to her tablet next to Ciara.

'Pull over now,' Ciara commands, her voice breaking with emotion.

Aimee brings the car to a stop two streets away from Kinloch. There's no one close by so Ciara sets aside the blanket and climbs out of the car and into the passenger seat.

Ciara had known deep down that all wasn't right with Morgan, but sleeping with her friend? They were neighbours, for goodness sake.

Anger pulsates through her body. This changed everything. She has the overwhelming urge to slap her neighbour's silly filler-filled face.

Aimee won't look at her. 'I'm sorry, Ciara,' she whispers. 'Neither of us meant to hurt anyone. It just… happened.'

Ciara snorts. 'What? Did you slip and his penis fell inside you?' she demands scathingly.

Tears run down Aimee's cheeks.

Outside, a well-dressed woman walks past with a black Labrador who pulls ahead, rummaging in the bushes as the woman talks on her phone. A man wearing a rugby supporters' scarf climbs out of a taxi. The tree-dappled Abbey Road is just ten minutes from Dublin city centre. This part of the city is also the home of some of the country's highest-profile politicians, barristers and sports stars. Here there were long driveways, tall redbrick houses, perfectly manicured city gardens. Lean luxury, an urban dream. Ciara had grown up here. She'd been given everything she'd ever wanted by her parents, but it was her mother's side of the family, who sold their construction business at the height of the boom, that had provided that wealth. Her father had worked hard, but they'd never have lived on this particular road on a Garda salary, or even a sergeant's or head of a unit. She has faint memories of hearing her parents argue about it once. She sensed the power imbalance between them when it came to money. The edge it brought to the husband and wife dynamic. Ciara's mother didn't work but controlled the purse strings. While Jimmy worked every hour of every day and still it never seemed to be enough.

Aimee's pleading voice brings her back to the horrible revelation.

'It didn't last long,' Aimee tells her, squeezing her hands together, her perfect nails glossy against tanned skin. 'It was a silly mistake, a fling... and... I'm sorry.' Her discomfort is obvious. 'I know Morgan wouldn't have done anything to hurt you or Sally.'

Ciara sits forward, ice around her heart. 'What about Sally?' she barks.

'I honestly wish it hadn't happened. I wish I'd never started spending time with him, if that helps.'

Ciara can't take her eyes off her friend's delicate features, those lips that Morgan had kissed. The blood rushes in her ears as she grow more furious. 'You were sleeping with my husband.' Her breath catches in her throat. 'And then he was murdered and you didn't tell the police about your relationship. Or the motive your own husband might have had when he found out about this.'

Aimee looks at Ciara, aghast. 'It... it... wasn't like that,' she stammers.

Why had Aimee not gone to the police about this?

'Why didn't you tell the detective?' Ciara manages to say.

'Tony understood how sorry I was, that it didn't mean anything. We went on a date night on the night... well, you know, when everything happened. Things were back on track, so when we heard about Morgan, I felt awful for you and Sally. Tony and I felt it was better not to involve ourselves, especially because it was... over.'

Ciara studies Aimee for a moment. 'How long was it going on?' she challenges.

Aimee squirms. 'Like, only a few weeks…' she manages.

Ciara's heart is hammering in her chest. Around the time he'd been acting weirdly. But picturing her Morgan with Miss Perfect Aimee… it didn't make sense. And what did it mean for the police investigation?

'Do you really believe you can get away without telling the police, Aimee? They'll need to know about this.'

Aimee shrugs. 'It honestly didn't mean anything, but then when Morgan died, it was such a shock.' She starts crying again. 'Tony could be dragged into this too. I can't have that.'

A police traffic motorbike stops at the lights opposite where they are parked. Ciara immediately ducks. Aimee spots it too and indicates back into the avenue. The bike passes them and Ciara exhales. They are only two minutes from her dad's house, but she needs to know more.

'How did Tony find out?' she asks. 'What's not to say he was so angry, he came over and murdered Morgan in his bed?'

Aimee shakes her head. 'That's not what happened, Ciara, and you know it. He was home, with me.'

'You need to take this information to Detective Inspector Clarke Casey. This could change everything for me.'

Aimee shakes her head adamantly. 'No. I won't, Ciara. I'm sorry. This could change everything for Tony and me too.'

'Aimee, you have to.' Ciara glares at the woman in front of her. 'I'd say I need a friend right now, but what kind of friendship is it when you were shagging my husband?'

They both stare at one another.

Aimee shakes her head. 'I can't risk anything coming back to me, Ciara. The way the media is about you… I have to think of Evie now too.'

Both women glance over at Evie who is still playing on her device, her tongue poking from between small, neat teeth.

Aimee sits up straighter. 'Get out of the car now, Ciara. I can't be here with you. I've done what you asked.' She turns away, biting her lip.

'Wait for me here and then take me to find Sally,' Ciara hisses, but with all the new information, the fight has gone out of her. No wonder Morgan was acting so strangely those last few weeks. She'd never have guessed about him and Aimee. She can't picture it at all. Then again, she knows how Aimee enjoys attention. It shouldn't surprise her.

'No, I'm not waiting. I can't be here with you.' Aimee is firm.

Ciara slumps back. There isn't much more she can do.

'If you tell anyone where I am, I swear to God...' Ciara glances at her. 'Please don't betray me again,' she says flatly. 'Promise?'

Aimee looks petrified. She nods quickly, clearly antsy to get out of there. 'I promise I won't tell.'

Ciara forces a laugh. 'As if I'll ever trust you again.'

Her hand is trembling as she opens the car door and climbs out of the BMW. She swings the backpack onto her back and watches as Aimee speeds away, doing a fast and illegal U-turn in her haste.

Ciara wonders if she'll tell Tony that Ciara was hiding in their mobile home. Or the police. Either way, she knows she doesn't have much time.

Pulling down an old black Nike cap she'd taken from Aimee at the holiday home, Ciara jogs towards her dad's house. The air is sharp and crisp and she notices Christmas trees in the front windows of all the houses, twinkling in the weak winter sunlight, their reds and greens reminding her of magic and childhood and all the joy that's supposed to come with this time of the year.

But her mind is spinning.

If her neighbours Aimee and Tony are involved somehow in Morgan's death, then perhaps it's not about Sally at all. Ciara should feel relief, but instead, her head hurts. She thinks of Aimee's husband Tony. Aimee said he was home but what if she was asleep? But then she can't imagine Tony being the type to lose it and come over to stab Morgan while he lay in his bed. But they did have a spare key to Ciara and Morgan's home in case of emergencies. Either way, Ciara knows she will have to let the detective on the case know what had been going on.

Affairs suggest motive – jealousy, revenge.

Ciara slows to a walk and crosses to the other side of the street.

But then again, it could also work against her. If Morgan was having an affair and she'd known, it might look as if she had an additional reason to kill him.

She feels cornered.

Ciara walks past the next avenue and then suddenly she has arrived. This is her road – the one she used to skip up as a child.

When she'd fled home to Dublin from Brighton with Sally, Ciara hadn't given the fact that money had helped a second thought. In fact, it was only when Morgan lost his job and they'd had to move out to the rental house in Kerryvale that she'd first felt that lack. It took her by surprise the impotence that came with not having enough money in the bank. Jimmy would have given her whatever she needed, but pride prevented Ciara from asking, even when things got really bad. Plus, she didn't want Jimmy's I-told-you-so quips. He'd long said to her that Morgan was trouble, an overgrown toddler, someone who wouldn't provide for her.

'I make my own money, Dad,' she'd shot back, disgusted at the idea of a man paying for her life, especially when she'd worked so hard for her degree. But when Morgan had lost his third job and started maxing the credit cards on ridiculous items like self-mowing robots for their garden, Ciara had begun to understand where her dad had been coming from.

She'd brought Morgan back to Kinloch on their third date. But the funny, quirky guy she'd met in a city nightclub seemed overshadowed by a new, arrogant persona. She'd put it down to nerves, but Jimmy hadn't taken to him from the get-go.

Kinloch is one of the largest houses on the avenue, imposing with its black iron electric gates hanging off curved granite columns. Statues of lions rest either side of the stone steps that lead to the arched front door, almost more cathedral-like than residential. Blond pea gravel stretches across the driveway, tucked beneath rows of low box hedging along the pathway.

It's not yet lunchtime but Ciara's stomach aches with hunger. She would do anything for some food, any food at all: warm toast; steaming soup; one of Jimmy's famous club sandwiches.

From across the road she surveys the situation. Oak trees arch overhead, wisteria coils around a wooden pergola next to where she'd buried at least two of her childhood pets. Ciara gazes at the gabled six-bedroom house she's always called home.

She'd walked through those same gates every single day during university, swayed over these same grey cobbles after nights out, had some boys from the nearby school sneak in and steal wine from the wine cellar during her eighteenth birthday party. So many memories that now feel so flippant compared to her current situation.

There are no cars at all driveway. With a jolt, she realises that her father's car is probably still with forensics. The car he was found in.

A sharp twist of grief in her gut. She pretends to be rooting in her bag as she absorbs the lie of the land. Inside the house, she knows, are a lot of her and Morgan's documents. As well as what Jimmy had been working on for Ciara.

The old white Mercedes Jimmy used to like driving on weekends with the roof down was likely in the double garage next to the large garden room. But there's no getting through the electric gates. The code was changed every month by Jimmy's security team. As a girl, Ciara had been able to shimmy over the gates at night when her father locked her out, but now Ciara opts for the more concealed option.

The laurel bush to one side hides the tall fence from the roadway. It is higher, but definitely a less obvious entry point.

Around these parts, it wasn't an exaggeration to say that many of the neighbours had binoculars in upstairs rooms to watch the comings and goings of some of the country's most well-recognised personalities. Glancing over her shoulder, Ciara waits until the street is clear and then quickly squeezes herself through the bushes, grateful her pointed cap shields her eyes from the backwards flick of branches. The padded material of her jacket also protects her from getting scratched by thorns.

Once inside the bushes, she reaches out and makes contact with the security fence. It's constructed from a tennis court barrier material, thin and criss-crossed, about ten feet high.

Sighing, Ciara claws her hand as high as she can and levers her body up. The small holes in the fence make it difficult to get her trainers wedged into the gaps, but she only needs a toe-hold, enough to propel herself higher.

Her backpack snags on the maze of branches as she moves higher, but she shakes it off, making progress.

Halfway up, she stops for a rest. Still hidden from view behind the bushes, Ciara can afford to do this part slowly so she doesn't fall. A trickle of sweat runs down her back.

At the top, Ciara attempts to kick one leg over, fails and eventually scrambles over. She twists her body and lies forward. For a moment she's lying horizontally along the thin frame of the fence, her centre of gravity struggling to rebalance. 'Woah,' she murmurs under her breath. 'Steady.'

Her foot hits off the wire on the other side clumsily, the soles of her trainers too smooth to find grip. For a moment, Ciara hangs, suspended only by the bloodless, sweaty grip of her fingers until her toe catches in an opening. She manages to lower herself further and then, looking down, drops into the soft flowerbed below, stumbling slightly, and landing heavily on her bottom next to the geraniums.

It's a painful landing, but also the chance to catch her breath. Both legs are scratched but it's nothing compared to the jumble of emotions assaulting her as she looks up at her home from her dirty perch.

There's no movement from the house, but Ciara knows that it is also the most obvious place police would expect her to come. There might even be officers inside the house, waiting for her, or a patrol going past.

She cannot be complacent.

Staying low, Ciara runs along the side of the garden until she gets to the steps that lead down into the basement of Kinloch. Some of the houses around here had converted theirs into separate accommodation for adult children or rented them out to those keen to have an address in this part of town. Jimmy used his as storage, mainly.

Ciara jogs down the eight or so steps and hesitates at the glass-fronted door. She rests her forehead against the cool, rough stone of the wall. Sudden tears surprise her.

She's home.

She's also an orphan.

A widow.

A criminal.

When she was in prison, Ciara had dreamt a lot about this house. How oblivious she had been to the privilege of growing up with loving parents and a beautiful house. How removed from the rest of the world. If she closed her eyes, she could almost picture her mother in the kitchen beyond these walls, cooking something on the Aga, a gardening programme on the radio in the background; or, when she was older, Ciara waiting for a friend to call in so they could lie on her bed and talk about what they'd wear to the Red Box disco that weekend or how devastated they were about Take That breaking up.

The memory blows cold as quickly as it arrives. There's no bridging the gap between then and now and besides, she has to hurry. Aimee may have immediately called the police on her. Ciara reaches inside her backpack for the crowbar and with a quick flick of her wrist, she smashes the glass.

An alarm immediately screams in her ears.

Fuck, fuck, fuck.

They never used to leave the alarm on – a bad habit, but it was because Jimmy usually had his own security around.

Ciara's entire body tenses. The sound of the alarm seems to grow louder as she removes the largest glass shards and stretches her hand quickly through the now-empty pane to unbolt the door. It's stiff but it opens.

She doesn't have long at all. The familiar scents of the place almost stop her in her tracks as she makes her way through the basement room towards the inner stairs. The smell of home is undefinable, really – everyone unique – but to Ciara, Kinloch always smelt like baking and furniture polish when her mother was alive, and of leather and grief once it was her father's realm.

She reaches the bottom doorway and wrenches it open. Ahead of her is a narrow staircase that leads to the main lobby of the house. Morgan once said it reminded him of an English five-star hotel – all black-and-white tiling, peach carpets, gleaming chandeliers. Ciara races up the stairs, taking two at a time, her hands over her ears as the noise intensifies. At the top of the stairs, she takes a left to the alarm pin pad. She knows there are only minutes before the police turn up. Yanking open the small white box, she tries the code they'd used for everything growing up. The alarm rings on. Frustrated, she taps in her birth date, trying to channel Jimmy's thought process. He was the type of guy who was always nostalgic about things.

The pin pad tells her she has one more attempt. She glances out of the hallway window to see if there are any police cars. The street is clear. So far.

With shaking fingers, she decides on another date – the date her mother died. It's a long shot but the alarm stops as abruptly as it started.

Ciara's ears are still ringing when the hall phone rings.

'There seems to be a disturbance there,' a male voice says. 'A gateway into the basement door was breached. Everything okay?'

It's the alarm watch company.

Ciara forces a smile into her voice. 'I'm so sorry. I'm the cleaner and the basement door was jammed so I had to really kick to get it open. I'm so sorry. I hope you will make sure there's no police coming out. It would be a waste of everyone's time. Plus my boss would kill me.' An awkward chuckle.

'No worries, love,' the voice responds. 'We get this all the time. But I'll need the password.'

Ciara prays it's the word they'd always used for emergencies – a code word Jimmy came up with when he'd first been promoted to gangland. Concerned she might one day be in trouble, he wanted a word that would signal distress or, in this case, safety. She had chosen it after watching one of their favourite movies together. A tongue-in-cheek reference to something you weren't supposed to say. It had to be something that didn't raise suspicions if she'd called him from school upset and wanted him to get her, or to collect her from a friend's house if things were a bit out of her depth when she was a teen. They'd laughed about it, but she'd had to use it a few times over the years.

Ciara takes a deep breath. 'Beetlejuice.'

The voice on the phone is satisfied.

She puts the phone back into the cradle and exhales. It might have bought her another few minutes, but time isn't on her side. She needs to find the documents Jimmy had been working on. She needs to see what her father's office is hiding and to find whatever documents of Morgan's that had been moved here after her rental house had been packed up.

Ciara puts one trainer on the first step and, glancing up, makes her way towards the top of the sweeping staircase of her family home.

Chapter 18

There's something about your childhood bedroom that grounds you – an instant time travel to the person you once were. Before children, before marriage, before life got so complicated. Ciara's former bedroom is all-white wicker furniture and a big double bed. There are still time-stiffened handbags hanging off the side of the bedposts, and inside the wardrobe when she pulls it open is her old deb dress, a pair of her old riding jodhpurs and a fancy-dress costume of when she'd dressed up as a clown one Halloween. All she wants to do is sink into that bed like she used to do whenever anything upset her – a heartbreak or a bad exam result or a day pining for her mother. She wanted to sink into that bed and stare at the ceiling with its familiar bumps and shapes formed out of the plaster. Her beloved posters and pictures of dogs and obsession with visiting the Greek isles. Ciara catches sight of herself in the bedroom mirror – all cropped black hair, pale with dark circles under her eyes, her usually round cheeks creating angles she hadn't had since she was a young girl. She has a moment where she cannot for the life of her figure out what got her to this place. Or how she'd allowed herself to get into a position where she was running away from the police, towards a child who wasn't supposed to be hers.

Ciara starts rooting in the wardrobe for a change of clothes. She throws a few old T-shirts and leggings into her bag and pulls out the drawers to try to find some cash. Her fingers land on a document: papers for her old apartment in Brighton; her old employment certificate for the hospital where she'd first met Alex Knight. He'd been the hospital psychiatrist and Ciara was working her first years in the neonatal ward. They'd instantly bonded. She pictures his rugged face, those kind eyes. She'd truly never known love like it.

And then Sally had come into their lives.

Thinking about how she'd come to have Sally was… complicated. It was perhaps too easy to say she hadn't had a choice. Of course,

Ciara had. She knew she had. She could have chosen to walk away empty-handed. Back to her simpler life with Alex in that Brighton apartment. How different might her life have been then? It's impossible to say. Because then Alex got sick, having Sally seemed like a balm for everything else that was happening. Maybe that's how Ciara had reconciled it to herself, like she was a benefactor – someone who took care of her sick husband and rescued a newborn. Instead of the truth – that she'd taken a child from its biological mother, perhaps even to appease her own dying husband.

Ciara puts a hand over her mouth at the discomfort of her nostalgia. The older Sally got, the bigger the implications of Ciara's actions seem to feel.

Regrets had always seemed to form a big part of Ciara's life. Regret that she hadn't been nicer to her mother. Regret that her father chose work over spending time with his daughter. Regret that she'd fallen in love with a man who would be diagnosed with cancer a month after she said 'I do.' Regret that she took a child from its family. And now regret that she had been framed for the murder of a man she'd probably not known as well as she'd thought.

Ciara swipes the tears angrily away and folds the paperwork back into the folder. As she does so, she catches sight of the picture of her mother that always sat by the bed, in a frame of seashells that she'd collected from the beach in Wicklow as a child alongside her mum. She remembers picking them up and hearing her mother's voice telling her what a clever girl she was – how beautiful the shells were. Even the damaged ones Ciara handed her, her mum had turned over in her hands, examining them carefully, finding beauty even in the breaks. Now those swirls of blush-pink and gritty white whorls surround the picture of her mum, who had the exact colour of blonde hair Ciara has.

Or had.

Regal and loyal, Ciara still missed her every single day. Her father used to tell her that Ciara had gotten her determination from her mother. Ciara loved it when he said that. She wished he'd talked about her mother more.

But there was no point in feeling sorry for herself. Ciara had made her bed, even if it was out of love and perhaps even naivety. Now she had to undo the mess she'd gotten herself into, one action at a time. She pictures her daughter crying for her like she always does when she's sick. The image spurs her on. As soon as she gathers the documents and other things she needs from here, she plans to make her way to the hospital to find out about Sally.

Ciara takes one last look at her bedroom, hitches the bag up on her shoulder, the shell frame bulky against the material, and pulls the bedroom door closed behind her.

Chapter 19

In the next bedroom, the sight of Jimmy's slippers so casually kicked off on the floor beside his bed is enough to make her grip the doorframe for support just to stay on her feet. Ciara stays like that for a moment, feeling stunned by the horrible realisation that her father currently lies in the ground, buried without her.

Then she forces herself to look around the room from the open bedroom door. It strikes her that Jimmy must have been in a hurry when he left. Her father was one of the most organised people she knew – a stickler for making beds and putting things away. Her mother used to joke that he'd throw her out if he could, given his penchant for decluttering. The fact that his bed is unmade, and his slippers cast so untidily aside makes her think he'd been in a hurry, wherever he had been going. Perhaps, she thinks, the disarray might have been caused by the police searching Jimmy's home after his apparent murder. But there aren't any signs of police tape or of forensics having been there – which also feels a little odd to Ciara.

Then again, maybe she'd watched too many episodes of *CSI* as a teenager.

She lingers at his doorway, remembering all the times she'd tip-toed into her father's room during the night, hungry for warmth after her mother died, and being sent back to her bed alone. Jimmy hadn't been cold or unloving, he'd just been grieving himself and found it almost impossible to know what do to with a little girl who wouldn't stop crying for her mummy. Her gaze falls to the next doorway, her father's office door. It used to be one of the spare bedrooms, but they'd converted it into his office when Ciara was a child. That way he'd have a view over the front garden, he'd told her, but actually she understood he wanted to keep an eye on the wider avenue, especially when he was in command of some of the biggest drug investigations in the state.

But she also knew it was on account of the break-ins. Jimmy needed to know the security team were always primed and ready to go. He couldn't have a repeat of the incident when someone had tried to shoot them both.

Ciara moves towards the office, and with a twist of the handle, she steps inside.

A huge mahogany desk sits facing the two large floor to ceiling windows. The wall to the left is completely covered in navy painted bookshelves. To the right is a burgundy Chesterfield couch next to a cream fireplace and to the right of that, two giant filing cabinets. The wooden flooring has been given some warmth by a huge colourful rug that to Ciara always looked a little out of place next to the staid grandeur of the rest of the room. On the panelled walls are paintings and prints; some of Jimmy out in his beloved Wicklow mountains hunting, others of Ciara at various stages of her life, always hiding behind that long fringe that almost covers her eyes.

This was Jimmy Mooney's domain and she'd never dared disturb him here. On his desk there are framed photographs: one of him and Emma, Ciara's mother, on their wedding day. The other, a picture of Ciara graduating university.

The two best days of my life, he used to declare proudly whenever they spoke of such occasions. But right now, Ciara doesn't have time for nostalgia; she knows she could be disturbed at any moment.

She tries to pull open the drawer of the first filing cabinet. Predictably it's locked, but when she turns to try the second one, she notices that behind the door of Jimmy's office is a huge corkboard with information about her case. She hurries towards it. A picture of Morgan, taken from his LinkedIn page, sits at the centre of the documents. Yellow Post-it notes chart the entire investigation. Although she knows most of it from David and from the updates her dad would give her when he visited her in prison, it's strange to see it mapped out like this in front of her. One of the notes is scrawled in Jimmy's handwriting and underlined. The Red Lion, a date and a name, Keith. Ciara knows Jimmy had been excited about a lead he'd had from the Red Lion pub from the lighter she'd found on the windowsill at her home on the night Morgan was killed. Ciara is convinced it belonged to the intruder who had broken in – the one she'd seen on the iParent screen – but from the note and date on the Post-it, Jimmy must have met this Keith person. Was that why he died?

Why hadn't the police removed it – surely they'd been here? She shivers suddenly. *Is this some kind of trap?*

Ciara pulls the Post-it from the board and throws it into her backpack along with her list of leads she'd worked on at Aimee's mobile home. Just as she turns back towards the filing cabinet, she spots something else sticking on top of the corkboard – Detective Inspector Clarke Casey's card. His name and phone number is printed in small letters at the bottom right. She throws that into her bag too.

Ciara wants to tell the detective about what Aimee had said about her affair with Morgan. Surely it had to be relevant.

The clock on the mantlepiece chimes suddenly, giving her a fright. A loud sound against the silence of the house.

It's already one p.m.

The sound of a car engine outside draws her towards the curtains. Her heart hammering in her chest, Ciara peers out, but it's just a taxi picking up a neighbour in the house opposite.

She resumes her drawer pulling, but every single one is locked.

Ciara's gaze falls to the rug. One Saturday, when she was eleven or twelve, she'd fallen in the garden quite badly and limped upstairs, biting her lip but needing her dad. She'd found him crouched on the floor of the office, jumping as she opened the door. Instead of admonishing her, he'd hesitated and then, perhaps reluctantly, told her to approach him. She'd spotted a small round circle built into the ground under the floorboards.

Inside had been a box with more money in it than she'd ever seen. Her father had explained to her that if anything ever happened, she must come here and take the money to keep herself safe.

Ciara peels back the fabric and jerks the floorboard. It's stiff but she worries at it for a minute or two until it jerks free. She reaches inside and her fingers brush against plastic. She guides the blue bag out. It's heavy and much bulkier than she was expecting. She opens the bag and gasps – a gun and a thick wedge of banknotes, folded once. She immediately recoils at the touch of the metal. Guns have always frightened her – ever since she saw a movie as a child where a police officer was shot. And then the incident here at Kinloch as a child. Jimmy had reassured her that Irish police didn't carry guns. 'This is our weapon,' he'd said and shown her his baton. 'It's better because we don't want any of the bad guys taking our gun if we had one.'

A few years later, when he started working in the armed garda unit in gangland, his words came back to haunt her. Ciara would stay up at night worrying her father would have some thug grab his gun off him and shoot him – that's why she was so reluctant to even hold the rifle when he'd taken her hunting.

She repacks the money into the blue plastic bag and slides it into her backpack. Now, as an adult, she understands her father wanted her to learn how to protect herself. But as a child it had felt... wrong. In the past two months, two men she'd loved have been murdered. There's no time to be anything but serious. She slides the gun into her bag too.

Tyres crunch on gravel outside and Ciara jumps up, kicking the rug back into place.

Remaining concealed by the curtains, she glances outside and freezes. A Garda patrol car has just pulled up outside the front door. Ciara glances around the room frantically. What else was there here that she needed? Without thinking she grabs some of the folders lying on Jimmy's desk and wedges them into her backpack.

Pulling the office door closed behind her, she races down the sweeping staircase, almost tripping in her haste. She can see the silhouettes of two Gardaí distorted through the front door.

Muffled voices. 'You'd better knock first,' a low voice suggests. The jolting static of walkie-talkies.

Ciara scrambles down the second set of stairs, into the basement rooms where her and Morgan's stuff has been stored. She closes the door behind her but, any moment, the Gardaí are going to come in and start searching the house. She tears at the boxes, leafing through documents, throwing out files, not even knowing what she's looking for. In a box marked *Morgan Work*, she spots files with the his old work logo and throws them in too. The backpack is seriously heavy now. In another box she finds a collection of old photos – she grabs a handful... an instinctive need to reconnect with who she once was. Next to the boxes is a container with old mobile phones and wires. They'd had a drawer in the rental house in Kerryvale where they'd kept their old phones just in case they hadn't transferred any photos. It was a jumble of wires that somehow had never contained the right one they'd ever needed.

A creak on the basements stairs makes her stomach flip. Ciara stuffs in as many of the phones and chargers as possible and turns to exit when she spots her father's winter scarf hanging on a coat rack in the corner. He'd always been a suit or a uniform guy – only wearing such clothes on a rare day off when he'd coax her into the garden or when Sally came to visit. But this one had been a gift from Sally to him and he'd worn it often to her delight. Without thinking, Ciara grabs it, balls it up and buries her face into it. This is all she has left of him now. She wraps it around her neck, trying not to think about his empty face and stiff hands at the funeral home.

There are footsteps in the passage outside the door – she knows that she has to move right now or she'll be caught. Ciara isn't sure if the police are there to investigate Jimmy's death, or because of the house alarm, or simply because the most likely place a fugitive daughter might flee is back to her own home. She's surprised this place hadn't been crawling with cops after what happened to Jimmy.

But there's no time to think. Ciara slides out of the back door, trying to avoid the broken glass shards at her feet, and closes it, just as the door to the storage basement opens. She stands against the outside wall of the house, heart racing, as the two Gardaí enter the room. She closes her eyes, her back pressed to the wall, praying they hadn't seen the broken glass just yet. She tries to make out what they are saying as she braces herself to run.

'…sighting on the avenue just twenty minutes ago…' one of them says.

Could fucking Aimee have called them? Ciara shakes her head. She knew she shouldn't have trusted her.

I promise I won't tell.

Those had been her exact words. But it was naive of Ciara to have any faith in someone who had lied to the police, and to Ciara's face – and slept with her husband. What else wasn't her so-called friend telling her? She probably called it in anonymously, so she didn't have to face any questions about how Ciara came to be there.

Ciara glances to her right. If she makes it up the steps, she should have a clear run towards the iron gates – they hadn't automatically closed after the garda car drove in. The voices are closer.

She hears one of the Garda exclaim when he spots the glass.

Now or never.

Ciara takes a breath, whooshes the heavy backpack onto both shoulders and moves quickly towards the steps. She launches herself up the steep stone steps, and runs at full tilt towards the gates, her shoes kicking up stones as she goes, waiting for the shouts. Pushing herself to go faster. Not daring to look back.

Chapter 20

Ciara's breath comes in short, sharp bursts as she stops to rest behind the pillar of an apartment block fifteen minutes later. Her trainers have rubbed against the thin skin of her ankles. Every step hurts.

Her clothes are ripped, her nails filthy, her legs stinging. She's pulled the scarf up over her head to conceal her face as much as possible, but the cold is snapping at her nose and fingers and worry about what's happening with Sally is making her panic.

Her heart rate refuses to slow down but she has to put as much distance between herself and those Gardaí as she can. Ciara forces herself to keep placing one foot in front of the other. She takes the back roads to try to stay hidden.

It's another half hour until she's in the city centre. Cars linger in traffic, their drivers completely oblivious to her plight as she walks quickly, head down. One foot, the other foot. Breathe. Find Sally. Ignore her blistered ankles and her growling stomach and the fear of hands suddenly gripping her shoulders.

Breathe, she commands her brain again, trying to work out how she'd contact Clarke Casey. Or this Kevin guy from the Red Lion. Or even if she should.

Ciara couldn't just walk into the police station, or even the hospital, and demand to see her daughter, but instinctively she realises that she's heading in the direction of the children's hospital. But she's not even sure which one Sally is being treated at.

By the time Ciara arrives at the city's main thoroughfare, her panic is at an overwhelming level. There are so many factors pulling her in different directions. Viscerally, she knows she has to be with Sally. But she doesn't know where her daughter is. Plus, she can't just present herself at the hospital, and she has to find information about who really killed Morgan so at least she can plant *some* seed of doubt in the prosecutor's mind.

There's no talking herself out of this one. Her heart hammers almost painfully in her chest, her breath shallow, palms sweating. The dread descends, just like it had on that last day, when Morgan and she had fought as he waited for his taxi to take him to the airport. The last time she'd seen him alive. The memory plays out in her head.

'Keep it down, Morgan,' she'd implored, closing the kitchen door, aware of Sally still trying to sleep upstairs. Morgan was angry that she kept asking him about when he was going to find work. She'd brought it up with him again that morning, asking all sorts of questions about who was paying for the flight to the UK, what work interview did he have? What was happening with the job?

'I've had to cancel the Netflix and Spotify subscriptions. Sally's school trip is due, and our health insurance has gone up and is due for renewal. When are you going to just get a bloody job?' She'd sat back at the kitchen table, reaching for her coffee… 'and keep it,' she'd added.

The blood had suddenly got louder in her ears. She knew she'd pushed things too far with him.

'What did you just say?' Morgan sprang towards her, bending low into her face, a dangerous voice. His reactions so much more intense than before.

A shiver had run up her spine, her shoulders tensing. This was usually the moment when she'd appease him, jump up and tell him to give it a rest, to de-escalate the situation, like she'd always done with Jimmy.

But more recently Ciara had been trying to find her voice in this relationship. For Sally's sake, as well as her own. And Morgan didn't like it one bit.

'I said…' she'd continued, gulping for air, bracing herself '…when are you going to get a job?' Then, softer, more pleading: 'Morgan, it's been three months. I've pulling double shifts at the hospital just to pay rent. I'm completely exhausted.'

'I've worked my fingers to the bone for this family,' Morgan had started. 'Have we ever gone without? Have we?' Then his face closer to hers. 'I said, have we?' he'd demanded. Flecks of toast crumbs were stuck to his stubble. His eyes were narrow and mean. When had he started to change into this person she barely recognised? It was as if, overnight, he'd become a completely different person.

Ciara was tired of dancing this recent dance, tired of allowing him this power over her. She'd held up her hand. The taxi was due any moment but there was something about her husband's swagger this morning that had disgusted her. Playing the big man when all he'd ever done was put her down. Once she'd started seeing how wrong it was the way he was treating her, it was hard to unsee.

'I'm done with your excuses,' she'd said, trying to push power into her voice. 'Man up or fuck off.'

Maybe she shouldn't have said it. Not only for the sexist connotation of those two words, but because Morgan had the kind of ego that couldn't handle being emasculated in any shape or form. Maybe that's exactly why she'd said it.

'Fuck you,' he'd shouted, slamming the kitchen cupboard, two bright spots appearing on his cheeks.

'Stop shouting,' she'd pleaded, thinking of poor Sally upstairs, no doubt curled in bed with the anxious knot in her stomach that she'd recently confided in Ciara about.

That's when Morgan's eyes had grown even meaner. He'd taken two steps towards her. 'I'm not shouting,' he'd said softly. So dangerously softly.

'Morgan, please.' She knew he had been pushed to his limit.

'Do you know what shouting is, you clown? THIS is shouting.' And then Morgan had leaned close to her, just inches from her face, opened his mouth and yelled at the top of his lungs. 'THIS IS FUCKING SHOUTING.'

The assault of his voice had stunned her.

It had rung in her ears, the sound violating her space in a shockingly violent way; his warm coffee breath; his once gorgeous eyes, so horribly hard; the flecks of spit that appeared in the corners of his mouth.

It was so sudden, so extreme. He hated her in that moment. She could see it.

Later, she'd gone over it in her head. Was it as bad as she'd thought? He hadn't hit her, after all. Being called a clown isn't exactly abusive. And yet, she'd felt as devastated as if he had slapped her. As violated, somehow.

Morgan was stressed, she'd told herself, he hadn't meant it. She'd pushed him to his limits. Of course he didn't hate her. Hadn't he brought her tea in bed that morning, and called her his sleeping beauty?

He was just struggling with this work situation and she'd riled him up. That was all.

But then he had gone off in the taxi, even texting her about putting out the bins later, like nothing had happened. His usual lack of account-ability and blame-shifting. And Ciara had sat at the kitchen table, tears rolling down her cheeks for half an hour until the panic attack took over when she finally realised that this wasn't love. This wasn't even close to the love she'd had with Alex. And, more importantly, it doesn't have to be a punch in the face that prompts you to leave a bad relationship. It can be just the fact that something isn't enough. Or that something is making you miserable.

'This isn't enough,' she'd whispered to herself later that morning, sitting on the couch, over and over. 'This isn't enough for *me*.'

She'd remained on the couch until Sally, mussy-headed and asking for cornflakes, found her a while later. That's when she'd sent him the text – Morgan. The one read out by police, leaked to the media. The one where she'd told him to fuck off and die. Then she'd dragged herself out to work to face her colleagues who faced possible suspension after baby Archie and his mother had died. It had been a bad day. The worst perhaps, considering what happened next.

A taxi honks at Ciara and she is brought back to the moment, walking through Dublin city, her feet aching, scarf wrapped tightly around her face, trying to figure out what happened in the time between that awful fight two months ago and Morgan being found dead.

Panic still swills around the pit of her stomach, and despite her long walk, she's freezing, starving and itching to get a look at the documents in her bag.

The sooner she gets something concrete that she can give to the detective, the sooner she can go and find out how Sally is doing. Or even where Sally is.

Ciara hurries down towards the McDonald's on Grafton Street and hesitates outside. There are CCTV cameras everywhere. She turns off into one of the alleyways that brings her into the small cobbled streets of the city.

At a smaller cafe, she uses the toilet, scrubbing her hands in the sink. The quiet room, and the simple act of applying the soap and rinsing, is enough to tamp down some of her panic. In the reflection from the mirror, a stranger stares back at her.

Ciara shakes her head at the absurdity of her new life. She buys a chicken sandwich and a takeaway coffee, using a terrible US accent and keeping a hand up over her face, grateful for the lack of interest the robotic staff show to a scruffy, middle-aged woman with a huge backpack, thinking her likely to be a tourist on the way to see the Book of Kells in the nearby university, she hopes.

Outside she stuffs the sandwich into her mouth, savouring the caffeine hit and the warmth of the coffee. She walks, head still down, feeling more alone in the world than she ever had. Aimee had betrayed her, and the only other person in the world who would drop everything to help her is dead. Still chewing, Ciara walks around the back of a clothes shop into an alleyway with three industrial bins, trying to find some respite from the cold. She finds a concealed spot next to some old boxes and breaks off a piece of cardboard. The temperature had dropped, and darkness will soon fall. There's no way she can do anything except try to figure out her next steps. But she needs something to go to the detective. Aimee sleeping with Morgan isn't enough, and possibly could even make things worse for her. It could be seen as reason for *her* to kill Morgan for sleeping around.

Sitting awkwardly, she rests her coffee between her legs, enjoying the heat against her legs and unzips the backpack, being careful with the sea-shell frame. Her fingers are stiff with cold as she pulls out the first file. A thick blue folder with the work logo of Morgan's old workplace. Her eyes swim, going through the detail as she tries to find anything at all about the projects he was working on. Nothing jumps out at her but then again, she's not exactly sure what she's looking for.

After a few minutes, Ciara tucks the documents back into the folder, and as she lifts out another, a photo falls out. It's a picture of her, Alex and Sally as a small baby. They are sitting on the balcony of their small apartment, the sun is shining and you would never know from how handsome Alex looks how sick he was – how close to death. She clutches it in her shaking fingers and can almost smell the scent of sun cream in the air, used during one of the hottest summers on record in Brighton.

Something else has fallen onto her lap. It's a mass card with Alex's face and a prayer that his family had chosen for his funeral. Ciara closes her eyes, presses it to her heart.

Being with Alex had been easy. He'd been as gentle with her as she'd been with Sally. And although what they'd done wasn't the choice everyone might have made, they'd been united in their determination to give the baby a more loving chance.

Ciara pictures his hands around hers, his twinkling eyes when he'd pop into the hospital nursery in Brighton and tease her about her 'baby bathing' as he called it. But she knew he'd felt it too – the joy of being around new life. Although he was charged with helping the mothers navigate the barrage of emotions they felt after giving birth, sometimes she'd see him looking at the tiny faces and understanding the magic of it all.

That's when they'd first come across Emmet Berg – Sally's real grandfather – and he'd told her all about his daughter Angela who was pregnant and needed help. Would Ciara be interested in working a private midwifery job?

A bang from the bin lid forces her back to the moment. It's one of the retailers from the shop throwing in old boxes and bags of rubbish. He's a young guy, about twenty or so. Trying to avoid his gaze, Ciara turns away and reaches into the backpack and takes out three of the phones. One is her very old Sony that she kept for the messages she knows Alex had sent. The other two are iPhones. She tries to turn them on, but their screens remain blank. She'd need to charge them. There's also one black Nokia, which is strange because she hadn't seen one since she was a teenager. She presses the power button.

The young man nods at her awkwardly. 'All okay?' he says politely, not meeting her eye.

She smiles back but keeps her head low.

'Yes, just taking a breather, thanks.'

She pictures herself through his eyes. Dishevelled, exhausted, grey with stress, her dirty clothes with papers strewn all around her. The obvious cold.

He's only wearing a thin white shirt himself. This is probably a college job. He hugs his own torso, long and lean with dark hair, curious eyes. Kind eyes.

He turns to go, but hesitates. 'I haven't seen you before...' he starts.

She keeps her eyes down, concerned he'll scrutinise her face too much.

'I know a few of the guys who hang out here during the day,' he says, almost apologetically. 'So you might not know, but St Anthony's hostel is just around the corner. They have extra volunteers at Christmas so there are a lot more resources.'

Christmas.

She hadn't properly registered the festivities, but thinks now about the trees in the windows near her dad's house.

The boy remains standing there and she understands the look on his face is pity, but even more than that, he genuinely wants to help her.

'I can show you, if you like.' He shrugs.

Ciara sighs. She's freezing cold and has nowhere else to go tonight. In her haste to uncover evidence to prove her innocence, she hadn't thought through exactly where she'd stay. Maybe the hostel would have internet, a hot shower. She doesn't dare try to check into a hotel, even with her cash. She'd probably need ID at a hotel too. A hostel would be perfect – not too many questions, no ID required and, in a strange way, Ciara felt drawn to the familiar unfortunates she'd aligned herself with in Logan.

She nods and starts to stuff everything back into her bag. The air is damp and the man's eyes are filled with concern. Now that she's stopped for a bit, her shoes are even more excruciating against her ankles. She straightens up painfully.

'It's not far,' he says, reaching to help her pack away her things.

'It's okay,' she says quietly, feeling a rush of shame. She pulls her coat around her protectively.

There's a small electronic beep. She glances down at her lap.

The Nokia has lit up.

Chapter 21

St Anthony's hostel is next to a fish and chip shop just off Crown Alley, the boy had said, giving her directions when she declined his offer to walk her there. A light snow starts to fall as Ciara walks past souvenir shops and bus stops offering open-air tours of the city, keeping to side streets and avoiding the Christmas shopping crowds. By the time she stands at the battered front door, her feet are soaking and tufts of her dark hair are plastered to her forehead. The phone burns a hole in her pocket. She needs to see what's on it and why it was stashed among her husband's things.

An older woman with pallid features and crinkly eyes opens the door. She's in a cheerful floral jumper. Behind her, down a long hallway, are some worn-out, carpeted stairs. A notice board on the wall next to the door offers curled-edge leaflets of support and assistance. A pile of hard plastic chairs is stacked in a corner. The smell of soup reminds Ciara of prison life at Logan, but the woman's face is so welcoming that she almost falls in through the door and into her arms.

'I'd like to see if there's a bed,' she manages, hyperaware of the pleading timbre of her voice. She adjusts it slightly. 'I've nowhere to go tonight.'

The woman steps forward and ushers Ciara through the cramped hallway to a small office with a large desktop computer and neat files stacked on the table, talking as she goes.

'It's a right night all the same,' the woman says, shaking her head. 'Nobody should be out in that.' She gestures at Ciara to sit in the small, misshapen couch to one side of the room. 'You'd catch your death.'

Ciara nods, her fingers tingling. She shoves them under her armpits, crossing her arms.

The woman lowers herself into the office chair and sighs with the effort.

Ciara waits patiently, too exhausted to think straight. All she wants to do is to tuck her legs up beneath her and sleep for days.

'Now, let's see what we have available,' she says, squinting at the computer. 'I'm Kay, by the way.' She types as she talks.

Ciara nods and attempts a smile, too tired to be polite. The room smells of lingering cigarettes and suddenly she's craving one.

'We've one bed left in dorm three,' Kay says, glancing up.

Her gaze lingers a fraction too long.

Ciara shifts on the sofa.

'I haven't seen you here before,' Kay says, her voice soft but probing.

Ciara lifts her backpack off the ground and hugs it.

'Do you have any ID?'

Ciara shakes her head slowly, her heart sinking.

'I didn't think I needed it,' she admits, hoping she doesn't sound frightened. 'I just need somewhere to sleep tonight.' She stammers. 'I've a friend I can stay with tomorrow. It's just been a difficult time...' Shame revisits, creeping up her spine, making her feel alienated for having such a desperate need.

But Kay smiles sympathetically. 'Everyone has something,' she says a little sadly, and goes back to writing something out on a piece of paper.

Kay's words resonate.

Flashbacks of Morgan's unkindness to her in the lead-up to his death assault her. Another memory strobes into her consciousness: the shouts from the journalists as she was led into court that first time. Then the noise of the first night in prison – desperate screams that remain lodged in her head. She'd wanted to join in, to yell and punch and fight against the unfairness of it all. Of being taken from her daughter. *Everyone has something*. But her something felt impossible to survive.

'Are you okay, my dear?'

Ciara shakes her head slightly, trying to drag her mind back to the small beige room.

Kay is looking at her with the same concerned look the boy outside the shop had given her. She lays her elbows on the table and leans forward, taking off her glasses. 'What's your name, dear?'

'Orla,' Ciara says, plucking one of the names of a girl in Sally's class out of the blue. 'Orla Matthews.'

'Are you okay, Orla?' Kay's kindness, her *mothering*, catches Ciara off guard. 'No,' she wants to say. 'Help me,' she wants to beg. But then she thinks of all the cruel shouts as she was lead into the courts for her arraignment. The headlines with that awful word they kept using: *butchering*. And even though she hadn't killed Morgan, she wasn't a saint. Nobody could absolve her of her previous sins.

'I…' she stammers. 'I'm fine,' she lies.

'Okay, Orla,' Kay says, sensing her reluctance. 'I just have to check your bag if that's okay. It's doors locked at eleven, no banned substances, no sexual relations, meals at eight p.m. and eight a.m. Doors are locked all day until six p.m. in the evening, okay?'

Ciara remembers Sally once asking why there were exhausted-looking people with huge bags waiting at the back of public library in the city centre when she'd taken her, and Ciara had looked around and realised that there were those without a home who had nowhere else to shelter from the rain. The hostels are locked all day, the cafe's too expensive place to linger, so the choice was to huddle behind commercial premises or find a public place to get some respite from the weather, from the streets, from the pain that had led them there.

Everyone had something.

'You okay with all of that?' Kay smiles kindly.

Ciara nods. Then, suddenly, she remembers the gun. Wrapped in the blue plastic bag at the bottom of the bag that is about to be checked.

'I'm so sorry.' Ciara feigns needing to be sick and jumps up, still clutching her bag. 'Bathroom, please?'

Kay purses her lips and points towards a small doorway. Ciara's meets her eye and shame once again floods her system. There's not much Kay can do though, Ciara supposes, if she suspects she is hiding drugs. She's not the police. But if Kay were to uncover the gun… that would complicate things.

—

Ciara locks the thin bathroom door and runs the taps. She slips the plastic bag out of the crammed backpack and turns frantically, looking for a hiding place. There's only a toilet, a mirror and a sink in the tiny space. Cracked tiles, an overflowing bin… Ciara remembers watching a Netflix show where someone stored a gun inside the toilet cistern. It seems ridiculous to her now that she's here, in a strange hostel, on the run from police, to be considering hiding a gun in a toilet. But then again, nothing over the past few months has felt straightforward.

The back of the white toilet cistern looks heavy. Ciara nudges it slightly but the immediate scrape of porcelain on porcelain makes her wince. Kay would definitely hear her. She didn't even know if the bloody toilet would even flush with something that heavy inside. Once again, being on the run is nothing like the movies. Ciara flushes the toilet, flustered. She looks desperately around the room.

Maybe they wouldn't frisk her. It wasn't jail, after all.

But she couldn't risk that either.

She only has a few seconds before Kay starts growing more suspicious. Ciara ducks down and feels behind the sink. It's grimy, the tiles here out of reach of the cleaner's mop perhaps. She uses her fingers to shuffle the base of the sink slightly forwards. Cobwebs lurk in the shadows. She forces the blue bag into the crevice and jams it into the space, her finger pads scraping painfully against the edges. Part of the bag is still visible. Shuddering slightly, Ciara uses the handle end of the toilet brush to wedge it further upwards.

Come on.

It's finally concealed.

She quickly replaces the brush, washes her hands, and dries them on her jeans before zipping her bag back up and unlocking the door.

Kay is still sitting in her chair.

'All okay?' she says lightly, glancing up.

A door slams in the distance and Ciara jumps.

'Yeah, just… you know.' She pats her stomach gently. Saying nothing and everything.

'Come on and I'll show you where you're going.' Kay creaks to standing and roots through her bag quickly. 'You've a few hours until dinner. I think it's stew this evening.'

Ciara's stomach rumbles as she's led upstairs to a dorm where six other shapes of women lie on their beds. Nobody speaks.

When Kay leaves, after giving her a key for a locker for her belongings and giving her a plastic bag containing a few toiletries, Ciara sits on the bed and exhales.

She feels safe here, warm, able to catch her breath and plan her next move.

She promises herself that if she ever gets herself out of this situation, she will come back and volunteer her time at such havens. Once again, she realises how oblivious she was to her advantages in life. She considers herself a compassionate and caring person, but she'd had her head in the sand in her privileged South County Dublin bubble to ever see the wood from the trees about how many people had to live their lives.

After a while, Ciara starts to go through some of the paperwork she'd thrown in the backpack from her father's house. There are bills and statements, letters, car insurance, tax details. She flicks through the sheets of paper, trying to understand what exactly she's looking for. The Nokia has immediately died after it had flickered on so it's on charge now, next to her small bed.

The first thing among the documents that gives her pause is a medical bill in Morgan's name.

It's a consultant's fee for €250 with an additional cost of one hundred euros for tests. Morgan hadn't told her anything about getting tested for anything. She checks the date – the summer before Morgan was killed. That was five months ago. What other secrets had he been keeping from her? She traces her finger down the page, as if she might be able to feel something of him, sense her husband captured between the pages.

'Were you sick?' she asks under her breath. But what she really wants to know is the answer to the question: 'Were you leaving me before I left you?'

The invoice is from someone called Dr Bridges at Blackrock Clinic.

She sets the piece of paper aside. It feels useful somehow.

Then she takes Detective Inspector Clarke Casey's card from the bottom of the backpack and adds this to her 'useful' pile.

Two more women join them in the dorm room, casting sidelong glances at one another as they heave themselves onto the thin mattresses. Kay's words come back to Ciara. *Everyone has something.* Whatever that may be, it's written across these women's faces.

Next, she turns to the mobile phone and switches it on. It illuminates and she's surprised to see it doesn't ask for a code. She doesn't recognise the phone – she and Morgan had iPhones which they got as part of a family bundle along with their internet at home. Why would Morgan have a burner phone? Her hand shakes slightly as she clicks into the messages section. Will she see messages from Aimee? She's not sure she can handle that. Besides, what other secrets had her husband been keeping? Could they be even worse than hers?

The messages are empty. Ciara closes her eyes, not sure what she wanted to find.

A smoking gun? Evidence Morgan was up to something? An obvious clue that would help her know what the hell to do next?

She finds herself absently twirling a pen in her hand – tumbling it between her fingers and over her knuckles. It helps her to think.

After a few minutes, the pen stops moving.

There *is* one person who may be her only chance at finding out who killed Morgan.

She pulls out Clarke Casey's card and steps out into the hallway of the hostel. Maybe this burner phone will come in handy after all. There's a of smell damp and the carpet is stained to one side. On the wall opposite her dorm there's a picture of a sunset scene that feels so alien to Ciara at this moment that she can barely look at it. All turquoise waves and white sands. It almost hurts to imagine a life that beautiful. The last time she'd taken Sally to the beach, she was just five. Ciara, Jimmy and Sally had spent the day on Dog's Bay Beach in Connemara, marvelling at the turquoise ocean and almost pink sand as Sally splashed about, trying to find crabs. Later that day they'd sat in Vaughn's in Roundstone and shared big juicy garlic prawns. Jimmy had had a Guinness and they'd chatted to a few American tourists who had come to see what all the fuss was about and had fallen in love with the area.

That felt like a million years ago now.

With a shaking finger, Ciara types in the number for Casey's mobile and holds the phone to her ear. She hears the TV evening news floating up from downstairs and catches snippets of the lead story about the ongoing search for the missing prisoner. Her heart rate speeds up.

'Hello, Casey?' Ciara stammers. The moment she started speaking, technically she upped her chances of being caught. Then again, she needs Clarke Casey to have all the information that Jimmy had and that Aimee has given to her.

'Detective Inspector Clarke Casey.' the voice repeats. 'Hello?'

Ciara remembers the man's gentle manner, his kindness with her the night of Morgan's murder.

She decides to take the chance.

'Casey,' she says, hoarsely. 'It's Ciara Duffy.'

Ciara bites her lip. She has no idea if they can trace the call or find out where it's coming from. She's hidden her caller ID but she knows she has to be fast.

'Mrs Duffy,' Casey immediately exclaims, his voice shocked. 'Where are you?'

'Listen to me,' she demands. 'I need to know where my daughter is.'

A hesitation.

'Where is Sally?' Ciara hisses, clutching the phone tight against her face.

'Ciara, Mrs Duffy, you have to tell me where you are. We will find you and this will go against you—'

She cuts him off. 'Tell me where my child is right now.' She starts to sob and her shoulders shake with the pent-up worry she's been carrying, devastated how clueless she is at this moment about what's going on with her daughter.

'She's in St Trinity's,' Clarke finally says. 'She's safe.'

Ciara takes a moment to compose herself. St Trinity's is the best children's hospital in the country so if Sally is there, she is being treated by the country's most skilled specialists. But she still feels the visceral need to be by her daughter's side.

A woman walks up the stairs and Ciara turns her back and speaks quietly into the phone. She knows she has to be quick.

'Listen to me,' she hisses. 'Morgan was having an affair with my neighbour, Aimee,' she quickly relays. 'I'm not sure what exactly that means for your investigation but it has to be relevant,' she continues. 'It's new information,' she reiterates. 'And my father was meeting with someone from the Red Lion pub the day he was murdered,' Ciara adds. 'Someone called Keith.'

'Ciara, please let me help you,' Casey urges.

'Are you writing this down?' she pleads. 'Morgan was also getting medical tests,' she is tumbling over her words now, 'with someone called Dr Bridges. At Blackrock clinic. Can you find out anything more about this?'

A strange beeping sound in her ear makes her jump. Could she be traced? But she has so much more to say. She needs someone to investigate some of the missing pieces of this crazy jigsaw.

'Are you getting all of that?' she begs, desperate for someone with the clout to help her understanding all this before she lands back in prison.

'I am,' Clarke says quietly in her ear and, for some reason, she actually believes him. 'Can you meet me,' he says. 'Are you in the city?'

He takes her silence as acquiescence.

'You'll bring an army,' Ciara says softly a lump in her throat.

'I'll come alone,' Clarke says and she wants to believe him but then again, why would a detective risk it all for her? 'I want to help you,' he promises, and Ciara leans her forehead against the wall, her entire body exhausted by the tension of holding it together for so long.

'I can't trust anyone,' she finally says. Then, ending the call, she turns off the phone.

Ciara looks at the time; it's almost eight p.m. Could she risk trying to get to Sally at St Trinity's this evening?

Absolutely.

Back in the dorm, she locks her bag into the locker, takes the well-worn towel that is on her bed and heads to the showers. It's a relief to shed her grubby clothes, ripe with the stink and grime of the day. She lets the hot jets punish her skin and scrubs her short hair using the soap from the dispenser on the wall, remnants of the cheap dye running down her legs as she contemplates the secret life her husband had been leading.

She stops scrubbing her hair for a moment. How had she missed Morgan having an affair with Aimee? Morgan hadn't liked Aimee at first, but as both couples got close, he'd become more friendly with her. Now Ciara has to look at everything in a new light. Aimee had claimed Tony was in bed at their house when Morgan was killed, but of course she would lie to protect Tony – she'd lied about plenty of other things. *Could* Aimee's husband have hurt Morgan in retaliation? And was the affair the reason he'd been behaving so strangely, or had it been something else entirely?

Back in the dorm, she pulls on the selection of the clothes she'd grabbed from Kinloch. Black leggings and an old hoodie with the *Friends* logo from her youth. As well as the towel, Kay had given her a toothbrush, a hairbrush and soft socks. Ciara sighs gratefully, and brushes her hair quickly as the other women file downstairs for dinner. She plans to slip out and try get to Sally.

Ciara thinks about Clarke Casey asking her to meet him the next morning. It would be such a risk. She'd be mad to take the chance. But... what other choices does she have? All other options don't look good. Ciara pictures his open face, his kindness that night. His willingness to take her words at face value. His promise: 'I will help you.'

Maybe Casey would help her. Maybe he'd help her once he knew what was at stake.

This is what she's thinking as she's walking down the stairs when a woman next to her does a double take. She studies Ciara's face and raises an eyebrow.

Shit.

Ciara glares at her, then drops her eyes quickly down. Her face is all over the news. She can't get caught now. Not when she has come so far. She drags her hood up over her hair.

'I recognise you,' the woman with the nose piercing says loudly.

A few women glance over. Ciara shakes her head, her mouth feeling like cardboard. She tries to screw up her face so she looks less herself. *So much for a safe haven.*

'No,' Ciara mutters.

'It is you... I've just seen a picture of you. With long blonde hair.'

Ciara leans towards her menacingly and puts on a thick accent. 'Nah, I'm not from here,' she insists, hoping a bit of attitude will shut this woman down. She channels her pal Paula from Logan.

The woman challenging her smells like chewing gum and stale cigarette smoke. She raises an eyebrow. 'Well, there's a bald fella downstairs with a load of tattoos. He an ex or something?'

Ciara tries to control her shock at this information.

'He's going around with a picture of you showing it to everyone. Asking if anyone has seen ya.'

Chapter 22

Ciara doesn't dare take another step further.

Swallowing nervously, she explains to the woman that it is indeed her violent ex and to please not say anything at all. 'Do not let him up here,' she begs, her knees shaking. 'He'll make up all kinds of lies just to try to get to me. Do not believe a word he says.'

Heartbreakingly, the woman immediately nods and squeezes her shoulder. 'We've got you,' she says firmly. 'We'll let Kay know too.' Even in her haste to run back upstairs, Ciara feels sad at the fact that this must happen a lot.

There's nowhere else to go.

In the dorm, she lies on her bed, staring at the bunk above her, trying to calm herself down. She feels guilty for lying about her situation, especially given the kindness of a lot of the women in her dorm. But as she lies there, Ciara probes whether or not she'd been in an abusive relationship with Morgan. Could she really belong in a place like this where so many abused women seek shelter? Would it have been easier to leave if she'd had confirmation of it? Lying in the dark, she shakes her head, shakes away the tears. Shouting at someone isn't abuse, she tells herself, like she'd always told herself when she was confused by Morgan's treatment of her. She pictures the hole in the bedroom door that Morgan had punched one night after a fight. She wasn't the door. He hadn't hit her. But the little voice in her head had been growing louder over the past few weeks. A voice that said emotional abuse is abuse. Verbal abuse is abuse. The putting her down, the fear of his moods, the unpredictability of his temperament… it had all chipped away at her already low self-esteem to the point where she hadn't even known who she was anymore.

I'm not the door, another part of her insists.

It was Dr Derry's advice, her colleague at the hospital, which had been so helpful in his letters in bringing her to understand that she deserved more. Even using the words 'abusive relationship' is a way of absolving the perpetrator of his actions, he'd explained. It implied there were two people abusing one another. That wasn't the case though. From what you've told me, Morgan is abusing you, Derry had explained to Ciara gently. Call it what it really is. But she hadn't dared think about the implications of accusing her husband of mistreating her.

Eventually, Ciara fell into a fitful night's sleep at the hostel, where she dreamt of Sally on a beach getting further and further away from her until she was just a speck in the distance. Ciara dreamt of giant manta rays that kept dipping below the surface as she pointed them out to her daughter who was beside her, then nowhere, then beside her again.

She wakes early, a heavy feeling weighing her down, her neck stiff from the pillow, eyes gritty, like she is hungover. Then comes the panic. Everything flooding back.

Ciara re-examines the contents of the backpack and wonders who had followed her to the hostel. Each new development just confuses her more. First Aimee's betrayal, and now a strange man tracking her movements. What did it all mean? If it was the police who'd found her, they'd have come up and dragged her out.

An icy fear runs down her spine at another thought. What if it's Sally's biological family? Ciara's name and picture have been in the news and that news could easily have made it over to Brighton.

As she shuffles through the documents as quietly as possible, Ciara knows what she's really looking for. She'd spotted it among the photos as she'd thrown them in. Her favourite picture.

A photo of Alex Knight looking dapper on the day he graduated from college, long before she'd even known him.

He's shielding his eyes from the sun, a wide grin on his face. She misses his fingers intertwined in hers as they walked their usual weekend walks with Sally in the pram, feeling like the luckiest people in the world.

After Alex's diagnosis, they'd been so hopeful that they could beat his illness. But cancer is one of the crueller diseases. The tumour could have lurked undetected for a decade the doctors explained, and Ciara didn't know if that was better or worse. It felt considerably more tragic that this tumour had been growing in parallel with their joy. A slow distortion of the wonderful life they'd known so briefly.

Alex stopped working; the treatment was too intense. An operation was suggested – a dramatic rejigging of his insides that wasn't covered on health insurance, so it would cost them. He lost weight, the tube in his nose a permanent fixture, the bile-coloured liquid food no match for this strong man with his soulful eyes. His easy-going nature began to condense into someone she stopped recognising. Someone so bitter they were being eaten away one sad day at a time. The only thing that had made him smile after a while was when she had brought her little charge around to see him. His face would light up at the sight of the tiny baby girl.

By this stage, Ciara was spending all her time with the baby, at Emmet Berg's request. His daughter, Angela, the baby's mother, wasn't able to cope, he'd explained.

'Can't you ask your family for the money for the operation?' Ciara had begged Alex one evening, when Sally was just a few weeks old. Between his diagnosis and her bond with the baby, she was all over the place. Ciara had even inquired about loans. But Alex hadn't wanted his family to know how ill he was and Ciara hadn't been working long enough to afford the kind of money an operation like this would mean.

When Emmet Berg has come to her with his suggestion, he couldn't possibly have known how desperate she was for the money. Not that it excuses any of it, she'd always thought to herself. But what he was offering was more than enough to pay for Alex's last-chance operation.

In the hostel, Ciara closes her eyes and clutches another picture to her heart. A picture of the little girl on the pier. She remembers snippets, like a dream. It was early evening in Brighton. There was a festival on – a fun fair. They'd had baby Rosie, who they'd renamed Sally, with them for six months by this stage. Alex was in a wheelchair – the cancer had spread to his spine. But there was still light in his eyes. The Ferris wheel had been turning slowly, the neon lights reflecting off the sea from the pier. In the photo, Ciara was pointing towards the candy-floss vendor and laughingly handing over a fiver, relishing the excitement in Sally's eyes as she tasted the sweet candy clouds for the first time. Ciara can almost see Alex weakly throwing the hoops to win Sally a huge teddy. He hadn't had the strength to get them over but the man in the cap behind the counter had manoeuvred them over the biggest teddy's neck as tears stung Ciara's eyes.

Back in the hostel, nobody else is yet awake. Ciara allows silent tears to fall at the memory of that day.

But she can't stop thinking about that day because of what happened next.

They'd been walking back down the pier, the sky a navy blue, Sally rubbing her eyes, Alex pale but happy, when the first shout came.

Ciara will never forget that look, like in slow motion, as she turned and locked eyes with Angela Berg – Sally's birth mother. She was still so young, still the same as Ciara had remembered her six months previously, when she'd helped her give birth privately, at home.

The indignant yelp of recognition.

Ciara's stomach had lurched, and she'd held Sally tighter and started to run through the crowds, Alex weaving in and out behind her in his chair.

She'd ducked into the festival medical tent, panting, and cited her husband Alex's illness to justify her need to be there. Alex turned up behind her looking desperately worried. Ciara had shaken her head at him. This was what she'd been afraid of. They should have left Brighton long before that, but Alex's treatment had kept them there.

The operation they could now afford but which, in the end, hadn't helped at all.

Outside the little medical marquee, Alex and Ciara had heard the woman's desperate cries: 'Rosie, Rosie,' she'd screamed over and over, until someone came to comfort her.

'Poor woman musta' lost her kid,' the nurse muttered under her breath, as she Velcroed the navy cuff around Alex's skinny arm to take his blood pressure.

Alex had glanced at Ciara, grim-faced. This was the price they knew they'd pay for taking someone else's child.

Later, back at their small flat, Ciara expressed her urgency of having to move back to Dublin. 'Dad will help us,' she said to Alex, who lay in bed, pain written across his face. 'We have to get out of here.'

But they had both known that Alex wasn't going anywhere.

Ciara jolts herself from her sad memories; she needs to stay focused on her quest. She turns the Nokia back on. It immediately beeps with a text alert. She dives at it, as one of the women curses at her for making noise. She peeps at it from under the covers.

> Duffy, I'm urging you to turn yourself in.

It's from Casey.

She types quickly back.

> I have information about Morgan's case. City library at 9:30
> a.m. If there's anyone there but you, I won't show.

She shuts off the phone before waiting for a response.

Ciara tucks the photographs into the bag along with the others and tiptoes out of the room wearing the same clothes she'd slept in.

She wants to get in touch with Courtney to speak to her about Sally, but Courtney doesn't have a phone, only a landline, and Ciara doesn't have her number. Morgan's family lived off-grid for much of his life. These days they'd be called 'Preparers' but back then, the home-schooled boy was just called weird. *Maybe that's why Morgan found being social so difficult. Perhaps that's why he needed to exert control over the people around him.*

Ciara jogs down the stairs and into the small bathroom in the hallway. Inside, she locks the door. For a moment she worries when her fingers brush nothing but porcelain, but then she feels the tip of the cold steel against the bag. She pulls out the gun and pushes it into her backpack. She tells herself that hopefully she won't need it, but if this bald man who's been hanging around wants trouble, Ciara needs something to defend herself.

She may have baulked at pulling the trigger that day with Jimmy, but the message had stayed with her: *Don't hesitate.* She pictures Morgan's knife wound. Whoever is involved in this means business.

Outside, it's another icy-cold day. As she zips up her coat she notices a large black car parked opposite the hostel. As she rushes past, she catches sight of one arm resting on the open car window – a generously inked arm. She quickly crosses the street and turns down an alleyway, turning to make sure she's not being followed.

Shivering, Ciara marches down the busy morning streets, making her way to her meeting spot with Clarke Casey, ducking into doorways when she can and keeping her eyes peeled for anyone watching her.

The library won't be open for a while yet, but Ciara plans to watch all the comings and goings to make sure Casey isn't setting a trap. Dublin city centre is busy, despite the early hour. Trucks pull up outside shops delivering goods, bin trucks honk and people in suits bustle towards the financial district. She lingers in the doorway of a café across from the library. It's half an hour until Casey's supposed to meet her, if he shows. But just ten minutes later, she spots him. Clarke Casey is jogging lightly, brown shoes, a long navy coat and a grey scarf neatly knotted at his neck. His hair is brushed to one side, a worried look on his face.

She can tell it's him by his long stride and sandy hair. She pulls her own black scarf around her face; her father's oaky smell lingers, making her feel slightly braver. She follows Casey with her eyes as he walks up and down the street outside the library. Morning traffic snakes along the narrow road that leads through the heart of the city, dividing it into north and south. A bus rattles heavily past and the smell of roasting coffee beans is overpowering. Ciara presses herself to the glass of the cafe, trying to keep out of sight. There doesn't seem to be anyone else with him but she can't trust that he didn't bring back-up.

She takes out the Nokia and types a quick message. She watches in the reflection of the cafe as he pulls his phone out and reads the message. He glances up and around, slightly confused.

That's because she's just changed the game.

Chapter 23

Ciara turns in the opposite direction, away from the library, towards a small chapel next to St Trinity's hospital, next to where she used to work. So close to where Sally is being treated.

The chapel is tucked into the older part of the original grey-stone hospital, once part of the prestigious university of Dublin, but its location – down a long lane – means that it remains mostly unclaimed by tourists.

Ciara had sought it out as a refuge a few times when things hadn't gone well at the hospital – especially after baby Archie and his mother had died. It wasn't about religion. But there was something about the dim interior, away from the bustling bright hospital lights, and the streets, that had drawn her in.

She'd found it a helpful sanctuary, where she could speak to her own god – the mother she'd lost as a child.

Ciara is saying prayers of a different sort now as she slips into the chapel ahead of Detective Casey and sits in one of the side pews, in the darkest part of the small church.

She is hoping that if Casey has organised some kind of trap, his plan will be out of whack now.

It's a risk, but then again, everything is a risk at the moment.

There are a few people at the front of the chapel lighting candles. Another woman sits at the back, head bent over her folded hands, rocking slightly. In sorrow or celebration, Ciara will probably never know. She remembers grown-ups bent the same sad way at her mother's funeral, all those years ago. Awkward pats on her back as she sat there in her brand new coat and stiff black patent shoes, waiting for her mother to come and give her lunch. But her mother wasn't coming and her father was broken. There would be no sandwiches cut into stars that day or ever again. Ciara had lost so much when her mother died. She'd lost a nurturing that she'd never regained.

Catching her breath, Ciara allows herself a moment to absorb the pretty stained glass designs dancing on the aisle of the church from a window so far up she can't see it.

She doesn't turn when she hears soft, urgent footsteps behind her. This is real faith – the belief that Detective Clarke Casey will keep his word to her. And that he'll believe what she has brought him here to tell him.

There are beads of sweat on his forehead, but his breath still causes fog in the slightly stale church air as he slips into the pew next to her. 'Mrs Duffy,' he states, his eyes searching her face.

She doesn't look up.

'Are you alone?' she whispers.

A curt nod. 'I told you I would be. But I'm here to explain that you have to come with me to the station. You can't think for one second that you can solve this case, as a fugitive.' His forehead wrinkles. 'Like this...' He gestures around, likely at the ridiculousness of the situation: sitting side by side in a church like clandestine spies.

Ciara glances around, still petrified that a team of officers will suddenly storm in and grab her. She has to hurry. 'Thank you for coming, but I don't have long,' she says. 'Tell me about Sally... please.'

Clarke looks away. He rubs a hand over his jaw.

'Please,' she repeats. She looks hard at him. 'What aren't you telling me?'

He meets her eyes. 'Your daughter isn't well at all, I'm afraid, Mrs Duffy.'

Ciara suppresses a whimper. 'You said to me that she was safe...'

'She was in the hospital, but I was informed this morning that late yesterday the child was taken to her aunt's house while a treatment plan is being put in place.'

Ciara lets her head fall into her hands.

'No,' she cries, and then clamps a hand over her mouth. 'Please, no.' She had been so close to her daughter. She should have gone to get her last night. It feels like she's slipping through her fingers all over again.

Clarke looks uncomfortable. 'Courtney is the wrong person,' Ciara sobs. 'She's mistrustful of hospitals and modern medicine. Sally shouldn't be with her,' she pleads.

'But you can't make those decisions for your child while you are on the run,' Clarke says gently. 'Which is why I want you to come with me to the station. Give a statement. Help your daughter. Besides, there's nobody else,' he adds, as Ciara slumps in the pew, the energy draining from her body.

'You could just be saying this to make me turn myself in,' Ciara says, but she knows Casey is right. She's completely caught between a rock and a hard place. Emerge and help Sally, and she'll end up back in prison. Or continue to try and prove she didn't kill Morgan, and then share that evidence, so she doesn't go to prison at all.

Casey's blue eyes meet hers. 'I promise you that your daughter is extremely unwell, Mrs Duffy. I found out this morning that she's been placed on a transplant list.'

'Transplant?' Ciara's hands fly to her face. 'What kind of transplant?' Her voice raises an octave.

'I'm sorry. I don't have that information,' Casey admits. He puts a hand on her shoulder. 'Listen, I have my own child, a daughter that's similar in age to Sally. Her name is Yvonne. I wouldn't lie about something like this. I promise.' He looks sincere. 'If you turn yourself in, we can try and take you to her.'

Ciara lets her tears fall, so tempted by the possibility of laying eyes on her sick child, of offering comfort. Even if it was only for a few minutes.

The dividing forces pull her in two opposite directions. Instinctively of course she'd do anything to see Sally but what then? How could she help her child if she's thrown back behind bars.

She straightens her back. 'I need to get to Sally, but in order to come back to her for good, I have to find out about what happened to Morgan,' she says, miserably but firmly. 'I need to get to Sally, but I have to clear my name.' Ciara imagines her frail daughter in that awful house in the woods where Courtney lives – Morgan's childhood home.

Courtney is a product of Morgan's unusual upbringing. They'd grown up with a devout mother and an abusive father in a remote house in the Dublin mountains where Courtney still lives. A woman suspicious of everyone and everything. A woman who believes the power of prayer will fix every problem.

'Why can't you just go and get Sally – remove her from her care. I'm here now. I'm her mother.'

Casey shakes his head. 'You are a fugitive, Mrs Duffy – you are breaking the law. You don't have the right to decide that. Since your father died, the state is responsible for Sally's care and they are in the process of trying to ensure Sally gets the help she needs.'

'But what if I prove I'm innocent? Does that change things?'

Casey considers this. 'I'm not a solicitor, Mrs Duffy, but I assure you it's a lot more complex than either of us imagines.' He moves closer to her. 'I'm sorry to say this to you so bluntly, but the bottom line is that if Sally doesn't get treatment urgently, she might not make it. And the longer you are on the run, the less likely it is that you can help her. It will take time for the state to convince Sally's aunt to bring her in for treatment, even if they mandate it. There'll be court cases... too much time will pass.' He hesitates, bites his lip. 'I'm afraid it's time Sally just doesn't have.'

Ciara is weeping quietly. 'Transplant sounds so serious,' she whispers. 'Oh Jesus, Clarke, is she going to die?'

Suddenly they aren't fugitive and captor, they are just two parents connected by similarly aged daughters.

'What should I do?' Ciara says shakily to herself, but aloud. Her tears won't stop. 'What the fuck am I supposed to do now?'

Clarke passes her a tissue and she scrubs at her eyes with it. 'Please, Mrs Duffy, the best thing you can do is to please come with me,' Casey urges. 'Together, we can try and help Sally.'

It's so tempting. He seems so genuinely sincere and willing to help. But Ciara knows that the moment she's brought to the police station, she'll be thrown back in Logan and have to wait, wait, wait for some appearance or appeal or motion. She'd never get to see Sally, not for more than a few minutes. The legal system crawled while women lost hope. She'd seen it too many times in Logan. The system had no regard for time, or gradually weakening bodies, or of all the lost moments.

Inside Logan Prison, she is useless to Sally. Out here, at least, she can fight for her. Out here, she can prove she has no business being anywhere near a prison.

As much as her heart is breaking to see Sally, she had to push forward with proving that she is not a killer.

She blows her nose and then quickly roots in her backpack and hands Casey the medical receipt for a Dr Bridges.

'I wasn't aware that Morgan was getting any kind of treatment, so this might be worth looking into,' she says.

Casey takes it from her and she watches as his eyes dart across the page.

'None of this was in his file,' he confirms.

'Another thing,' Ciara adds, her words tumbling out in haste, 'my neighbour, Aimee, I told you about her on the phone. Did you look into her?' She raises her eyes to Clarke. 'She told me she was sleeping with Morgan.'

'When did she tell you this?' Casey raises an eyebrow.

Ciara shakes her head. 'It doesn't matter when. But she said her husband Tony knew about the affair.' She glares at Casey. 'Are you writing this down?'

He pulls out his notebook.

'We can't do it like this,' he insists. 'You have to come to the station with me. I can get you a car – you still have time to minimise the damage you will do to your case when you are caught. Because you will get caught. Make a statement, let me and the team look into this for you.'

She gazes into his blue eyes – she can tell that he's an intelligent man, a kind one too. She can see he looks troubled – that he'd be the person who would urge her to do the right thing – but the right thing hadn't served her well so far.

Ciara is now comfortable operating in the margins.

She watches the woman at the back of the church unfold herself from kneeling and shift a little in the pew. She looked sad, Ciara thinks. *Inconsolable.*

Ciara glances at those lighting the candles and they have the same look on their face – of desperation, of raw hope. She knows that feeling – that push–pull of emotions.

As Clarke scribbles in his notebook, she takes in his wedding ring. 'You're married?' she says, pulling her dad's scarf tighter around her neck.

Clarke nods. 'Five years ago.' He seems like he'd be a good husband – concerned, fussing, but in a nice way. Protective. A little like her Alex. Maybe that's why she'd warmed to him.

She wants to ask Clarke if he's ever told his wife to go fuck herself. Or screamed in her face. Or called her an asshole under his breath. Of course, he hadn't. Of course, most people's loved ones don't do that.

That's not love, she reminds herself. *Sleeping with your wife's friend isn't love.*

But Ciara has been in this cycle for so long, she isn't sure of anything anymore. She isn't sure of anyone any more either.

The door to the church opens and another few visitors walk in. Ciara tenses. 'There's one other thing,' she says, rushing now, knowing she's spent too long there. She hands Casey the Post-it note with the name 'Kevin' written and 'Red Lion.' 'My dad was working on this lead the day he was killed. I found a lighter with this logo in my kitchen the night Morgan was killed.'

'I know this place,' Clarke Casey says, glancing up. 'It's known as a bit of a criminal hotspot.'

'I think my dad was trying to arrange to meet someone from there around the time he was killed,' Ciara whispers. 'What's happening with that investigation? Into my dad?'

Clarke looks awkward. 'There isn't one,' he says gently.

Ciara leans forward. 'What do you mean?'

'Your dad's death is likely going to be ruled suicide,' he says quietly.

Ciara exhales. 'This must be some kind of joke. He had a meeting with this guy that same day.' She taps the Post-it note. 'He was shot in the stomach, Casey.'

'With his own former service gun.'

Ciara spreads her hands in desperation. 'Don't you think it's strange that both my husband and my father were murdered within a few months?'

'Your father had many enemies,' Clarke agrees. 'He put a lot of people in jail, but, ultimately, his only daughter was in jail for murder. The working theory, and this isn't my case by the way, is that he couldn't handle it.'

'This is fucking crazy.' Ciara drops her head into her hands.

Footsteps behind them stop. A chill runs the length of Ciara's back. She doesn't know why but instinctively she turns around.

There's a man standing behind them. A bald man with tattoos. Next to him is another guy, also squat, but with a nose that takes over his face and long, dark hair hanging into his eyes, giving him the look of an angry scarecrow.

Clarke immediately jumps up. There's something familiar about one of the men.

The bald man takes a step forward. 'We just want to talk to Mrs Duffy,' he says in a low voice. 'We don't want any trouble.'

Ciara freezes, searching for any weapons in their hands. Are these the guys who killed her father? Or could it be something to do with her taking Sally from the Berg family? Was it all catching up to her now?

For the past ten years, she's been petrified that the Berg family would catch up with her and try to take back their daughter. But what was she supposed to have done? Left poor Sally with them? To an unknown fate? Not taken the money to help Alex?

No.

NO.

She hasn't realised she'd shouted the word out loud until the people lighting candles look around. Her voice echoes along the vaulted church roof. It feels as if even the saints in murals on the walls are staring at her expectantly.

'Now, if I could just...' Casey is saying, arms out to try and calm the escalating situation, but Ciara barrels forward, surprising the bald man, as well as herself, as she pushes into him with all her strength and starts to run out of the door of the church.

If they take her, it won't be to Logan, and it certainly won't be to find the truth.

Risking a glance over her shoulder, she sees the man has staggered backwards, both hands over his stomach protectively. Casey has leapt to his side. But Ciara is already pushing through the heavy doors, gasping for breath, searching both directions to try and decide which way is better.

She spots a pedestrian laneway to her right and starts to sprint towards it. It leads under an archway next to a bike shop. She pushes some of the parked bikes that are outside the shop over as she runs past them, trying to block the path of the bald man, now racing behind her, and gaining on her. He's shouting something at her but the blood is rushing in her ears and she's too focused on getting the hell away from him to hear.

Heart hammering, mouth dry, Ciara darts into another street as cars honk at her. Weaving through the traffic, she sees the park – St Stephen's Green. The centrepiece of this huge city park is a lake with swans, next to it is a children's playground and a pretty bandstand where people now sit sipping takeaway coffees. She pushes past a group of mothers rocking prams back and forth, who cry in indignation as she dashes past, her legs feeling as though they are on fire. A girl with her phone in a tripod dances on the grass – content creating. Ciara knows that if she can just make it to the other side of the park, she can disappear into the crowds of students who regularly spill out of the English Language school there.

She weaves past a row of benches where tired parents watch toddlers throw bread for the ducks. Ciara is glancing back to see just how far away the man is, when he grabs her.

She spins in mid-air and crashes heavily to the ground, banging her head hard on the tarmac. A concrete feeling envelopes her, and she immediately tastes blood. Her ankle has buckled beneath her too. The man is saying something to her, but everything grows foggy. *Don't faint, don't faint*, she tells herself.

Ciara feels for her backpack next to her on the ground as she crawls backwards, away from him. The bald man stands above her. Through the haze of pain and shock, she manages to pull out the gun and holds it in her shaking hands. 'No,' Ciara yells. 'Leave me alone.'

The bald man holds his hands out in a defensive gesture, clearly surprised.

Ciara's hands shake, her arms twitch. Sticky wet liquid drops into her eyes. The taste of blood. 'Back off,' she shouts, and the man starts to retreat.

She lowers the gun shakily, the world still feeling so far away. Suddenly, the bald man goes to grab her again – but Detective Clark Casey is there. He puts out his arm sidelong, and with a flick of his elbow stuns the man with a punch to the nose. Casey then turns and somehow flips the man over onto his back, even though he must weigh twice what Casey does.

Ciara takes the opportunity to scramble away, on her bottom, stuffing the gun back into her bag.

Casey crouches over the bald man. They are both talking angrily at one another, but Ciara can't process anything. There's a loud ringing in her ears. A disconnect between her and her surroundings. Everything still feels foggy and slow.

Only Casey's words echo in her ears – *Sally will die without treatment.* An unbearable statement.

A crowd starts to form around them. Ciara refuses their offers of help, shaking her head, disorientated, more frightened than she's ever been. The seriousness of her situation overwhelms her. She wants her father. She wants to be held by him while she clings to her daughter. She even wants Morgan. She wants her old life back before everything fell apart.

The moment that poor, newborn baby had died in hospital on her watch, everything had started going wrong.

Disoriented, she pulls herself to standing and lets herself melt into the crowd. While Casey is preoccupied with the man on the ground who tried to hurt her, Ciara drags herself away, tipping her fingers to her forehead, observing the blood, falling dizzily against trees and then the railings of the park as she tries to flee. She puts one excruciating step in front of the next, knowing there's only one place in the world she can go right now.

She only has one place left.

Chapter 24

By the time she sees the entrance to St Trinity's Children's Hospital, Ciara is close to fainting.

The pain in her right ankle radiates up her body and her head feels as if it's double the size. The black scarf has slipped down from where's she's tried to stem the worst of the blood from the wound on her forehead.

She leans against the concrete wall opposite the hospital and tries to formulate how she's going to do this. She needs to speak to Dr Derry Cunningham – to find out more about Sally's illness and to find out more about the man whose wife and child died in St Trinity's the week before she was framed for her husband's murder.

But as Ciara limps towards the shiny hospital entrance, she knows that she also just needs a friend, and her colleague Derry had been the closest thing to that since she'd moved back to Dublin and started working as a midwife here. Derry would know what to do, even if she had been writing a statement that rendered him negligent. He was the kind of person that always did the right thing.

St Trinity's hospital had two wings – the maternity and the children's hospital. Most of the sickest babies in the country were transferred there after complicated births or during difficult pregnancies. The building itself was huge – recently renovated, it was all curved glass and huge coloured walls that rose next to newly planted trees.

The Taoiseach had come and cut the ribbon – even though he'd overseen the massive overspend and decade-long delay. Ciara had booked in for a blow-dry for the occasion, and turned up at the drinks reception afterward with some of the other midwives. In fact, that was where she'd first met Dr Derry Cunningham.

Ciara catches a glimpse of herself in the glass reflection of the sliding doors as she drags herself towards them, trying to mop the worst of the blood away from her face. She'd been drawn to Derry's commanding presence, his amused face when she mistook him for one of the Taoiseach's press people. She'd enjoyed chatting to him as he leaned against a table, a sparkling water in his hand, his full lips strangely captivating as he explained about his work as an obstetrician. After that, she'd spotted him around more – he was hard to miss with his owlish glasses and always-busy energy.

Yes, Derry would know what to do.

Derry was calm in a crisis – even after that horrible day.

The sliding doors open and the energy changes. The reception is a hive of activity. Large pictures of Disney characters on the walls give Ciara a shuddering reminder of the murals at Logan in the visitors' centre, but here, everything is new and oversized. Ciara immediately grabs a facemask from the dispenser to the right of the reception desk and puts it on. She continues walking, trying not to wince with the effort.

She crosses the waiting area and past the small shop where concerned parents gaze distractedly at soft pastel teddy bears, their shaking fingers kneading the small bodies, their minds elsewhere, as if they need as much solace from the soft fur as the children they are buying them for.

Ciara has always felt for these people. She's seen them first-hand, like dazed zombies walking quietly down corridors, or at the chapel, sometimes hand in hand with someone, always a haunted look on their face. There were no special corridors for those who weren't celebrating the birth of a child, or clear test results. Parents passed one another, shoulder to shoulder, some ecstatic with joy, others hunched in unimaginable grief. The same corridors, the same love, just vastly different outcomes. That's the range of emotions Ciara had come across every single day at her workplace. And while her particular job meant it was mostly joy-filled, she couldn't forget the days, like with baby Archie, where the colour was leeched from life if a child never gave its first cry.

–

As Ciara reaches the doors for the stairs into the wards, she realises that she is now a parent like that. An only parent to a very sick child.

The noise of activity and the overpowering smell of fear and disinfectant almost makes her gag. Without checking to see if anyone's looking, she types a code into the door. It's reset on a daily basis. Always the initial of the day of the week followed by the date, followed by STH – St Trinity's Hospital. The door releases and Ciara tries to move as fast as she can, using the banister of the stairs to lever herself upwards. More blood drips down her face. She knows that Derry's office is located on the third floor.

She'd started spending more and more time in that office in the lead up to Morgan's death. In fact, Derry was the only one who knew about how badly Morgan had treated her. Ciara doesn't know how it came up, or why she'd ended up telling a colleague something so personal, but it had created an intimacy between them – especially when he'd jumped up, shaken his head and laid a hand gently on her arm.

'I'm here if you need me, Ciara. But please consider making an escape plan. What you are describing is emotional abuse.'

Those words again. The words she couldn't reconcile with her relationship.

Dublin was supposed to be a sanctuary for her when she'd come back. When she fled from Brighton, she never thought she'd end up in another dangerous situation, albeit for different reasons. Dr Derry's kindness that day was the beginning of a spark that had ignited between them.

'Excuse me?'

Ciara freezes.

A young junior doctor has entered the stairwell. He looks absolutely grey with exhaustion. 'May I help you?' he offers, looking in confusion at her injuries.

She looks at him, grateful for the continued use of masks in the hospital setting since Covid times. She tries to think quickly. 'I was told to come this way for X-ray,' she lies. 'The nurse put in the code and let me come this way.' She hesitates and he raises an eyebrow – unsure of the protocol perhaps. She winks. 'Fear of lifts.' She shrugs.

Relief floods the young man's face. He doesn't seem like the type to invite a fuss. He nods knowingly. 'Yeah, I'm like that with planes,' he confides, and continues down the stairs, yawning. As a midwife, Ciara was stationed at the other side of the hospital – the maternity side – and with the rotation of staff, she didn't except to see anyone she knew here. It was only Dr Derry she is familiar with from this part of the hospital.

Once she reaches the third floor, adrenaline overtakes. What if Derry isn't here? What if he takes one look at her and calls the police?

Ciara eases open the stairwell door and pokes her head out into the corridor.

It's a long, windowless corridor with four wards – two each side. To the right is the nurses' station, to the left a set of bathrooms and shower rooms for patients, a separate one for parents. Derry's office is at the opposite end – a bright carpeted room with a sofa that overlooks another well-known Dublin park.

In his letters written to her in prison, he'd mentioned that he'd been promoted to chief attending. It had surprised Ciara, especially as he'd been so close to having his licence suspended over the death of baby Archie. It turned out that her not being able to testify had gone a long way to helping Dr Derry save his job.

But Ciara had never resented that. She hadn't welcomed the idea of influencing her friend's career, even if he had dropped the ball with that one devastating case.

The bleeding from her head is getting worse as she hurries down the shiny hallway, the beeps from machines, the squeak of laminate flooring, all familiar and comforting in their own way. They were the backdrop to her days working as a midwife.

A few nurses are gathered around a computer as she eases past. There are a few parents milling around the wards and she's glad she managed to coincide her surprise visit with visiting hours.

Ciara holds her breath at Dr Derry's door, his new title written in neat silver writing. She is about to knock when she catches herself. She's on the run from prison. She's been attacked. Her head is pounding, her foot injured, her heart aching for her daughter. She has nothing left in the tank. She leans on the handle and gently pushes it open.

Derry Cunningham is sitting with his back to the door. He turns as she steps into the small office, pen poised in his hand as he writes notes.

To one side of the room are filing cabinets below a line of framed accolades hanging on the wall. On the other side are shelves full of books and a coatrack. Derry Cunningham is a meticulous surgeon but his workspace charts the other side of his personality – maverick and yes, even a bit charming. He immediately drops his pen when he sees her. His face seems to drain of blood as he takes her in.

He jumps to his feet. 'Oh, Jesus Christ, Ciara.'

Ciara stares back – she'd always thought he was quite aristocratic-looking with his gold-framed glasses, strong nose and shock of black hair. Although he's been divorced for more than five years, he's remained single, much to the delight of some of the other midwives – who joked about him being the most eligible bachelor in the hospital. Ciara hadn't focused on his looks. It was more about his presence with patients, his careful consideration of his colleagues' opinions that she'd admired most.

But when they'd found themselves on a long, quiet shift one night back when she'd first started in St Trinity's, they'd spent the time between patient visits enjoying the simplicity of each other's company – the witty remarks and interesting conversations. Ciara could almost feel the energy between them, even though they were at opposite sides of the staff area writing notes.

He'd felt it too, she knew he had, because a few days later, she found that he'd moved his shifts to match hers. Again, the conversations between them crackled with the kind of chemistry she'd have loved to have enjoyed with Morgan. But she'd also known it was a dangerous game, and Ciara had had enough of dangerous games, so she'd tried to quell the rising flirtation between them, taking his careful inquiries about her safety at home at face value.

He was just a concerned colleague.

At first.

Derry seems to recover his momentary shock and immediately crosses the room and steers her by her elbow towards the chair. Her shoulders start to shake, and the room grows blurry. 'I'm sorry,' she's repeating. 'I'm so sorry.'

Derry murmurs softly as rubs the back of his hand across her forehead, smooths back her hair. 'It's okay, Ciara. Oh, my God. I can't believe you're here. What happened to you?'

Tears roll down her cheeks. It's the first act of tenderness she's experienced in a long time.

She cries even harder. Grateful as he rummages behind her and hands her a plastic cup of water from the cooler and she drinks thirstily, every last drop.

'Sally,' she whispers, as Derry reaches into a cabinet and starts to clean her head wound gently with gauze.

'This will need stitching,' he says, frowning in concentration.

Ciara removes his hand and holds it in the air, forcing him to look at her. 'What do you know about Sally?' she insists.

'Wait,' he says. 'First tell me what you are doing here. I saw on the news that you'd... absconded.'

Ciara wants to tell her story but even her face is tired. She has no words left. 'I need to get to Sally,' she says, pushing his hands away as he tries to help her. 'Please...'

The air feels so thin suddenly. She tries to stand up but the room spins. Nausea overpowers her.

'Derry, I need to know about Sally.'

Heat rises quickly through her body, then drops. She has an overwhelming urge to throw up. Ciara claws at her neck. 'I can't breathe,' she suddenly pants, panic overwhelming her.

Derry stands, looking at her, his hands suspended in air. He takes a step back. That confuses her. Why isn't he helping her?

'Ciara,' his voices comes from somewhere.

Air will not fill her lungs. Ciara gulps, her throat tightening as she attempts to control her breathing. She starts to shake, her head aching with every judder as she bends her head forward and tries to get some oxygen into her body.

'I can't...' she attempts, flailing her arms, needing help, beads of sweat gathering on her forehead.

Derry turns back to his cabinet. He roots through it slowly as she wheezes for air.

'Please, Derry,' she implores. 'What's happening?' Amid her panic, she's wondering why Derry is so calm in the face of her overwhelm.

When he turns to her, he's holding a syringe.

Her eye widen.

Heart racing, a feeling of dread descends, low and dark and extremely frightening.

What's going on here exactly?

She opens her mouth to try to muster even one breath, but nothing happens. Her heart is a hammer, banging horribly against her chest. Pain floods her mind as Derry starts moving towards her.

Everything edges on black. Ciara can think of nothing but Sally. Of holding her daughter once more. She tries to push him away but she's got the strength of a kitten.

The fluttering in her brain grows stronger as Derry grips her, and with strong unyielding hands, injects her.

She looks up at him mutely, shock and horror written across her face.

He doesn't meet her eyes.

She'd trusted that her friend Derry would take care of her.

'What are you doing?' she tries to say, but Derry is staring straight ahead, biting his lip. 'What are you doing?' she tries to repeat, but the world has started to swirl.

'I'm so sorry, Ciara,' she thinks he says. Or has she imagined him speaking? It's as if she's behind glass, everything taking on a dream-like quality.

Ciara feels Derry's arms pull her to standing. She's aware of being half dragged, half carried down a set of the emergency stairs. Every step hurts. Her brain doesn't seem to work. The next thing she's aware of is that she's in a basement car park.

She rests her lolling head against the seat of a car and lets herself be taken over by the movements as Derry navigates his Mercedes SUV out beyond the car park barrier, and over the speedbumps. She closes her eyes. Every bit of strength flows out of her body.

As she loses consciousness, she wonders if she might be dying.

Or being killed.

Chapter 25

Open your eyes.

A crack of light makes Ciara wince. Her eyelids flutter, heavy and unwilling.

It's too bright. She is completely disorientated. A jolt of panic hits. She remembers Sally is sick. She remembers prison. Maybe she's back there?

A wave of dread pulls her back under.

'Open your eyes, Ciara.'

A male voice, sharp and urgent.

It's Derry.

Hands grip her shoulders but she tries to push him away. He hadn't helped her. He'd hurt her.

'Ciara, are you okay?'

Derry's voice cuts through her confusion. She struggles to open her eyes. She's in a bright room, a bedroom with a light on. The world around her spins, the edges blurred.

'Can you stand?'

Ciara blinks at him as she tries to engage her brain. Derry is sitting next to her, his hand holding hers. He looks exhausted. Next to the bed is a lamp, a jug of water, a sick bag.

'My backpack…' she croaks, her fingers clawing at the air.

'Shhh, it's okay, Ciara. Everything is okay. You are at my apartment.' Derry strokes her hair out of her face.

Ciara touches her throbbing head and comes in contact with a bandage.

'I've stitched your cut,' he says softly, helping her sit up. 'It might hurt a little.' She is suddenly so thirsty. He holds a glass to her lips.

Then she remembers. 'You injected me,' she whispers, fear fraying the edges of her exhausted mind.

'You were having a panic attack,' Derry explains, refilling the glass and handing it back to her. She gulps the whole thing down. 'I was afraid you would attract attention because you were verging on hysteria. I gave you a sedative. I'm sorry, Ciara. I couldn't risk you shouting out. I was trying to protect you.'

She takes some deep breaths but a wave of nausea crashes over her. Can she really trust him?

He hasn't turned her into the police, but had she really been *that* hysterical? Bad enough to drug? Ciara surveys the room. It's not like she has too much choice about matters. She's at his mercy here. It's a large room with floor-to-ceiling windows overlooking other apartment blocks. The blind is half pulled down, but it's dark outside. She can see other people in their homes, eating dinner, ironing, Christmas trees twinkling. She's always liked apartment life – it has given her comfort, especially in Brighton. There's something so safe about being able to live your life while watching others live theirs – the shawl of monotony and ordinariness a balm to her own extraordinary situation.

The bedroom is hotel-like, opulent – a large double bed with dark sheets, oak wardrobes, an ensuite, modern art on the walls. She remembers Derry told her he lived alone after his wife had left a few years before.

She lets her head land back against the pillow and falls back asleep.

–

When Ciara wakes again she makes her way unsteadily to the bathroom and shakily splashes water on her face, trying not to put weight on her right ankle. In the bedroom, she pulls on an oversized sweater and tracksuit bottoms that Derry has left on her bed, and she shuffles towards the kitchen where Derry is at the cooker stirring something that smells incredibly good.

'What time is it?' She sits at the marble island where there's a fruit bowl with apples, a few newspapers with the sports pages opened, a half-opened bottle of red wine. The TV is on in the corner, some police procedural from Netflix she's probably seen. Derry is wearing a shirt and jeans. He's barefoot.

'It's after six.'

He sets a plate of something steaming in front of her. 'Here, eat something.'

And though her entire body aches, her head throbs and she has a million things swirling through her head, Ciara eats every last noodle, relishing feeling sated for the first time in days. She accepts the glass of wine he offers too.

He watches her, his own glass in his hand, the curl of a smile on his face as he leans against one of the slick kitchen cabinets. 'I'm really sorry I had to do that,' he says. 'Back at Trinity's.'

She shrugs. 'Better than getting caught,' she offers. But a niggle of doubt remains whether she can really trust him.

'So, what do we do now?' he ventures, and it occurs to Ciara that he seems a little unsure of himself. 'I'm here for you, Ciara, you know that, but after everything that happened, I can't be involved in this. I can't risk my job.'

He looks pained.

The wine has helped her relax. 'I know, Derry. I know.' She exhales, rolling up the long sleeves of the sweater he'd given her. 'I needed to get out of Logan to find out who killed Morgan. And who killed my father...' Her voice breaks. 'And Sally is alone. She's very sick. Derry, I had to do something.'

Derry sits next to her.

His face is close to hers. His kindness is intoxicating. She realises how much she's missed him.

'Yes, Sally is a very ill little girl.'

'Tell me,' she commands, attempting to push his out-stretched hand away – but he clasps her hand in his. His touch is electric.

'Ciara. We can't treat her. Her aunt won't give permission so the state will have to get a court order.'

Ciara shakes her head.

'That could take weeks.'

'Tell me what she needs,' Ciara says, the words lodging in her throat, choking her. 'Tell me why she needs a transplant.' She finds it hard to say the word.

'Sally has severe aplastic anaemia, or SAA. It's a condition where her bone marrow doesn't produce enough blood cells.' He gently squeezes her hand between both of his. 'It can be treated with blood transfusions and medications, but so far Courtney refuses.'

'What's the prognosis?' Ciara stifles a sob.

Derry sighs. 'Without treatment, severe aplastic anaemia can cause complications from infections, bleeding and organ failure.' He shifts uncomfortably. 'Ciara, the average survival time is reduced ranging from a few months to a couple of years depending on the severity and access to care.'

'Can it be cured?' Ciara asks in a small voice.

'Currently, Sally's at risk from strokes and seizures, and renal damage is a risk too, due to decreased oxygen supply. Sally's immune system is weakened, which makes it difficult to fight off even minor infections.'

'That would explain her exhaustion...' says Ciara, explaining to Derry how Sally couldn't shake the virus going around when school started.

'Exactly that.'

'But can it be cured?' she insists.

'Yes, but she needs a bone marrow transplant or what we call a stem cell transplant.'

'But how?' Ciara stammers. She yanks her hand away from his. 'How did this happen? Is it genetic?'

'An inherited gene mutation is possible,' he explains. 'And that's most likely, in Sally's case.'

'Did you see her?' she whispers.

Derry nods slowly. 'I studied her chart and stayed by her bed whenever I could, Ciara. I knew it's what you would have wanted. I told her, though she was mostly sleeping, that her mum loved her and that I was a messenger for her so she didn't feel so alone.' Derry looks emotional and Ciara has never felt so grateful. She squeezes his hand, tears rolling down her cheeks. Sally was so pale and not herself those last few weeks before Ciara ended up in Logan. She should have gotten it checked out.

Ciara accepts the tissue Derry hands her.

'So, is she on a list?'

Derry hesitates and Ciara's heart sinks.

'They wouldn't just let her die on some waiting list, right?'

'Ciara... I'm sure you know the importance of genetics in these cases. For children, a bone marrow donor that's a relative is often considered to be the ideal,' he explains. 'It's for compatibility. Relatives, particularly siblings or parents, are more likely to be a close genetic match. It reduces the risk of rejection. A closer genetic match also means the child's immune system is less likely to attack the new marrow – a common complication in transplants. Studies have shown there are better... survival rates.'

Ciara buries her head in her hands. They are sitting on the kitchen stools opposite one another, knees touching.

'Oh god. It's too much to take.'

He lays a hand on her head. 'But the good news is that now with you here, Sally has a much better chance. We can see if you are a good match. They'd have sent for you in prison either way, but it's only been in the past couple of days that she got her formal diagnosis.' Derry raises her chin. 'Now she has a really strong shot, Ciara.'

But Ciara shakes her head. It is yet another cruel trick the world is playing on her. She's been running from Sally's blood relatives since the day she'd stolen her from them. And now she might have to pursue them instead, in order to save Sally.

But Derry doesn't know any of that. Nobody in the world does, now that Jimmy is dead.

Derry gathers her into his arms. She rests her face against his chest, sobbing. He strokes her hair.

'You've been through so much,' he says.

She thinks of Sally lying pale and weak in that awful place Courtney owns in the mountains, waiting for her.

Waiting for her to help her.

Derry is right. It's too much to bear alone. 'I need to get to her. Can you take me Derry, please?' Tears roll down her face. 'Can you take me to her?'

Derry gazes at her sadly. 'I can't, Ciara. I'm so sorry.'

'I need to get to Sally.'

'I know, but you can't do anything for her there. You need to come into the hospital and get tested to see if you are a match. That's how you can help her. And you can't do that while you are a fugitive, Ciara.'

She knows he's right. He's always been right. But what he doesn't know is that it's impossible that she's a match. Sally isn't biologically hers.

He pulls her towards him and holds her against his body in a hug. 'It will be okay, Ciara,' he murmurs into her hair, but all she can do is cry as if her heart is going to break.

'You didn't reply to my letters,' he says, as he strokes her back. 'I wrote to you almost every day at first, telling you I knew you were innocent, but you never replied.'

'I couldn't let anyone know about us,' she whispers back. 'I couldn't risk having it come out during a trial.'

It was on an overnight shift when Derry had first kissed her, after a particularly nasty fight with Morgan when he'd brought up her weight gain. Derry had noticed Ciara was not her usual bubbly self while on shift. They'd gone to the hospital roof where there was a makeshift garden and Ciara had confided in Derry about the problems in her marriage. It had been just four months before Morgan was killed.

'You need to leave him,' Derry had urged. But nothing in life was that straightforward. Sometimes Ciara wished Morgan had just punched her in the face. It would have been easier to figure out she was in a toxic relationship rather than having to rely on researching on the internet and Googling 'Am I in an abusive relationship?'

She had felt foolish and weak and unable to escape the situation she found herself in. Derry had made her feel beautiful, competent and strong. It had been a beautiful, balmy summer evening and as she'd stood there, telling him about the wreck of her relationship, he'd stepped closer, bending his head to find her lips. And she'd let him. She'd let the tension that had been building between them for months spill over, craving tenderness, comfort, touch.

He'd moved his lips to her neck, gently trailing kisses down towards her collarbone and she had leaned into it, shivering at the first physical contact with another person in almost a year. A soft moan as his hand slid under her jumper. Her breath hitching somewhere in her throat.

'Is this okay?'

She hadn't wanted him to stop. Ciara had nodded, pulling him closer – forcing herself for once not to think, but to just surrender to this urgent desire.

He had kissed her deeply then, his arms wrapped tight around her body – and then she'd jolted away, frightened by the intensity of her feelings. Frightened by the idea of Morgan if he found out. But it was impossible to stop what had started.

'I have to be careful with you, Ciara,' Derry had said that night 'You are in a vulnerable position. I never want to think I'm taking advantage of that.' He'd sounded so worried when he'd said that, so caring, but she'd pointed out that his presence made her feel less alone in the world, more cherished, and that couldn't be a bad thing.

They'd caught moments here and there when they could, even booked a hotel room one night. But after she'd been arrested, Ciara had been petrified information would come out about her affair – she wouldn't be able to defend herself against the perception of what it would look like if it emerged she had been spending nights at the Four Seasons while her husband ended up dead in his marital bed.

After all, it was already a trial by media. She was a the 'butcher bitch' who was locked up for knifing her husband to death. It didn't matter that she hadn't done it, or that he was a cruel, cruel man to her towards the end. That part wasn't as sexy. It didn't sell as many papers as the narrative of a murderous nurse. But she couldn't let them add 'adulterer' to their slam list.

So she'd ignored Derry's letters. She'd tried to push him out of her mind as she navigated her new life at Logan.

But now, she is here with him, curled up in his apartment as she cries for her daughter, and he tries to console her with kind words and sweet promises that everything will be all right. 'I'm here now. Everything will be okay, Ciara.'

And she wants to believe him.

She wants with all her heart to believe him.

Chapter 26

That night, after Derry has helped her to bed and given her more medication for her pain, Ciara starts to talk and doesn't stop. She's known this type of trauma response before – the need to state aloud every detail to make it real, to ground oneself or perhaps steel against the shock of a situation. She'd never spoken aloud about the trauma of what had happened. Not even to the prison psychologist. After all, she knew that her notes could be requested by the prosecutor and read aloud to the court. Another unbearable betrayal. So as Derry holds her hand, Ciara starts to talk and as she does, some of the weight she's been carrying lifts ever so slightly. Derry is a good listener. He traces his thumb up and down her hand as she lets everything out in a jumble of words.

She describes the fear of searching her house the night she saw someone on the baby monitor app. 'Every time I lifted the sheet or looked under a bed, I thought I was going to be murdered,' she whispers, eyes to the ceiling. 'I felt so responsible for both the girls.' She shudders, and Derry's grip grows tighter. 'They were so vulnerable... We all were.'

'But it was when I woke up and felt someone in the bed next to me that I can't stop thinking about.' Ciara can feel her heart rate shoot up as she speaks but she needs to share the burden of what she's been through.

Derry keeps on stroking her hand. A silent support of all she needs to say.

'He was so...' She gasps for air. 'He was so sad-looking,' she finally says, crying. 'Everyone asked me about how gruesome it was, but I just remember thinking that his face looked so sad. He didn't even look like himself. He looked softer somehow, in death.' Her voice is thick with tears.

'I felt so sorry for him in that moment.' Ciara turns her head to look at Derry. 'Even though I hated him sometimes.'

'That he lost so much?' Derry asks gently.

'That he didn't know how to love,' she whispers.

'But then it was hard because I was so angry at him the last time we'd spoken. I'd practically wished him dead.' Ciara glances at him again. 'So I also felt a huge amount of guilt. As well as confusion and grief and… relief.'

'Of course you felt all those things, Ciara,' Derry says. 'How could you not? And fear and isolation, especially when you were accused of murdering him.'

Ciara nods, and fresh tears fall. 'They were suggesting I had been responsible for taking a life. Everyone thought I took a life… Can you imagine how that felt?'

Derry nods quietly. 'I can.'

Ciara remembers baby Archie and his mother and how Derry feels responsible for it.

He clears his throat. 'It's not the same because in that case, I was responsible. But I live with that feeling every single day.'

Ciara knows Derry is eaten up with guilt over the loss of that baby because he delayed the C-section. 'We are all just human,' Ciara says, but it feels inadequate for the magnitude of what they are talking about. 'When I was in Logan, looking around at that waiting room, it struck me how much these mistakes cost us. Cost children too.' Derry hands her a tissue and she blows her nose. 'One the first day Sally came to visit me in prison, she wanted to hug me, but I had to ask for permission, and they said no. Try explaining to your child she can't hug her mother.' Ciara shakes her head. 'And everywhere I looked in that room there were mothers and sisters and wives just crying out for some love or affection or validation or forgiveness or compassion, and none of it was given. And those children who had to be restrained in case they passed drugs to their mothers through their hugs, what will they look for when they are older? What scars will those circumstances inflict on them? What scars will Sally have from seeing me in that place? Unable to be a mother to her…' Her voice cracks.

There are no answers to the slipstream of inequality at Logan, to that which is going on around her. A cycle born of reduced opportunities, and reduced understanding, leading to daughters and mothers caught up in the same warped system, resulting in entire families experiencing the same circumstances time and again.

She thinks about Paula whose older sister had left Logan just a few weeks before Paula came in. How to stop that cycle? Who was going to stop it?

Ciara starts to drift off as she opens up to Derry about some of what she experienced at Logan. She is never going to be the same person again, that is without a doubt. But for the first time in a long time, Ciara feels heard. Less alone.

Derry had eventually promised he'd help get her to Sally in the morning. She's not sure how long Derry sits there next to her, holding her hand, listening to her sobs, but she finally falls into a deep sleep.

Where a tiny glimmer of hope begins to float.

Chapter 27

When she opens her eyes, Derry isn't beside her. The room is bright and she's groggy from sleep. On the bedside locker is a hurriedly scribbled note from Derry:

> *Got called in for an emergency C-section. I wanted to let you sleep. I'll call you later this morning about getting you to Sally.*
> *X Derry*

She slips from beneath the duvet, gathers her leggings and *Friends* hoodie that Derry had washed, and dresses quickly.

Derry had warned her last night that she was pushing herself too hard: 'Ciara, you need to rest,' he'd advised her after redressing her wound and adding antiseptic cream. 'Lay low, at least for a few days. Your escape is all over the news.'

But she had to get to Sally. She didn't have the luxury of time on her side.

The digital clock on the oven tells her it's just after nine a.m., and she feels a lot more refreshed than she has in days. And still more hopeful. She takes a glass of water from the kitchen tap and spreads out the documents from her backpack on the kitchen island as she waits for Derry to return.

She takes out one of the iPhones and charges it. The Nokia has a series of messages from Clarke Casey when she powers it on. Ten missed called too.

'I can't protect you, Ciara. You had a gun in the park today which makes you appear dangerous to the public. It's escalated things. Let me take you in. It looked as if you were injured. Please. I can come and get you wherever you are. It's for the best.'

There are a few more in a similar vein urging her to contact the police incident room number. Then there's one that makes her sit up.

'I did some digging and discovered that the Kevin your dad was supposed to be meeting the night he died was Kevin Bradshaw who frequents the Red Lion pub. Kevin is a known informant. But he's been in jail for the past two years so it couldn't have been him your dad was meeting so someone may have been posing as him to get to your dad. Another contact I have in that place admitted that someone came in asking about a termination job they needed doing just before Morgan's murder. I'm tracking down CCTV.'

Ciara rubs her eyes and then turns off that phone. If someone was inquiring about a murderer for hire, and Casey got footage of them, it might point them in the direction of who killed Morgan. Or Jimmy. Just one bit of footage could give her the doubt she needs to plant in the prosecutor's case.

She considers calling her solicitor but decides against it. She has to have something concrete to give his team first. She makes herself a coffee from Derry's fancy frothing machine and pads back to the kitchen stool.

Her head still aches and her ankle is tender but the idea of seeing her daughter sends a fizzle of excitement through her. Her heart aches to hold Sally.

She's just finishing the last dregs of her coffee when the phone in the apartment rings. She answers and remains silent.

'Ciara.' Derry's voice immediately soothes. 'It's me. How are you feeling?'

'Holding up,' she answers, taking a look at some of the photos stuck to his fridge. 'I'm just going through some of the documents here.'

'I also managed to get Courtney Duffy's landline for you.'

Her heart soars as she writes down the number he gives her.

'Thank you so much. When will you be back?'

Ciara hears the smile in his voice. 'I'm just finishing up here but I've another patient to see. I don't think it will be until later this afternoon but I'll hurry back.'

With trembling fingers, Ciara dials Courtney's number. She needs to hear that Sally is okay and to urge Courtney to bring her back for treatment. She wants more than anything else to hear her daughter's voice. She hasn't heard that gorgeous lisp since Sally visited her in Logan over a month ago.

Ciara checks the date suddenly as the number rings in her ear. It's 24 December. Christmas Eve. Imagine if she could be reunited with Sally this Christmas somehow?

Butterflies dance in her belly as she wills the phone to pick up, picturing the small shabby bungalow in the heart of the Dublin mountains.

She can see in her mind's eye the phone in the hallway by the front door. She'd only been to Glenavon a handful of times since she'd met Morgan. His childhood home wasn't a happy place growing up, he'd admitted. But hopefully Sally was being taken care of by Courtney. Even if Courtney Duffy was a little batty, she'd always been fond of her step-niece.

It rings out. A pang of acute disappointment floods through Ciara.

She hangs up and tries three more times before giving up, planning to call again later. But now that she knows how serious Sally's condition is, there's a new urgency to her situation.

Derry, under serious probing from Ciara, had admitted to her that every day Sally wasn't in hospital was seriously damaging her health.

Helplessness overwhelms her.

There had to be something else she could find out. She turns her attention to the phones lined up, charging in front of her.

One of the iPhones has a cover on it she doesn't recognise. She turns it on and waits for it to illuminate. The screen saver is of a pretty woman on a beach, laughing. Was Morgan having an affair with this woman too? Ciara goes through the camera roll. There seems to be a lot deleted from the phone but of those left, there are a lot of the same women. Ciara clicks into the Gmail icon and the account is for someone called Bill. Why does Morgan have someone else's phone? She searches for more information and comes across an order for flowers sent to someone called Lana Naughton. The address isn't far from here. Could this woman know something about Morgan or who this Bill person is?

Ciara looks at the clock. It's only 9:45 a.m. and Derry won't be back to take her to Sally until after lunchtime. She can't sit still, just waiting.

Ciara looks at the phone again and runs a hand across her face, second-guessing herself. Is she grasping? She gets her piece of scrap paper and writes down her new list.

Dr Bridges: Why was Morgan going for genetic testing?

Then she writes: *Red Lion Pub*. Did this Kevin person that her dad was supposed to be meeting on the day he was shot have something to do with Morgan's murder? Who was pretending to be the informer? Maybe the CCTV Clarke Casey has requested from the pub will offer some clue as to who was trying to hire a hit man. She wonders if the bald man with the tattoos is that person. She knows central to the prosecution's case is a financial motive – that she would stand to gain a lot from Morgan's life assurance when he died. Was someone perhaps trying to frame her for Morgan's death and then take whatever money came her way?

She writes down the thing she fears most. *The Berg family*. Are they involved in some way because they want Sally back?

Finally, she writes: *Aimee* and the word *affair*. Clarke has promised her he'd look into it. Now a new question. Why did Morgan have someone else's phone, and who is Lana?

Had he been living a lie all these years? Was that why he'd been so horrible to Ciara towards the end? Did this woman have something to do with his death?

Frustrated and irritated, Ciara tries Courtney's number once more, but it rings out again. She sees the bin trucks outside making jerky staccato stops at every block entrance and makes a decision.

A new feeling has descended on her – indignation. What a fool she'd been the whole way through her marriage.

She sees that Lana Naughton lives on the north coast of Dublin in a small port known for its excellent fish restaurants. She remembers Morgan taking her and Sally there one Sunday for a fish and chips supper. That memory, like many of her memories recently, takes on new nuance, now.

Has her whole life been built on lies and falsehoods? Was any of it real?

As she gathers her belongings and writes Derry a note, she watches people in the apartments opposite – blinds rising, window movement, kids milling about.

'Who the fuck are you, Lana Naughton?' Ciara whispers to herself as she hauls on her backpack, making sure her gun is still there. 'And what did you do to my husband?'

With the address from the Gmail flowers delivery carefully written down, she limps towards the door. It shouldn't take her more than about an hour to get there and back.

A fine rain darkens the concrete as she limps out of Derry's apartment door and into the freezing morning. Ciara is so focussed on finding Lana and figuring out what to do next that she doesn't notice a black car slowly trailing her as she slips in and out of the jagged shadows.

Chapter 28

Ciara stands outside the front of the pretty house with its clean, strong lines, huge glass windows and metallic number eleven screwed to the wall.

Lana Naughton's house. The woman whose picture is all over the phone Morgan had in his possession.

The winter air is tissue-soft.

There's a trampoline to the right of the front garden, its safety net slightly torn from use. A child's scooter lies on its side beneath it, a layer of frost giving everything a milky, ethereal vibe.

A child.

Ciara feels loose somehow, a little overwrought, as if anything could happen.

The gun in the bag makes her feel braver than she might otherwise. And a little bit dangerous.

If this woman Lana has anything to do with Morgan's murder, Ciara prefers to have it within reach.

The taxi driver had dropped her off a few doors down, just after eleven a.m., pleasantly surprised by the crisp fifty-euro note she'd handed him for the twenty-minute journey to the other side of Dublin Bay.

'Merry Christmas,' he'd called cautiously after her, perhaps not expecting an answer after the entire journey in silence, the passenger's head bent low.

Ciara takes in the twinkling Christmas tree in the front room of the house, the bicycle with a basket on the front leaning against the porch. A picture of a perfect family life.

Bitterness creeps in. It's everything she thought she'd had before the incident with Morgan.

She finds herself growing angrier about the fact that someone else might have taken it all from her.

Ciara tries to hold her emotions in check, but since she'd surrendered herself to Derry in those few hours, a floodgate of feelings has opened up in her. If she's being honest with herself, what's coming out is overwhelming. Holding everything together had kept her upright, now she feels as if she's unravelling.

Ciara slowly pushes open the white swinging gate and pads around the side of the house. She just needs to get a feel for this situation. To ask this woman some questions. It might be entirely innocent, but Ciara's gut is telling her something else is going on.

Around the back of the house is a small, neat garden with astro turf, a set of kids' swings, a little playhouse and a built-in fire-pit.

Again, a surge of something venomous overtakes her. Sally should have been playing innocently like this in her own home.

Logically, Ciara knows she cannot invent a parallel universe where everything would have been fine if Morgan hadn't died, but right now she's agitated. She's lost everything.

She's resentful.

Vengeful.

Ciara is sick of people taking advantage of her – it's happened her whole damn life. Even Derry hadn't been honest with her about his feelings until she was behind bars. But she has come too far to walk away now. She has to keep going if she is ever going to find the truth and make her way back to Sally.

On a whim, she tries the back sliding door of the little house.

She just wants to see if this Lana person knows anything about her dead husband. Or why he had pictures of her on a phone.

The door slides gracefully, and silently, open.

Ciara steps gingerly into the warm kitchen. The house is sleeping. It's the Christmas school holidays, and she imagines any mother might try to take Christmas Eve off work.

The phone she's been using to communicate with Detective Inspector Clarke buzzes in her pocket on vibrate mode but she cuts it off and powers it down, cursing herself she'd left it on.

Ciara slides the door shut gently behind her.

The curiosity that compels her forward is as powerful as a magnet.

On the fridge there's a paper plate painted in brown with black antlers and a red reindeer nose bobble made out of wool. 'Lacey

Naughton' is written in sensible teacher's black pen beneath. A box of Rice Krispies rests on the cream kitchen counter.

She stops, stretching her listening. The sound of a TV comes from the next room. Ciara tiptoes towards it and peers through the glass doors that connects the living room and kitchen. A small girl sits sprawled across the sofa, wearing colourful pyjamas. Her legs dangle over the seat rest.

On the floor is a bowl of milk with a spoon resting in it – a few lone Rice Krispies float at the top. The child watches cartoons, a half-smile on her face.

She's completely unaware of Ciara standing behind her.

In another life, it could be Sally lying there. Ciara wants to reach out to her. To touch the child. As if in some weird way, it would close the gap between her and Sally. She wonders for a second if she's the victim or the perpetrator. After all, she's a stranger who has just broken into someone else's house.

There's a sudden thud from upstairs and Ciara breaks from her trance. She lowers her hand and quickly retreats from the living room, creeping out of the kitchen door and back around the side of the house.

She takes a deep breath and rings the doorbell.

Her fingers are shaking as she hears footsteps thunder down the stairs.

What the hell is she doing here?

What's she supposed to say?

An older child opens the door. He's about eleven, wearing a snowman onesie, his face sleep-swollen. He blinks at her.

Ciara rights herself. 'Eh, sorry, is your mum here?'

The boy shouts 'MUM!' over his shoulder so loudly that Ciara winces.

'One second,' a female voice calls in the distance.

'Come in, I guess.' The boy shrugs, leaving her in the hallway as he retreats into the kitchen to join his sister on the couch.

Ciara loiters in the hallway, avoiding the hall mirror. There's an overflowing coatrack smothered with parkas and raincoats; a dark coat hangs lower, that looks as if it belongs to a man. For a second, Ciara's stomach lurches. What if she has all this wrong? What if this family has nothing to do with hers?

Maybe she's losing her mind completely.

She's just about to pick up a family photo that sits on the hall table alongside keys and coins, when a woman appears at the top of the stairs.

It's the woman from the pictures on the phone Morgan had: Lana Naughton. But this version of her is wearing a faded pink bathrobe and her hair is a mess of fuzzy blonde. Without makeup she looks slightly erased.

'Oh, hello—?' she says, a question in her voice. After all it's Christmas Eve, and Ciara is now a stranger inside her home. 'Everything okay?'

Still no plan.

'Hi.' Ciara smiles, putting on her friendliest voice. 'I'm one of the mums at Lacey's school,' she lies.

Lana's face relaxes momentarily, but she's still confused.

Ciara sees Lana's eyes dart to her backpack.

'Ah, okay,' she decides. 'Come in, come in.'

Ciara waits for her to descend the stairs and follows Lana through to the kitchen.

'Coffee?' she asks politely, but it's clear she's concerned with this strange morning call. 'Sorry, I don't know your name—?'

'No, thanks,' Ciara declines, feeling increasingly awkward. How to change gear from this to 'Were you having an affair with my dead husband?'

'I'm… Sally.' Ciara stretches out her arms self-consciously, like she's yawning. 'All set for Christmas?' she starts.

But Lana, who has poured herself a coffee from the percolating jug, has turned back around to face her. 'I'm sorry to seem rude, Sally, but is there a problem with Lacey or something?'

Of course, a mother's mind would go straight for the most obvious. A disgruntled parent is the conclusion Ciara may have jumped to herself in this situation.

'What did you say your daughter's name was?'

Ciara hesitates. She opens her mouth and closes it again.

It's enough to trigger alarm bells in the woman's mind.

'Excuse me,' Lana says, her fingers twitching nervously on the mug of coffee in her hands. 'I'll just call my partner down.'

Lana has moved towards the hallway. 'Darling?' she calls, but even Ciara hears the note of fear in her voice.

Ciara holds out her hands to try and keep the situation under control. 'Okay, I'm not here about a child,' she admits. 'It's just that I found some pictures on my husband's phone.' Lana's eyes widen. 'And I think they were from you.'

It's Lana's turn to gawp. 'Are you being serious?' Lana starts to say. Her concern has turned to anger.

'Well, it's not his phone, it's someone else's. Someone called Bill.'

There are heavy footsteps on the stairs. Ciara knows she should just leave this place. Leave this family alone.

This is lunacy.

'This is crazy,' Lana mirrors.

Ciara admits defeat. She starts for the front door. What was she even thinking, stalking someone, breaking into their home? With a gun.

'Mummy?' a little voice says, and Ciara hears Lana bark at her daughter.

'Lacey, not now. Go back to the living room.'

The air is thick with something tense – it crackles with it. Ciara is suddenly horrified she's brought this awful energy into the family's lovely home.

Lana follows closely behind her into the narrow hallway as Ciara fumbles with the door latch. She needs to get out of there immediately.

'Who are you?' the woman says sharply. 'What do you want from us?'

The steps on the stairs grow closer. Ciara's back is to everyone. She doesn't want a scene. The fucking door won't open.

'I'm calling the police,' Lana threatens.

'Sorry, sorry,' Ciara whispers, the latch finally coming undone. Lana's partner is now behind her. She can feel his presence. Ciara tugs the door open, her entire body tingling.

'What do you want from us?' Lana cries again.

Ciara swings around desperately and she's suddenly face to face with the man on the stairs.

Her breath hitches in her throat. She cannot move. She's paralysed in utter shock.

It's Morgan.

It's her husband.

And he's very much alive.

Chapter 29

Ciara runs out onto the driveway in a blind panic, the world around her spinning.

Morgan?

Morgan is *alive?*

But she'd watched him die.

She'd seen him dead, at least.

The murder scene flashes through her mind as she stumbles onto the roadway. The puddle of blood, the knife embedded in his chest, those lifeless eyes. You couldn't fake that. The paramedics were there. They'd declared him dead.

How was this possible? Perhaps she was seeing things. For the first time in her life Ciara is genuinely frightened by her confusion. Had she lost her mind completely?

She runs without thinking about the direction she's going in. Tears sting her eyes and she pulls out the Nokia, feeling as if she's in a nightmare that she's bound to wake up from.

It immediately vibrates. She presses the answer button, her breath coming in ragged sobs as she tries to find the direction of Derry's apartment. It's Detective Inspector Clarke Casey.

'Ciara, thank god. Are you okay?'

Ciara breathes heavily into the receiver. She has no words.

'Where are you?' Clarke demands.

She cannot speak.

'Ciara, I'm going through the paperwork needed to get Dr Bridges to hand over results of the tests Morgan had carried out. But it's not simple to obtain medical records. It could take weeks.'

Ciara shakes her head. 'Clarke, I've just seen the man I'm accused of murdering.' She almost laughs because everything is so ridiculous. 'I've just seen Morgan,' she repeats.

Clarke is silent. 'What did you just say?'

'Morgan is here in Dublin. He's alive.'

More silence. Then: 'I'm afraid I'm not sure what you are saying,' Clarke admits. 'But I wanted to tell you that we just got the CCTV from the Red Lion pub. The person who went in the week before Morgan's murder and who was asking for a hit for hire... well, and I'm sorry to tell you this, but it was... Morgan himself.'

Ciara blinks. Nothing makes any sense.

She turns down another avenue. Everywhere looks the same around here. Homogenised houses; clones of one another. The sense of order everywhere is so isolating when she's in disarray. She has crossed so many lines already since walking out of Logan. Theft, criminal damage, assault. She's done some terrible things.

Christmas lights dazzle at every turn, assaulting her with their tacky faux cheer.

'I've also decided to run forensics on your dad's car after we spoke. Morgan's DNA was found on the gun.'

'This is what I'm telling you, Casey. Morgan was still alive when he killed my father. He knew my dad used someone called Kevin as an informant, so he must have gone and posed as him. He *is* still alive.'

Could that mean that Morgan most likely killed her father?

Jesus Christ. That meant that Morgan wasn't a poor dead victim this whole time, Morgan was a very much alive killer.

But how?

'I saw him dead, Clarke. We both did. Didn't we? Oh god, what is happening to me? Tell me we saw Morgan dead.' For a moment the Detective Inspector doesn't answer. Ciara feels like she's spiralling further away from reality. 'Clarke?' she shouts into the phone.

But it's Clarke's next four words that bring her back. They validate the fact that that she's not crazy. 'I know we did. But there's no way your husband is still alive. I was there the night he died, remember?'

She remembers what Clarke had told her the first time they'd met in her kitchen: 'When I build a case, Mrs Duffy, I forget everything I'm told,' he'd promised her. 'I ignore all the agendas. I start from scratch and build it from the ground up, only with facts. I always keep in mind that the simplest explanation is usually the best.' She remembers that he'd leaned forward then. 'My job is to tell the story that someone somewhere doesn't want to tell.'

She doesn't know what's happening but having Clarke on her side helps.

'You have to believe me,' she insists.

'Ciara.' Clark Casey's voice in her ear calls urgently. 'Where are you now?'

Ciara turns to check if Lana or Morgan are following her. It's that moment that she spots the black car. The same one that was outside the hostel.

She freezes.

The car stops.

She can see the bald man's face behind the driving wheel. They lock eyes.

She's still holding the phone up to her ear. A new idea hits her with such force that there's a roil of nausea in her stomach. Maybe what she's about to do might make up for the terrible things she'd done in her life. It's a mad idea. But it might be her last chance to tell the truth. It might be Sally's only hope.

'Clarke,' she says, her voice shaking with emotion. 'I have a story. A story I didn't want to ever tell.'

'Ciara, where are you? What's happening?'

'But I think I have to now,' she says softly. 'I think you need to know my story.' Ciara takes a step towards the black car. The bald man gets out.

'Tell me,' Clarke urges. 'Tell me where you are, Ciara. I'll send a car. Please, Ciara. I can help you.'

'Maybe...' Ciara continues, 'maybe you can help me save Sally's life, Clarke. My story is about my daughter. It's about a little girl who was once called Rosie.'

Baby Rosie. Taken from her family home when she was just ten days old.

'Sally is Rosie Berg, the Brighton Baby,' Ciara admits. 'And it was me who took her.'

Clarke's shocked silence tells her all she needs to know.

That case had made international headlines. Angela and Roger Berg had made appeals every year on their daughter's birthday.

Baby stealer.

Butcher.

She remembers Morgan's last words to her under his breath before he'd left for the airport.

Bitch.

Ciara is so many things. And now she has to do the bravest thing of all.

She has to make sure she saves Sally. Otherwise, what has all this been for?

She hangs up the phone to Clarke and, narrowing her eyes, she walks straight towards the bald man.

Chapter 30

The Brighton Baby case, a decade ago, was all anyone talked about. Ciara had even joined in the conversations, expressing shock and anger at the missing child, even though all the while baby Rosie, now renamed Sally, was at home in her and Alex's tiny apartment squawking prettily, oblivious to the fact that she'd been separated from her parents. Ciara and Alex would lock eyes over the baby's head shocked at the magnitude of what they'd done. They'd lie in bed with Sally between them and talk about the circumstances that had led to this situation.

'I'm scared,' Ciara admitted the day after they'd taken her, but Alex had reminded her they were doing the right thing.

'A child should be with its biological family,' Ciara had pointed out, but they'd been over it so many times since Angela Berg's father, Emmet, had approached Ciara and asked her to intervene.

Being a private midwife at a stunning house in Brighton had started off well. The pay was excellent, and the new parents overjoyed at the birth of baby Rosie. But over the following days, it had become clear that, despite their incredible wealth, Angela and her husband, both in their twenties, had serious problems with drugs. The baby was often left alone, wailing, and on a few occasions when Ciara came to spend the night, both parents were passed out and only wanted to play with the baby when they woke up and got high.

It was Emmet Berg who'd first brought up the possibility of Ciara and Alex taking the baby. Ciara couldn't have her own children. She'd known that since she was a child. But when Emmet had heard that Angela and her husband were planning to go on a round-the-world trip with the baby, he'd come to Ciara, concerned. 'They won't cope with her.' He'd started to weep as he spoke. 'They don't have the tools.'

Ciara privately agreed with him. She'd come across cases where babies like Rosie were left exposed, suffering sunburn or malnutrition because of parents' addictions. She'd spoken to Alex about it and he'd seen Angela Berg for a few sessions and was concerned about her mental state. 'Ciara, I'm really concerned about this child,' he'd admitted. 'Those parents are not equipped to care for her.'

'So we can call social services,' Ciara said, but her heart had hurt because she'd spent nearly every hour with the child in those early days and felt a maternal pull to the baby. Normally she kept a professional distance from her little charges, but the lack of care Angela gave her child awoke every emotion and mother's instinct that Ciara had.

And that's when Emmet Berg had begged them to take her. He travelled for his own work and couldn't bear Angela's child put into care.

Despite her worries, Ciara had refused to be involved in something so harrowing and underhand. But it all changed the night Angela and her husband has taken the one-week-old Rosie out to the beach for a party. They were found by Emmet passed out in the sand, the waves almost at Rosie's toes where she was propped up in a sleeping bag, freezing cold and inconsolable. Any later and the tiny girl wouldn't have made it. He'd called Ciara immediately and it had taken her hours to settle the baby, who had had cuts all over her tiny newborn feet.

Ciara had been determined to ring the police, but Emmet had begged her to reconsider this suggestion – if the police got involved, Rosie would go into care.

When she had told Alex, he had been upset. He told Ciara some of the harrowing things he'd seen occur in the foster system. He'd spent a lot of time with baby Rosie by then, on walks with Ciara and visits to their apartment. He'd bonded with her and was adamant that the care system was nearly as bad as staying with the Bergs. 'She'll be harmed one way or another, Ciara. Angela's dad is right to say the baby will be better off with you.'

'We'd be criminals.' Ciara shook her head. 'We'd never be able to even get her a passport.' But she couldn't get the look in Alex's eyes out of her head. His sorrow and pain, and worse, his disappointment in her.

The following week Alex had been told his cancer was terminal. No chance of recovery and no treatment likely to buy much time, except maybe the specialist operation. Ciara continued to go to work finding respite in the soft baby skin and gentle snuffles of the tiny bundle she cradled. Angela was going out more and more, and baby Rosie needed Ciara nearly around the clock. She found herself wondering how wrong it would really be to nurture the child whose parents couldn't take care of her and who barely registered her existence.

When Emmet Berg learned of Alex's diagnosis he was sympathetic, but also knew how to weaken Ciara's resolve. He offered the money which they could put towards Alex's treatment.

'Rosie can go home with you. That way you can be with Alex too. When Angela and Roger get better they can take her back,' Emmet promised. He was trying to get his daughter into a treatment centre away from her Brighton circle. So, after hours and days of talking, Ciara and Alex agreed to take Rosie on a temporary basis, discreetly, to keep her from the authorities who could place the child just about anywhere. And Emmet's money was used to fund the operation for Alex which they hoped would give him a chance at life.

By the time the case blew up in the media, Ciara was struggling to make anything work. Alex was getting worse and she didn't dare leave baby Rosie, now Sally, with anyone else. She became overprotective and obsessed with staying in. The day Angela spotted them on the pier was the day Ciara knew she'd have to leave Brighton. She'd called her dad that same night. Despite his tough guy career, Ciara knew he was a man with a big heart, and he'd seen enough of what the world could do to vulnerable kids to know landing the baby with two active drug addicts was the worst choice of all, but the care system barely any better. Plus Ciara knew she had so much love to give this little girl who seemed to reach for her. Who seemed to *need* her.

Despite the operation, Alex got progressively worse, his only consolation little Sally. And as the Brighton Baby case detectives closed in, Ciara knew Emmet Berg had no intention of his daughter ever having the baby returned. Ciara was stuck.

As Alex neared the end, Ciara fulfilled the promise she'd made to her husband: that he wouldn't suffer unnecessarily. She knew she'd never forget his beautiful eyes on hers as she gave him his wish for a painless death.

After initially being questioned over Alex's death, Ciara leaned on Jimmy who was the one who helped her get back to Dublin with Sally. But since then, Ciara has been looking over her shoulder in case Angela or Roger Berg ever caught up with her.

Or decided they wanted to punish her.

And who could blame them. After all, she'd snatched their baby right out of their arms.

Chapter 31

Ciara slams both hands violently against the bonnet of the black car.

The bald man doesn't flinch. He remains where he is, leaning against the passenger door, arms folded like he has all the time in the world. Measured and calm.

'Take me then,' Ciara demands, her breath coming in short, sharp bursts. If this is it – if she's next, she at least has to try to get to the bottom of what the hell is going on.

Nothing makes sense. The bottom has dropped out of the world she thought she was in, a world where Morgan had been killed. But she'd just seen her husband's face, the same wary eyes, the same scornful curl of his mouth. Alive.

The bald man tilts his head, observing her reaction. 'Mrs Duffy,' he says, his accent Northern, his tone calm. 'I need you to listen to me. I've been trying to talk to you for some time.'

She stares at the man who is probably in his early sixties, anger coursing through her veins. If this guy had been hired by the Berg's to kill her then he also has answers.

She bangs the car bonnet again. 'What happened to my dad? Why is my fucking husband still alive?'

He presses his lips together. 'Ciara,' he says slowly. 'Don't you recognise me? Your dad's old security detail, Gabriel.'

He pauses, waiting for recognition.

A memory stirs – the man who used to drive her father, the one who used to pull coins from her ears when she was just a little girl. That was a long time ago.

'Gabe?' The name feels foreign in her mouth. There had been so many different Gardaí tasked with keeping her father safe over the years.

'Jimmy hired me back out of retirement after you were arrested,' the man says. 'To keep you safe. Your father's instruction, should anything happen to him, was not to let you out of my sight.'

Her heart expands in her chest.

Jimmy was still protecting her even now.

Mistrust instinctively kicks in. Could she really trust what this man is saying is true?

But she does remember him. Her dad had been fond of Gabriel because he'd been kind to Ciara as a child.

'Gabe,' she finally says. 'It's you. I'm sorry... it's all been so difficult.'

'I've worked with your da for a long time when I was a Garda.' His body sags slightly. It was clear that Jimmy had meant something to him. 'He helped save my son's life back then. I owe him the same favour back.'

'So you are definitely not working for the Bergs?' she checks. His brow furrows. 'The Bergs?'

The knot in her stomach tightens. If he's telling the truth, she's still no closer to finding the answers.

Ciara blinks back tears.

'I'm sorry. I don't know which way is up,' she explains. 'And dad...'

'I'm sorry if I scared you,' Gabe says, apologetically. 'But you kept running off. Jimmy was close to finding out what happened with your husband. Then... well, then he was killed.' Gabe shakes his head, the devastation on his face obvious.

Ciara swallows. 'So now you want to help me?'

Gabe nods. 'More than anything, your dad wanted to find out who really killed Morgan. He'd have done anything to get you out of that prison and back to him. And now I want to know who killed Jimmy.'

Ciara hesitates. Then, in a voice barely above a whisper, she tells him: 'I think it was my husband.'

—

'Get in.'

Ciara slides into the passenger seat of Gabe's car, grateful for the warmth. She stares ahead, her mind still trying to process everything that had happened in the past hour.

Morgan. Alive.

The moment she'd seen his face had sent her reeling. That instant recognition. His angry retreat. She puts her head in her hands.

Gabe looks over at her, his jaw clenched.

'Tell me again,' he says sharply. 'What you said just now. About Morgan.'

Ciara runs a hand over her face. 'I'm telling you that I just saw him.'

He shakes his head, incredulous. 'No, you saw *someone*. Someone who looks like him'.

Ciara sits up straight and turns towards him. 'It was him,' she insists.

'Ciara,' Gabe gives her a sidelong glance, his voice edged with something close to frustration. 'Morgan's dead. I saw the police report. Your dad and I studied it. There was an autopsy. Morgan was identified. Morgan was *buried*.'

'I know what I saw,' she says, her voice tight. 'He looked right at me. And he knew I recognised me too.'

'Could it have been…'

'It was *him*.' The certainty in her voice makes him go quiet for a moment.

Then, he asks more carefully. 'Did he speak to you?'

'No,' she swallows. 'But he looked right through me. So angry.' She shivers at the thought.

'So if he's alive then you couldn't have killed him,' he says, running his hand across his jaw.

He sees her expression. 'I mean, we know that obviously you didn't, but if we can prove Morgan's still alive, then there can't be a case against you.'

Ciara can't allow herself to get excited by the prospect because everything feels so surreal.

'That's why we need to get the police involved. Before he disappears again.'

Gabe pulls out his phone.

'Hang on,' he says suddenly. 'If someone went to the effort of having everyone believe Morgan was dead, they won't want him found.'

'We could go back over there?' Ciara suggests, but the way Morgan had looked at her, she's not sure she could handle seeing him face to face until she understood exactly what the hell was going on.

'I'm texting Casey, the detective on the case,' she decides. 'He needs to get to that house before Morgan is gone.' She types fast, sending the address.

'It doesn't add up,' Gabe shakes his head.

'I know Jimmy was looking into this,' he says. 'He must have uncovered something. He told me Morgan had been seeing a medical specialist before his death. If we find out why, maybe we will get some more answers.'

'Is this someone called Dr Bridges?'

Gabriel nods.

'Clarke Casey, the detective on the case, has requested the doctor's medical records. But it's going to take weeks,' Ciara sighs.

Gabe smiles wryly. 'I already have his home address.'

Ciara looks at him sharply. 'Are you suggesting we just go to his home?'

Gabe nods, typing an address into his sat nav.

'What about Sally?' Ciara insists. 'I have to get to my daughter. She's up in Glenavon with Morgan's sister.'

'I'll take you to Sally,' he says, 'But first we should talk to Dr Bridges to try and understand what's going on.'

She considers this plan. The thing is, Gabe knew her dad. He was loyal to him. He's been digging into the case on her behalf.

He's on my side.

They needed to know how Morgan was now walking around living and breathing. Had he taken some kind of drug that mimics death to fake his own murder? Does that kind of thing even exist? Her mind spins at all the possibilities and none make any sense. *Why would he have done this?*

'Okay, let's go talk to this doctor,' she finally relents and Gabe starts the engine.

The fact that Gabriel knew about Dr Bridges brings her comfort. Plus, she's running out of options to figure out what had really happened that night.

As Gabe drives past Mount town, he explains that he now runs security on oil-based projects in the Middle East, but has been home in Dublin a year now, since the birth of his grandchild. He shows her a picture of a toothless smiling toddler and Ciara smiles.

'Your dad had been insistent that the police had overlooked certain strands in the case of Morgan's death.' Gabe tells her. 'He was devastated about your arrest. It was almost as bad as when your mum...'

'You knew my mother?' Ciara asks quickly.

Gabe nods. 'She was one of the kindest people I ever met,' he remembers. 'She used to bring us out tea and sandwiches sometimes when we did overnights.'

Gabe guides the black Lexus into the dual carriageway.

Ciara's eyes fill with tears. 'Your dad felt like he let you down.' Gabe says quietly. 'He couldn't bear to see you in that place, away from your child. Since then, we've been doing everything we can to figure out what happened.'

'He didn't let me down,' she says, brushing tears away. 'Dad always did what he could to help me.'

Even now, she wants to add.

'He loved you so much,' Gabe confirms softly and they drive for a while, both in sad silence.

–

Park Avenue is an upmarket address twenty minutes away. The street screams wealth and order, the kind of place where everything has its place, right down to the perfectly aligned Christmas lights that drape across the grand facades of the homes. Snow has begun to fall, covering the pavements in a clean, undisturbed layer. But Ciara barely notices any of it. Her hands clench and unclench at her sides as she and Gabe make their way to the largest house on the road, a towering three-storey townhouse with a huge wreath hanging on the front door.

She presses the doorbell, its chime elegant and understated. Gabe shifts beside her, glancing toward the street as if he expects the police to come screeching around the corner any second.

Finally, the door opens and a woman appears. She's in her mid-fifties, wearing a perfectly tailored cardigan and a slightly startled expression. Her grey hair is styled neatly, the same shade as her cool eyes. She looks like she belongs in a magazine spread.

Ciara forces herself to meet her gaze.

'Can I help you?' Her tone is polite, but her eyes narrow slightly as she takes in Ciara's tense face and Gabe's looming presence.

'We need to speak to Dr Bridges,' Ciara says quickly. She isn't there to exchange pleasantries.

The woman blinks, caught off guard. 'I'm sorry, who did you say you are?'

'It's about a patient of Dr Bridges'. A man called Morgan Duffy,' Ciara sys, her voice steady now, every word precise. 'It's extremely important.'

The woman bites her lip. 'It's Christmas Eve. This is our private home. He doesn't see patients here.'

'It's urgent police business.' Gabe steps forward authoritatively, he flashes a Garda ID.

The woman's eyes widen. 'Let me just see…' She hesitates, her brow furrowing slightly. Then, without a word, she steps back and calls over her shoulder, 'Phillip? There's someone here for you.'

A few seconds later, Dr Bridges appears, adjusting his glasses as he walks to the door. A tall man in his sixties, his face is lined with the wear of age and stress, but his expression shifts into polite confusion as he looks at them.

'What is it?' he asks, looking from Gabe to Ciara quizzically.

Ciara wastes no time. 'We need to talk to you. About Morgan Duffy.'

Dr Bridges frowns, his gaze flicking between her and Gabe. 'I… I'm sorry, I don't think I know that name.' He's dressed as sharply as his wife. Black suit, white shirt, blue tie.

'Don't you?' Ciara's voice has an edge now. 'But he was under your care.'

The doctor opens his mouth to protest, but then something in his expression shifts, recognition, followed by a flicker of unease. 'Duffy?' he murmurs, as if testing the name. 'I… I think I remember now. He was a patient. But that was a while back.'

'Yes,' Ciara said, stepping forward. 'And now he's dead.'

Dr Bridges blinks, his eyes widening slightly. 'Dead? My God, I… I had no idea.' He glances at his wife, who is standing just behind him, her arms folded tightly across her chest. 'Well, he was…' Ciara corrects herself.

The doctor looks frazzled. 'I've been away for the past few months, on secondment. I haven't kept up with my patients – what is this about?'

Ciara pushes past him into the hallway, her desperation overriding any sense of decorum. Gabe follows close behind, his eyes scanning the pristine interior. The house is immaculate, all polished wood floors and tasteful Christmas decorations.

Ciara turns to face Dr Bridges, her voice rising. 'You treated Morgan. My husband. You know something. Something no one else will tell me.'

Dr Bridges closes the door after a nervous glance at the street, then turns back to her, his face pale. 'I'm afraid I don't know what you're talking about. I treated him, yes, but only briefly. He was... difficult. He stopped coming to see me. I informed the Health Authority of Ireland, as is required, and that's all I know.'

'Don't lie to me,' Ciara says, her voice cracking slightly, and she takes a deep breath to steady herself. 'He was murdered, and I was blamed for it. And now it appears he's not dead at all. I need answers,' she pleads.

Dr Bridges hesitates. He looks cornered. 'I... I don't know what you expect me to say. This is highly irregular. You can't just...'

'She's not going anywhere until you talk.' Gabe is unsmiling. 'And I really don't think you want your wife to start making that call.' He gestures towards the woman, who has her phone in her hand. 'Or this won't end well.'

Dr Bridges swallows hard, his hands trembling as he gestures toward the sitting room. 'Fine,' he says, his voice tight. He shakes his head firmly at his wife. 'Let's sit. But I don't know how I can help you.'

As they move into the next room, Ciara's heart pounds in her chest. She can see the fear in Dr Bridges' eyes, but beneath it, something else. He knows something.

The living room is an old-fashioned room with slightly dated furniture and some antiques. The doctor doesn't sit at first so they don't either. He folds his arms in front of his chest nervously and waits for them to speak.

'Did you treat my husband, Morgan Duffy?' Ciara repeats.

Dr Bridges sinks into a chair by his desk. 'I'm sorry, but I can't discuss patient information without proper authorisation.'

Ciara leans over his desk, her voice low and urgent. 'My husband was murdered a few weeks ago. But today, I saw him. Alive. Please talk to me.'

Dr Bridges flinches at her tone.

'I found a medical receipt from your office among Morgan's things. I need to know what you were treating him for, or what tests you were running.'

Dr Bridges sighs, rubbing his temple. 'Mrs Duffy, medical records are confidential. I'm afraid I can't...'

Ciara's hand clenches around the strap of her backpack. 'Please stop.' She surprises herself with the sharpness of her voice. 'I just saw my dead husband alive. My daughter is really sick and I need to get to her. Please, Doctor. I need to understand what's happening here.' She steeples her hands over her nose, trying to steady her breathing.

Dr Bridges studies her for a moment, then gestures to a chair. 'Okay, sit down.'

Ciara collapses into the nearest chair. 'Morgan Duffy was a patient of mine,' the doctor begins. 'He came to me because he started experiencing alarming symptoms and his GP referred him to test for a genetic condition.'

Ciara's eyes narrow. 'What condition? What symptoms?'

'Fahr's disease,' Dr Bridges says reluctantly. 'It's a rare disorder that causes abnormal deposits of calcium in areas of the brain that control movement and cognitive functions.'

Ciara's breath catches. 'And Morgan had it?'

The doctor nods. 'I'm afraid so.'

Ciara sits back in her chair.

Morgan had been sick.

'What does this disease do to a person?' Gabe takes a seat next to her.

'It leads to a range of symptoms,' Dr Bridges explains. 'Initially it's mostly a movement disorder, but it causes a form of dementia, psychiatric issues. The disease is progressive and quite debilitating, unfortunately if it's not caught.'

'Could it cause someone to disappear? To fake their own death?'

Dr Bridges hesitates. 'In some cases, the disease can cause significant cognitive decline, hallucinations, paranoia. It's possible Morgan's behaviour became more erratic. I only saw him a few times. But faking his own death... that's quite extreme. I'm not sure how one would do such a thing.'

Ciara's voice trembles as she remembers. 'He was acting very strangely in the weeks before he died. Paranoid, confused, angrier than usual.' She thinks of the affair with Aimee. 'Risk-taking. Just not his usual self.'

Dr Bridges nods. 'Yes, that sounds consistent with Fahr's. In some cases it can change someone's personality entirely.'

'Can it kill you?' Gabe asks.

Dr Bridges frowns. 'The progression of Fahr's disease can vary widely. Some individuals may remain relatively stable with mild symptoms, while others may experience severe disability over time. The disease's impact on quality of life can be significant due to its progressive nature and the wide range of potential symptoms. In this case, Morgan's presentation of Fahr's was much more pronounced than...'

The doctor trails off, stopping himself from continuing. His face turns red.

Ciara feels her own face flush with anger. 'Than what... what aren't you telling me, Doctor?'

Dr Bridges glances at the door, then back at her. 'Mrs Duffy, I'm telling you everything that I can.'

Ciara has come too far to be fobbed off by this guy. She's so close to finding out something important. 'No more lies,' she says. 'I need the truth. Morgan's condition was much more pronounced than what?'

She feels a surge of fear about what this man is about to tell her.

'Morgan's presentation of the disease was not more pronounced than *what*... but more pronounced than *who*.' He meets her gaze.

Ciara glances at Gabe. What is this guy on about?

'There was... an unusual circumstance,' Bridges continues, his voice catching slightly. 'As I said, Fahr's disease is extremely rare. I've only ever come across a handful of cases in my entire career. One was in the US and the other two... well, both of them became patients of mine.'

Ciara sits forward, her heart racing.

'Both of them here.' The doctor meets her gaze.

'Both in Dublin.'

Ciara's mind is racing. 'What are you trying to say?' she asks sharply, her voice growing louder.

'That both cases were related to one another?'

Time, which has been slipping away from Ciara so fast for days, slows to a crawl. She feels it unravelling, each strand separate and static.

Blank spaces, missing time, her mind skips backwards, conjuring up all kinds of scenarios.

'What do you mean "related"?' She says, her voice barely a whisper. Surely Courtney wasn't sick too?

'Mrs Duffy, during our consultations… Morgan discovered he had a brother. A twin brother.'

Chapter 32

The doctor puts his hand out towards a laptop on a table near him, then looks at Ciara questioningly for permission.

She nods stiffly for him to continue, her heart pounding.

'Morgan had an identical twin named Bill Emerson. Neither of them knew about the other until recently. Morgan discovered all of this because of a mix-up I made during an appointment. I called him by the wrong name and it came to light. Both of them had Fahr's disease. I'm the only specialist in the country, you see.'

'So, you're saying it was Bill I just saw, not Morgan?' Her head is spinning at the revelation. But Ciara knows her husband. She knows his expressions off by heart. Everything twists once more. She thinks back to the night she saw Morgan murdered – the face so very slightly different. She'd figured it was death that had distorted his features like that. Could the man who died in her bed next to her have been his brother, Bill?

But how would that have happened? And why?

'It's possible,' Bridges admitted. 'But I've no idea, I'm afraid. I was just their doctor. I do know that when Morgan found out he had a twin he was shocked, as you can imagine. And he was most keen to meet up with his brother.' He pauses. 'I do know they'd arranged to meet and I personally encouraged it. I felt the support would benefit them both. It's important to say that Morgan refused to take medication for the condition. In fact, the diagnosis had upset him greatly. Maybe it was Bill Emerson you saw this morning. It could explain why you thought you saw your husband Morgan alive.'

Ciara's eyes prickle with tears. She's filled suddenly with an irrational kind of hope – if Morgan is alive, she couldn't have murdered him. And maybe he wasn't horrible to her over the past few months because she was worthless. Maybe it was his illness affecting him. If he is alive... maybe... but she catches herself.

If Morgan is alive, he'd killed her father, and possibly his own twin brother.

Disorder or not, he could be a killer.

Ciara tries to catch her breath.

'I'm truly sorry, Mrs Duffy,' Dr Bridges says softly. Gabe rests his hand on her shoulder. She starts to cry, overwhelmed and confused.

For a few moments, the room falls into a tense silence, the weight of the revelations pressing down on them all. Even the doctor looks shellshocked, but that is likely because of the interruption to his day and the devastated woman sitting in front of him sobbing. But there's no time to process anything. Ciara feels the urgent tug that has been spurring her forward. She needs to get to her daughter. She looks up at Gabe pleadingly, wiping the tears away. 'I need to get to Sally now.'

–

Ciara is badly shaken as she leaves Dr Bridges' house. The snow is getting heavier, giving the afternoon a dark, melancholic feel. Gabe guides her to the car and sits her in it, her face is smeared with tears.

'Are you okay?' he asks as he slides into the driver's seat next to her.

She shakes her head numbly. Her hands clenched on her thighs, she stares out of the windscreen. 'A fucking twin,' she finally manages.

She steals a look at Gabe but he's focusing on the road, his face unreadable. The car speeds along the sleet-slick road, the Dublin mountains looming closer.

Ciara sits rigid in the passenger seat, her arms folded tightly across her chest, her thoughts a whirlwind of disbelief.

The revelation about Morgan being alive has left her feeling as if she's suffocating. And then there is Sally – waiting for her in a cottage somewhere in the mountains ahead.

Beside her, Gabe keeps his hands steady on the wheel, his eyes scanning the dark road ahead. The faint glow of the dashboard illuminates his face, which is set with a calm determination.

'Fifteen minutes, maybe less,' he says, his deep voice breaking the tense silence. He glances at her briefly.

'Thanks, Gabe,' Ciara mutters, her voice tight, her foot tapping against the floor mat.

'I know you're worried,' he says.

'It's all too much,' is all is she manage.

His fingers tighten on the wheel, his expression thoughtful. 'You know,' he says after a moment, 'your dad once told me there's no such thing as "too much". No such thing as too much love, too much fight, or too much loyalty. That's why he did what he did for me.'

Ciara turns her head to look at him. 'What do you mean?'

'Jimmy,' Gabe says, his tone softening. 'I told you he saved my son's life, right?'

She nods.

'Liam,' Gabe says, a faint smile flickering across his lips. 'A few years ago, he got caught in some trouble he didn't even understand. Your dad stepped in, put himself in harm's way, no hesitation. He didn't know Liam. But he cared. He just... acted.'

Ciara blinks, the intensity of his words cutting through her spiralling thoughts. She'd known her father had a reputation for sticking his neck out for others, but she hadn't heard this particular story. 'I didn't know.'

'He didn't like to talk about it,' Gabe says with a shrug. 'But I owe him, Ciara. Big time. And I told myself if there was ever a way I could pay it back, I would.'

'That's why you're here?' she asks, her voice quieter now.

Gabe glances at her again, his face serious. 'I'm here because your dad was the kind of man who didn't think twice about helping someone who needed it. And I can see you're cut from the same cloth. Your daughter needs you. I know what it's like to be a parent staring down the barrel of something terrifying, and I'll do everything I can to get you to her.'

Ciara feels her throat tighten, a rush of emotion rising unexpectedly. She looks away, out of the window, the darkened trees blurring past. She *is* cut from the same cloth. She is... brave.

'Thank you,' she whispers.

Gabe gives a short nod. 'It's nothing. Just keep it together for Sally. She's what matters right now.'

They see the sign for Glenavon up ahead. Courtney's town. Ciara's stomach flips. 'Quick,' she urges Gabe. 'Please, faster.'

Gabe puts his foot down, and as the car climbs higher into the mountains, dread fills the pit of Ciara's stomach as Gabe manoeuvres the car past farmland and dense forest, every minute bringing them closer to finally finding Sally.

But the truth is that neither of them have any idea of what really lies ahead.

Chapter 33

When her phone vibrates a few minutes later, Ciara grabs at it, her stomach churning with anxiety.

'Ciara, we received a 999 emergency call a few moments ago,' Detective Casey tells her, tension radiating from his voice. 'From Courtney Duffy.'

'Oh, my God.' Ciara doubles over, her voice slow and laced with desperation.

'Ciara…' Detective Casey is speaking urgently. 'I don't want you to panic but she's also asked for the ambulance service.'

'Sally,' Ciara cries, a painful guttural groan, like some of the mothers at her hospital when they were giving birth.

'Where are you?' Clarke demands. 'I turned up to that address you sent but there was nobody there. The house was empty. Now Courtney says that her brother Morgan has turned up outside her house in Glenavon. Courtney says he's acting extremely erratically. She's afraid to let him into the house. She's obviously in shock too – she thought her brother was dead up until a few moments go. We all did. What the hell is going on?'

A whoosh of air leaves Ciara's body. She's so mired in fear that she can barely speak.

Gabe grabs the phone from her. 'Detective Inspector, I'm Gabriel Long, a former Garda and long-time associate of Jimmy Mooney. We've been informed that Morgan had a twin brother. They were both suffering a rare neurological illness which may cause them to become violent.'

The car bounces in a pothole and Gabe corrects the steering, Ciara hitting her head on the window.

'Casey, it's looking increasingly likely that Morgan might have killed his twin brother, and possibly tried to switch lives with him.'

Ciara can just make out fragments of the rest of the conversations between the two men. The blood surges in her ears. She pictures Morgan ahead at Courtney's house hurting for Sally.

'Faster,' she hisses.

Morgan had always been a wonderful dad to Sally, but this version of Morgan is unpredictable and paranoid. She'd seen it in his eyes at that woman's house. He'd seemed capable of anything.

Gabe informs the detective inspector that they are on their way to Glenavon and are just minutes away.

Casey explains that he is about twenty minutes away. 'Do not approach him,' Casey warns. 'I'm serious. We've sent a patrol unit, but with the skeleton Christmas staff, there's no telling how long it will take them to get there. I'm already in the car.'

'What about the ambulance?' Ciara stammers.

'Hard to say. It's Christmas Eve and the snow is pretty bad up that way.'

Ciara wraps her arms around her torso, her knuckles white.

Five minutes, Gabe tells her.

Ciara remembers a warning from Dr Bridges before they'd left his home. 'Mrs Duffy, I must caution you,' he'd said. 'An individual with Fahr's disease can develop extreme paranoia. It means they might perceive benign actions as threats, potentially leading to aggressive or defensive actions to protect themselves from such imagined threats.'

'And had Morgan been showing any signs of this?' Ciara had asked, her voice tight.

The doctor had sighed, looking once again at his notes. 'Morgan was becoming progressively more paranoid and had started complaining that he was experiencing vivid hallucinations and delusions. He believed that people were conspiring against him and that his house was under surveillance. He felt family members were imposters sent to harm him, which is why I escalated it to the health authorities. It's conceivable that he viewed someone who looked just like him as an extension of himself, or even as a threat that needed to be eliminated.'

If he'd seen his own brother as a treat to eliminate, thinks Ciara, *then he's definitely capable of harming Sally.*

–

A series of hairpin bends greets them as they approach the section of the mountain where Courtney lives. It swirls this way and that as Gabe speeds along the country roads in the snow, trying to keep the car safely on the road.

The air darkens around them as daylight slips beyond the horizon. Ciara close her fists at the thought of Morgan harming Sally.

Come on, come on.

Outside, it is all thick forests, barren hills, fir trees stretching into the thundery sky like black-toothed combs.

'Do you think the person who you saw today is Morgan or his twin?' Gabe asks Ciara suddenly.

Her entire body is tense as she sits forward, eyes ahead, willing them faster.

The engine strains as they climb higher. The snow is coming down faster and thicker.

'I know that it's Morgan,' she states, remembering the small pock mark on his right cheek he told her he'd had from picking a chicken pox lesion as a child. She was almost sure she'd seen it on the man in Lana's house.

Plus, he'd recognised her. If it had been his twin, he wouldn't have known her.

Gabe's face is in shadow as night falls. 'So, you think Morgan killed his own twin and placed him in your bed?' He turns to her. 'But why?'

'You heard what the doctor said,' Ciara says. 'He was paranoid. He was angry with me. We were headed towards divorce. He'd been fired for messing with money in some fund at work and… well, I've never said this to anyone,' she confides, 'but Morgan wanted his own child. He badly wanted a child. We tried, but I'd already explained to him that I couldn't. It seemed odd when he said he wanted to try again…

'Then, abruptly, he changed his mind again. I wonder if finding out he had a genetic condition had an impact. But he grew more resentful. He was much angrier at me. And… at Sally. I think it all just came to a head.'

Ciara chokes back a sob. 'Morgan had no money left and knew Dad did. Maybe he just wanted me out of the picture and thought he'd find a way to claim the insurance money somehow. If he wanted to start afresh, this twin revelation allowed him to do that relatively seamlessly.'

'Biological fraud,' Gabe mutters.

'What's that?'

'Biological fraud,' he repeats. 'Nature is full of creatures that take one another's place – sometimes to the detriment of the original, and sometimes as a necessary part of their survival.' He glances over at her. 'These social replacement strategies can be as straightforward as one we are all familiar with; the cuckoo. Or it can be as insidious as the deception of some insects who mimic and blend in with the rest of the swarm before doing them harm once they gain their trust. Disarming peers by hiding in plain sight and then doing them harm for their own benefit.'

Ciara digests this. She'd slept every night next to this person who was slowly suffering with this serious condition.

'I know it's awful,' she says to Gabe, 'And I shouldn't, but I just can't help feeling sorry for Morgan that he was struggling so badly with his diagnosis and probably had nowhere to turn. He must have been so isolated to have taken things this far. Why couldn't he have just spoken to me about it?'

'Ciara…' Gabe says gently. 'I can tell that you are an empath. My wife is the same, but right now you need to turn that compassion inwards. Protect yourself. If what you are saying is true, Morgan is the reason you went to jail.' He glances at her sideways. 'The reason you have been separated from Sally. And possibly the reason Jimmy was killed.'

Another ache in her heart.

Morgan had never liked her dad, Jimmy. He'd felt Jimmy could see right through him. But killing him…

'And it's the reason Sally may be in serious danger right now,' Gabe adds, softly. She notices that his speed has increased. 'Sometimes a disease can change someone so entirely that you don't recognise them anymore. It's devastating, but it's also dangerous. I know it's not exactly the same, but when my Liam was in the worst of his addiction, we couldn't trust he wouldn't hurt himself or others.' Gabe's voice breaks slightly. 'It was like he was another person entirely.'

'I'm just scared what we'll find up ahead,' Ciara admits.

A sign, this time for the Derrycairn road, flashes white against luminescent headlights. The road has narrowed dramatically and is soon barely enough for even one car. Branches scratch along both sides of the Lexus.

Ciara clamps both hands over her mouth as they approach the small cottage. There are no lights at all from inside, just a small porch light that flickers eerily as they pull up. Ciara's heart sinks. She'd hoped somehow that the Gardaí may have arrived before them. She'd hoped she'd see the comfort of lights, of Morgan in handcuffs, of her little girl waiting to run into her arms.

Instead, a horrible silence. The snow is thicker up here.

She tightens her grip on the gun now in her hand. Gabe stops the car, leaving the engine running so they can use the lights to guide their path, and Ciara tucks the gun into the front pocket of her hoodie. All her focus is on the house.

The first thing they notice when they approach is another car parked awkwardly up on the grass verge a few metres away. It wasn't Courtney's little yellow Mini. As they get closer, Ciara realises the car has been badly crashed. The bonnet is crumpled awkwardly against a small stone wall, the tyres suspended over a ditch. Undrivable.

Night sounds puncture the freezing air: the clack of winter branches, the whisper of the canopy overhead. Ciara gets closer to the house, her feet crunching on the snow-covered gravel. Trees stretch up around her, willowy shadows barely visible against the inky night.

Gabriel remains next to her – swivelling this way and that. She feels safer with him beside her, and tries to forget the fact that he's more of a bodyguard than an experienced SWAT team member. He's not properly trained for this type of scenario. Would he be any match for Morgan?

She says a silent prayer that Detective Inspector Clarke Casey will arrive soon with back-up. But there is no way she is waiting another second to get to her child.

In the light from the headlights of the Lexus, Gabe tries the front door. It's locked. He taps gently, but there's no answer. Ciara feels light-headed, petrified of what they'll find inside. Gabriel is beside her, leading her now around the side of the house. Her breath comes out in short, sharp bursts.

Gabe peers in through the back window and then recoils in shock. Ciara clutches his arm.

'What?' she cries, as quietly as possible, ice running through her veins. 'What have you seen?'

He shakes his head, grim-faced. He tries to pull Ciara back, away from what he's just seen, but she shakes free of him and looks in through the dirty pane.

A pair of human legs lie on the floor of the kitchen, stretched out, lifelessly. Tights and a skirt.

Ciara moans in anguish. Gabe has his arms around her shoulders – trying to ground her.

'Oh god.' She turns towards him and buries her face in his chest. 'No...' she cries. 'I can't bear this.'

Suddenly, Gabe stiffens. He brushes her off and hurries to look again. One leg is moving, slowly. Gabe taps the window gently. 'Hello? Courtney? We've come to help,' he hisses. Ciara joins in. 'Courtney, it's me, Ciara. Let us in,' she pleads, trying to keep her voice to a whisper.

Suddenly, Ciara senses movement behind them.

From somewhere in the forest comes the snap of a stick. Fear coils through Ciara's body like a snake. She feels the hairs rising on the back of her neck. She knows she's being watched.

Inside the house, a shape moves slowly across the kitchen towards the back door. There's the sound of a lock turning, and the door opens a fraction. It's still pitch black around them.

'Quick.' Courtney's voice is dry and scratchy. She sounds terrified. 'I've been hiding under the table,' she tells them.

Gabe and Ciara slide in through the gap in the door and Courtney closes it quickly behind them, turning the lock with trembling hands.

The only light is a small-beamed torch the fifty-four-year-old recluse has placed under the table where she's been cowering.

'Where's Sally?' Ciara demands of her sister-in-law. They'd gotten on despite their differing approach to the world: Courtney suspicious and fearful of medicine, while Ciara embraced the life-changing miracle of drugs that can save lives. Courtney had once confided in Ciara about what life had been like growing up in this remote cottage: regular beatings from their father, while their mother knelt praying in front of the hearth with her rosery beads, allowing it to happen despite her children's pleas. Morgan had left home as soon as he could, while Courtney had remained as a carer for her aging parents until they had died a few years ago, within a year of one another.

'Where's Sally?' Ciara repeats, pulling Courtney's arm as she ushers them into a corner of the kitchen.

'Shhh,' Courtney begs. 'He's out there somewhere.'

Goosebumps run along Ciara's arms at the fear in her voice. 'What happened, Court?'

Her sister-in-law grips Ciara's hand.

'Morgan turned up and started banging on the door,' she whispers, her face ashen even in the dim light. Courtney's hair was much longer than the last time Ciara had seen her. She was thinner too. A shy woman, Ciara always felt it was a great pity she'd never met anyone. She'd doted on Sally but would always point out that Morgan and she should have their own children too.

A huge taboo subject for Morgan.

'I thought it was a ghost,' Courtney continues. 'He was shouting about a brother, and I didn't know what he was going on about. I thought he'd lost his mind. Then while I was hiding, I remembered my mother had told me when she was dying about another child that she'd given up. She couldn't manage any more kids, she'd said. Father wouldn't let her. But I had no idea that there were twins.' Her entire body is trembling. 'Ciara, he's saying crazy things. He wants to take Sally away from here.'

Courtney's voice breaks in anguish. 'He said he'd killed that other fella... his brother.'

Ciara shudders. So, Morgan *had* killed Bill. 'What does he want now?'

'He wanted me to give him Sally. He said she was the only one who loved him.' In her peripheral vision, Ciara sees Gabe moving into the other rooms. He's obviously looking for Sally. But Courtney still has Ciara's arm in a vice-like grip. 'I don't even know who he is anymore,' she says, face uncomfortably close to Ciara's, the whites of her eyes showing.

'Courtney,' Ciara pulls her arm away and checks the gun is still in the pocket of her hoodie. 'Where's Sally? I need to get to her,' she says desperately.

'That poor child is upstairs,' Courtney says shaking her head. 'I did my best for her, Ciara. She's not well. I called the ambulance, and you know how I feel about hospitals.' A tear rolls down Courtney's cheek.

Ciara immediately turns. She feels her way into the middle of the house, despite the gloom and clutches the banister, her legs starting to buckle beneath her.

She can hear Gabe upstairs, walking about. It's a tiny house, one that a big bad wolf from Sally's stories could easily blow down.

She hears Gabe talking as she tries to get up the stairs, but her legs are useless. Adrenaline surges through her and she crawls commando-style up one step at a time.

Gabe appears at the top of the stairs. 'She's here,' he says, but his tone is cautious. 'Ciara, Sally's here but... it's not great.'

Ciara scrambles up the last few steps, using the banister to hold herself upright.

Gabe reappears on the landing with a tiny bundle in his arms. Sally wrapped in a blanket. 'We have to get her to a hospital,' he says, panic in his tone.

Ciara reaches into the mound of soft covers and finally touches her daughter.

Sally's paler than any living person should be, eyelashes fanned out across her gaunt cheeks, mouth slightly open. Unconscious or sleeping, Ciara can't tell, but definitely alive.

'Hi lovie, it's Mummy,' Ciara whispers, her tears trickling down both cheeks. 'Sal, it's Mum. I'm here now. I'm going to take care of you. Mummy's going to keep you safe.'

She holds her daughter's tiny, lifeless hand as Gabe carries her carefully down the rickety stairs. Sally's fingers are like silk, feathery light. The only light comes from the torch on Gabe's phone in his front pocket. It dusts everything in a ghostly filament.

Shallow breaths, weakening pulse, fluttering eyelids.

They have to get her to a hospital. Sally seems to be dying right before her eyes.

Just as Ciara's about to open the front door for Gabe, the roar of an engine cuts through the night. She flings open the door. The Lexus is being reversed at speed back down the driveway, the headlights slowly disappearing – their only way to get Sally to the hospital.

The darkness crushes everything around her.

'No,' Ciara roars. She can almost feel the energy leaving her daughter's hand. 'No,' she screams again, as she starts to run towards the car.

Chapter 34

The gears crunch painfully as Morgan tries to turn the Lexus in the narrow driveway. He's close to the bottom of the narrow lane when Ciara catches up with the car.

The first thing Ciara sees is Morgan's eyes staring at her from behind the steering wheel. It's as if he's not there. Like a stranger has taken over his body.

'Morgan,' she screams.

She stands in front of the car, illuminated by the bright headlights. Shadows stretch and grasp, the heavy snow making her squint. Morgan, on the other hand, looks right through her.

'Stop,' she shouts.

He revs the engine, still staring at her with that blank look in his face.

This is the man she'd shared a bed with for the past few years. A man who'd promised her the world and then torn it away from her. This is the man who'd probably murdered her father. It's unfathomable that it's come to this.

It's only a split second before she realises what he's doing.

The Lexus screams with the thrust of his foot on the pedal. The engine is a beast, snarling and spitting. Stone-cold eyes bore into her, both Morgan's and not Morgan's at the same time. The dim lights from the dashboard cast strange shadows across her husband's face.

The car moves towards her at speed. The lane is too narrow. She has nowhere to jump to safety. Ciara barely has time to grasp the pocket of her hoodie as the car gets closer.

The car is nearly on top of her. Her mind whirs.

The gun.

Ciara holds her arms straight ahead of her, the gun pointed straight towards Morgan.

She hears her father's voice clearly in her ear. '*Do it now, Birdy. Do you hear me?*'

Do it.

Do it, she urges herself.

The car barrels towards her.

She's about to squeeze the trigger but at the last minute, she jerks her arms up, firing into the air instead, her entire body shaking.

The sound of the gun reverberates through the night. The car veers erratically to the right and scrapes noisily along the crumbling stone wall which slows its pace, before stopping just inches from where Ciara has dropped to a crouch. She wraps her arms tightly around herself, trying to hold herself together somehow.

For a moment, there's no sound except her own panting, the echo of the gunshot, the desperate ticking of the engine. The only feeling, the searing pain in her leg, the urgency to get Sally out of there.

Then Gabe is behind her with the little girl in his arms.

'Got her?' he asks, handing Sally to her, as Ciara drags herself to her feet. She feels the lightness of her daughter in her arms. So fragile. Just like the first time she'd ever held her.

'Mummy's got you.' She bends her face close to Sally's. 'Mummy's going to help you now,' she promises, rocking her baby in her arms.

From behind them, Courtney suddenly screams.

Morgan is dragging himself out of the car, his nose streaming with blood.

He moves towards Sally, but Gabe puts himself between Morgan and Ciara, deftly sliding the child from her arms as he does so. Sally appears lifeless, her head lolling back. Her long hair falls over Gabe's arms as he moves.

'Get the fuck away from her,' Morgan says in a frighteningly flat tone. 'She's mine.' He tries to grab the unconscious child.

Ciara doesn't wait to hear the rest. She jumps on Morgan from behind, trying to stop him from getting anywhere near Sally. But he's too quick, elbowing her to the ground and going after Sally again.

Ciara falls to the ground, her injured ankle so painful that she cries out. She spots the gun which fell from her grasp after she'd fired it a few moments ago. It's just a few feet away from the wall. She tries to reach for it in the dirt, dragging herself towards it, but Morgan is on top of her again. He lifts her roughly to her feet to stop her from grabbing the gun. His face is mere inches from hers.

'Why, Morgan?' Ciara asks, trying to hold back tears, wanting more than anything else for her husband to appear as himself – not this stranger with dead eyes staring back at her. Completely unreachable.

'Why?' she pleads again and as Morgan hesitates for a split second, it's just enough time for her to throw into his face the snowy mud she has clutched in her hand. When he staggers backwards, momentarily blinded, Ciara drives Morgan's head into the car bonnet – a move Jimmy had taught her. A wet crunching sound comes, followed by a loud moan from Morgan.

She stands in the driveway panting, her breath misting in the cold air. The mountain wind tugs at her thin clothes, but she barely feels it. Her entire focus is on getting Sally out of there.

Morgan staggers a few feet away, and pulls himself to standing, his posture now coiled and dangerous. One eye has swollen to twice its normal size, giving him an even more monstrous look. Gabe is behind her, holding Sally tightly against his chest, her small, feverish body trembling under the thick blanket wrapped around her. Morgan keeps coming.

Ciara looks around frantically. *Where are the fucking police?* They need Sally in an ambulance now.

'Call the police again,' she yells at Courtney, who is standing further up the lane sobbing, but the older woman doesn't move. She continues to chant prayers.

Morgan's face is now a mask of cold fury, his eyes flicking between Ciara and the bundle in Gabe's arms. 'Sally's coming with me,' Morgan growls, his voice low and menacing. 'You're not taking her anywhere.' He staggers towards them once more, a little disorientated now. Blood runs down his face and pools onto the snow.

'She's sick, Morgan,' Ciara pleads, stepping between him and Gabe. Her voice is firm, but her heart pounds in her ears. 'I need to take her to the hospital.'

'She's my daughter,' he shouts, his voice rising, echoing off the nearby trees.

'Yes,' Ciara tries to appease him, her hands raised in a peace gesture. 'You love her and I know you want to help her, don't you, Morgan? Together we can save her.' Despite the situation, Ciara searches in his eyes for the man she'd married. She searches for the father he'd been to Sally.

But any trace of empathy or compassion seems to have been leeched from Morgan and replaced by this stranger with narrowed eyes.

'You turned her against me, Ciara. Against her own father. Just like the others.'

Morgan takes a step forward, his fists clenched, and Ciara instinctively raises a hand, as if that could hold him back. Behind her, she can feel Gabe tense, his grip on Sally tightening.

She flashes him a warning look. She wants to do this her way.

'You think you're going to get away with this?' Ciara calls to Morgan.

He takes a slow step forward. 'This isn't about me. You think I'm going to let you take her away from me and live happily ever after?' He curls his top lip in a rictus grin. 'I tried that,' he continues. 'And look where it got me.' He touches a hand to his face and smears the blood across his sweater.

'Why did you do this?' Ciara says, keeping him talking as she tries to spot where the gun is on the ground.

'I needed a new life,' he says. 'I tried with that stuck-up bitch Aimee next door, but I needed to get further away. I needed to start fresh. I needed cash. Finding out I had a brother meant I could do it all seamlessly. It was easy. After I met him, he told me all about his life. I just started chatting to his girlfriend online. Lana hadn't a clue. They'd only been dating a while. Then I just had to get rid of Bill and I had a shiny new life.'

'Get rid of him? You murdered him,' she cries. But all this is just wasting precious time that Sally doesn't have.

Come on, Clarke.

Ciara sees something out of the corner of her eye just as Gabe puts a hand on her shoulder.

'Get Sally out of here,' she hisses.

Gabe hesitates. 'Ciara—'

'Just go,' she says, her eyes never leaving Morgan. 'Take the car and get Sally to a hospital now. Please, Gabe.'

She hears the faint shift of gravel as Gabe moves toward the car, then the sound of the door opening, then closing. Courtney has scrambled in too. The engine roars to life. Ciara uses the distraction to take a step closer to the gun.

Morgan's eyes snap to the car, his body jerking towards the sound – but his movements are slow, laboured.

Behind her, the car tires spin against the gravel, then grip, the vehicle speeding down the driveway. Ciara's shoulders sag. Her girl is on her way to safety.

Then it's just her and Morgan, both of them covered in the red hue of the receding taillights. The only sound is the whispering of the trees as the snow continues to silently fall.

Her heart hammers in her chest.

Where are the police? Where's Clarke?

'You let them take her from me,' Morgan says softly.

Ciara is achingly close to where she thinks the gun is. It's still on the ground but closer to Morgan, she thinks. Darkness envelopes them both. She uses her feet to feel around the ground as she faces him.

'They want to take everything from me,' he says, even his voice seeming alien to her – flat and robotic.

'Who is "they"?' Ciara asks, trying to keep him talking until the police come. She takes a step closer, only a single flickering bulb from the cottage porch offering any light at all. Her foot connects with an object.

They both leap for the gun at the same time.

Morgan gets there first. She sees her father's gun in his hands. Fear overtakes everything. This is the worst possible outcome.

'I knew you were sleeping with that doctor,' Morgan sneers, walking towards her, bolder now. 'Did you think I would just let you leave me?'

Ciara turns and bolts toward the dense forest lining the driveway, her feet slipping on the loose gravel before hitting solid, frozen ground. She immediately hears Morgan's heavy footsteps behind her, his voice ring out in the cold air. Her ankle is so sore it feels like she's running across glass.

'Ciara,' he shouts. 'You can't outrun me!'

She doesn't respond. She darts between the trees, her lungs burning, her mind focused on one thing: survival.

Somewhere far off in the distance, she hears the wail of sirens. *They're coming*, she thinks, relief surging through her. *Oh, thank god.*

Branches scrape her arms, the uneven ground threatens to trip her, but she keeps going. Behind her, Morgan's footsteps crash through the underbrush, his shouts echoing in the darkness.

'You think you're clever?' he sing-songs at her. 'You think they'll save you? They'll shoot you on sight, Ciara. You are a prisoner on the run.'

But Ciara doesn't slow down. She can't… The sirens sound closer now, red and blue lights flash faintly in the distance. But she doesn't let herself stop. Her injured foot snags again and she swallows down a scream of intense pain. The muddy snow cloys and tugs at her, slowing her down.

And then, suddenly, she stumbles into a dead end, the lights from the police cars ablaze in the distance.

Please hurry.

Her legs give way, and she drops to her knees, gasping for breath. She's exhausted and trapped.

Morgan bursts through the trees a moment later, his face contorted with rage.

'Stop,' Ciara cries, her voice hoarse. 'It's over, Morgan. You need help.'

The whir of a helicopter sounds above them, between the dark tree-tops. Her husband's chest heaves as he looks at his wife, his expression a mix of frustration and something else – something almost like fear.

She straightens, meeting his gaze. 'It's over,' she repeats. 'Nobody else needs to get hurt. Please, Morgan…'

There are flashlights cutting through the darkness. The forest is alive with the sounds of pursuit. The gun in his hand shakes.

'Morgan, you aren't well. We can get you help. It doesn't have to end like this.' She's crying now, genuinely devastated that it's come to this. Her once lovely husband now a shell of himself, puffy and disorientated and clearly very unwell. She sobs for what they once had.

She tries to get her bearings. Her heart sinks as she sees where she is. It's the valley edge. And beyond the high fence that marks Courtney's land – she knows there is a sheer drop into the violent water of the Glenavon waterfall below. She pictures the water crashing against jagged rocks, their roar competing with the pounding of her heart. Their ears are filled with the sound of the helicopter overhead. She presses her back against the damp wood of the fence, her mind racing.

Beyond them, the piercing wail of sirens and dogs barking is getting louder.

Morgan glances around frantically, also a cornered animal.

Ciara knows this is the most dangerous state of all.

Morgan faces her, his eyes wild. He stops a few feet away, his chest heaving, his gaze locking on to her. 'You know I loved you,' she says, trying to melt the ice in his eyes. She digs her nails into the back of her hand.

'Don't give me that crap,' he bellows back. 'You wanted to leave me.'

'You gave me no choice,' Ciara answers, but she understands that it's too late now for reasoning.

'You've got nowhere left to go now,' he says, shrugging. 'Guess we are both fucked.'

He raises the gun.

'Please Morgan,' she begs. 'Don't do this. I need to take care of Sally. Please don't do this.'

Another step closer, his movements clumsy. 'You're weak, Ciara. You always were.'

'You killed your own brother,' Ciara sobs. 'You shot my dad. You don't have to kill me.' His grip seems to tighten on the gun.

'You lured your twin to *our* home and then you killed him.' She can't understand how anyone could have hatched a plan like that.

'If I hadn't, he would have killed me,' Morgan says, his words sounding more and more garbled. 'He would have killed me and taken over *my* life. That's why I went to the Red Lion. I tried to hire someone, but they laughed at me. So I had to do it myself. It helped that you were passed out drunk,' he sneers.

She thinks of Sally and her friend being in the house in Kerryvale at the same time as Morgan murdered his own brother and placed him in their marital bed.

'If I hadn't gotten rid of him, everything would have been taken from me,' Morgan shouts at her now.

'Everything *is* lost,' Ciara says softly, as tears sting her eyes.

'Yes,' he says. 'Now, it is.'

His eyes have taken on a dead quality – like an attack dog. The hairs on the back of her neck stand up. She's seen this look before. On her father's face, right before he had killed a man in her childhood home when she was eleven. Just after she'd snuck out of bed that night. Jimmy had been a talented detective but he was also a killer. Maybe that's why he'd been so good at catching them.

But what warped mission was Morgan on?

He suddenly cocks the gun and Ciara's instinct takes over.

She lunges forward. There's a scuffle in which she's aware that she's very much fighting for her life. She manages to wrestle the gun from Morgan's hands, and this time there's zero hesitation.

When the gunshot cracks through the night for a second time, it's deafening and final.

Morgan staggers backwards, his eyes wide with shock as he clutches his chest. Blood spreads across his shirt as he stumbles a few feet before collapsing to the ground.

Ciara freezes. The gun falls to the ground. Her breath comes in ragged, uneven gasps.

'Oh, Jesus Christ,' she whispers. 'Jesus Christ. I'm so sorry.'

Morgan stares lifelessly up at her. His fingers twitch. What has she done?

'I'm so sorry,' she repeats. 'Oh, my God.'

The police are so close that she can now make out their shadows between the trees. Florescent uniforms shouting. Sirens screaming.

But she knows what's coming next.

They'll find the gun and Morgan's body, and they won't care why she did it. They'll drag her back to that cold, empty cell. They'll take her away from Sally. She's proved them right. She's now a murderer.

Her gaze shifts to the fence.

Her fingers grasp a jutting crack along the unyielding barrier. It's just enough. She pulls herself up with everything she has left. Her muscles quiver, her eyes closed tight as she scrambles painfully up. At the top, she clambers over, risks a glance back.

Her chest tightens as the thought takes root. It's insane, reckless, but it might just be her only option.

She can hear the police shouting behind her, their torches sweeping the ground. Morgan lies motionless.

Below her on the other side is only darkness. She breathes it shakily in. She looks down at the water, her whole body trembling. The wind howls around her. Her voice is barely a whisper. 'I'm so sorry, Sally,' she tries to say, but the freezing wind snatches her words away.

A fleeting memory comes to her. A fairground, colourful neon lights, the tinny music of a Ferris wheel in the wind, wiping coral beads of wet candyfloss from a tiny face... It clouds over again, disappearing into nothing, like the fog of her breath dragged into the night.

'Ciara Duffy,' one of the uniformed Gardaí calls out. 'Stop. Don't move.'

There's no other option.

Ciara closes her eyes.

She pictures her little girl.

She lets herself fall.

Chapter 35

Ciara hits the water hard, the freezing cold immediately wrapping itself around her like chains. Shock radiates through her whole body. The current grabs hold of her, pulling her under, spinning her in darkness. Her limbs flail, her lungs scream for air, but she can't fight it. She's sinking. Ciara clings to the memory of Sally, safe in Gabe's arms. She has to believe in the possibility that Gabe will make sure her daughter lives. She has to believe there is still good in the world.

And then, through the chaos, she hears it − a shout. She throws her arms up. Against the rushing water, a car engine. Headlights sweep across the water, and moments later, strong hands reach for her. She gasps, choking on water, her body trembling violently. It occurs to her that this might just be a drowning vision. She's heard about euphoric moments when those dying feel a glow of what they are hoping for as they near death. The water fills her lungs, heavy like lead. She tries to cry out but more water comes.

The hands are gone. Ciara panics, moving this way and that but her strength is leaving her. She starts to sink deeper.

'Ciara.'

A voice cuts through the panic. Gabe drags her out of the water. He kneels beside her on the rocky shore, his face pale and frantic. 'You're okay,' he says. 'I've got you.'

Ciara coughs violently, water caught in her lungs spurting out as she clutches his arm. 'Sally,' she croaks, her voice barely audible. 'I told you to—'

'She's safe,' Gabe promises firmly, his hands steady on her shoulders. 'She's in the car. We couldn't leave you,' he says simply. 'I promised your dad I'd take care of you too.'

Ciara sags against him, her whole body heaving. 'Hospital,' is all she manages, coughing violently. Tears stream down her face, and when she eventually can talk, it comes out in a jumble. 'I have murdered him, Gabe. I killed Morgan.' She cries softly against his shoulder as he pulls her to her feet.

'It's okay,' he says quietly – but she can hear a note of uncertainty in his voice. 'It's okay, Ciara. He was trying to hurt you. That's self-defence. Let's get you both to the hospital.'

All Ciara wants to do is lie down and close her eyes, but they are not out of danger by any means.

Keep going, Birdy, she hears her dad say. *Don't give up now.*

Gabe drags her, half walking, half being carried, towards the battered car and Ciara climbs into the back seat where Sally lies. Her daughter's head is turned to one side, her eyelids fluttering, her heart still beating. Courtney is holding Sally's hand and praying.

Ciara wants to pull her daughter close but she's soaking and freezing and doesn't want to make her daughter any colder, so she just murmurs sweet words into her ear.

Gabe turns the heat in the car up full blast, but she's shaking badly. The flashing lights of the Gardaí fade into the distance, but the weight of what's happened doesn't lift.

For now, she tells herself, Sally is safe and she's there with her and Morgan can't hurt them.

And that has to be enough.

Murky black shadows of the trees blur pass. The snow still falls heavily. She buries her face in her hands as Gabe slides around corners, his face set in a grim expression, a vein in his jaw twitching.

–

A convoy of blue lights greet them as they approach the Dublin ring-road farther down the mountain side. Gabe slows down and stops, flashing the only headlight that works in the Lexus which is now painfully wheezing after all the battering it took in Courtney's driveway.

Ciara sees Detective Clarke Casey jump out from one of the cars, approaching the driver's side at a run. 'My god,' he says, when he sees Ciara's appearance.

Ciara is bloodied and torn. She's reopened the stitches in her head running through the forest and the cold feels as if it's seeping into her bones. 'Morgan's dead,' she says to him flatly. 'And Sally is in a bad way. You need to let us get her to the hospital.'

'No ambulances can make it up this far in this weather,' he confirms.

Clarke flicks his eyes towards Sally who is curled up on the back seat next to her. Ciara knows there is no need for hyperbole.

Clarke looks shocked by the child's appearance and steps away, speaking quickly into his radio. Ciara leans her head back against the car seat, praying the police won't detain her. There'll be police procedures and questions. So many questions. She tries to stop the shivering but her body is just so exhausted. Courtney is helped out of the car by one of the officers and is led away crying.

Clarke paces as he talks, his body coiled for action. In the front seat, Gabe is a ball of nervous energy. He clutches the steering wheel, twisting his hands on it, turning his knuckles white. Ciara understands why. After all, he made a promise to Jimmy and so far he'd demonstrated that he'd do anything to keep it.

A moment later, Clarke hurries back to the window. 'Are either of you armed?' he asks quickly. Two more Gardaí join him. Ciara shakes her head. The gun remains thrown beside Morgan's body in the forest. She pictures her husband, motionless, sprawled out like a star under the trees and feels… nothing but sadness and relief.

Gabe also confirms he's not in possession of a gun. 'Detective Casey,' Gabe pleads. 'Can you please get this child to the hospital? Then we'll answer any and all questions you may have. She really isn't well.' He jerks his head to the back of the car.

A thick trail of blood is running down the side of Ciara's face from her wound.

But she's entirely numb to pain – her sole focus is on Sally.

Clarke shakes his head. 'I'm sorry. There are twenty-five officers out there searching for you,' he says to Ciara, indicating the mountain behind them. 'And now a body has been found which presumably is Morgan. You are on the run from prison. I'm sorry, but I have no choice but to rearrest you.'

Ciara's shoulders slump as Clarke opens the door of the car. Something silly pops into her head. She'd read about it once: a fish that cradles its babies in its mouth, keeping them safe, hiding them from the sharp teeth of predators. But now she understands it; every instinct she has is screaming to keep her child close, to shield her from the dangers in the world – from people and illnesses.

Running, protecting, sacrificing – all for Sally.

But then Gabe speaks up. 'Morgan tried to kill Ciara – and I... I shot him. It was me that pulled the trigger.'

Ciara's mouth drops open. But she's too overwhelmed to protest. She remembers Gabe's words: *I vowed to Jimmy I'd protect you. No matter what.*

He'd protect her, and she'd protect Sally.

'Which means that Ciara didn't kill her husband today, nor last October,' Gabe tells Clarke. 'Ciara has been dealing with a partner who was, at best, extremely unwell, and at worst, a violent killer. Let her go and be with her daughter and do what you want with me.'

'You'll have to come in for questioning,' Clarke explains to Gabriel. 'But I can accompany Ciara and the child to the hospital if what you are saying is true.' He turns to Ciara. 'Is this true?'

Gabe catches her eye and dips his head.

Ciara hesitates but then turns back to Clarke and nods.

–

Ciara watches as Gabe is led from the Lexus towards another police car by two officers. Her body is hunched with cold as Clarke quickly carries Sally into his car. As he places the child gently inside, Ciara turns towards Gabe. The blue lights flash across their faces. You didn't have to do this, she wants to say to him, but she knows he's too far away to hear her, so she clasps both hands together over her heart in thanks.

He'd saved her life. He's done everything he could to protect Sally. He's protected her from Morgan. But most of all, he loved her father almost as much as she had. They shared that. Both lucky enough to have been loved back by the legend of a man who now lay in his grave.

Gabe meets her gaze as he's put into the back seat of the police car. She imagines him as a playful grandfather, young enough to horseplay and swing around a little boy who he'd described to her as 'a wonderful little fella', pride beaming from his eyes when he'd described how his son Liam had gone on to be a great father.

'Thank you,' she mouths, and just before she turns and gets into Clarke's waiting car, Gabe nods his head a fraction in acknowledgement.

She knows that once she's sure Sally is safe, she'll explain the truth to Clarke but, for now, she is immensely grateful to Gabriel Long for making sure nothing stands in the way of that mission.

Clarke puts on the lights and siren and tells her to hold on. He's given her a blanket which she's wrapped tightly around her shoulders. Sally is cocooned inside another one next to her in the back seat. Ciara grips her daughter tightly as Clarke speeds along the roads. It's Christmas Eve and traffic is light but the roads are icy and the conditions poor.

Once they've made it to the M50, Ciara leans forward and asks him a question she's been afraid to ask: 'Did you find the Berg family?' Ciara says quietly. 'Did you tell them that Sally is here?'

Clarke frowns in concentration as he overtakes a minivan and two trucks. Ciara feels a strange sense of relief now that she'd told Clarke that Sally was the Brighton Baby. There'll be more questions, of course, but the main thing is making sure Sally is in the best place to get her transplant. 'Did you find the Bergs?' Ciara repeats, dread and hope roiling and colliding in her stomach.

The blood from her head is really gushing now, she notices, even though she's used a corner of the blanket to quell the worst of it.

Clarke glances in the rearview mirror. 'Are you okay?' he asks.

She nods.

'And Sally?'

Ciara glances at her child. Her translucent skin, those cold fingers. 'We need to hurry,' she urges.

'We did find them,' Clarke says, after a moment. 'They are on their way over. They should be in Dublin soon.'

Ciara's lower lip trembles. 'Thank you,' she says, a strange feeling washing over her. Maybe Sally has a fighting chance – even if Ciara has to confront the parents whose child she took.

Maybe she'll lose Sally all over again. But at least her child will be alive.

Sally moans softly and Clarke shifts gears, driving even faster. Ciara soothes her, pushing her long blonde hair out of her closed eyes.

'Okay, not long,' he reassures. 'We're only a few minutes away. They've rung ahead and let them know you're coming.'

For the next few minutes, Ciara wrestles with what's about to happen.

The moment she walks into the hospital, Sally won't be hers anymore. Ciara could be arrested for child abduction.

In every scenario, she is going to lose Sally. Either to her birth family. Or to death.

There's a moment, as they speed along, that part of Ciara wonders if maybe all of this is the universe punishing her for taking Sally from her real parents in the first place. The question she keeps asking herself is if she would she do anything differently.

Would she still have taken the child if she had known what was to come?

She bends towards Sally and kisses her cheek gently. 'Hold on, my sweet girl,' she whispers.

The answer is always yes. A million times yes.

Clarke catches Ciara's eye in the mirror. 'How is she?' he says.

She glances at her daughter's grey face. Everything is quiet. No more jerky breaths.

Fear pools in her stomach. 'She's not breathing,' Ciara says frantically, as Clarke screeches up to the hospital.

Ciara tries to shake her daughter awake. 'Stay with me, Sal,' she cries.

'Please,' Ciara sobs desperately, linking their smallest fingers together. 'Remember we pinkie promised we'd be okay?'

Sally's fingers go limp.

Chapter 36

Clarke pulls the police car to a stop outside the emergency room entrance. The sound of wailing sirens from an arriving ambulance clashes with the sounds of paramedics rushing a stretcher inside. Clarke throws the car into park and jumps out, but Ciara is already ahead of him. She wrenches open the back door, hands trembling as she gathers Sally's slack body in her arms. The child's head lolls against her shoulder.

'Sally,' Ciara chokes, her voice cracking, 'Stay with me, sweetheart. Please.' Inside the corridor of the hospital, lights glare down harshly as she staggers towards the sliding glass doors.

Clarke runs ahead, shouting for assistance at anyone he sees. 'We need help here,' he pleads to a nurse, clipboard in her hand.

With Sally now on a gurney, together they jog alongside the nurse as she barks orders to the nearest medical staff. Casey quickly tells them about her condition and being on the transplant list. The words blur for Ciara, who is still clinging to Sally's hand.

'Ten-year-old female,' someone explains, pushing the gurney into a room. A mask gets strapped to the child's face. Suddenly there are people everywhere – paramedics, doctors, nurses – closing in with practised frenzy. 'Unresponsive,' someone calls, 'start chest compressions,' and that's when Ciara feels arms around her shoulders, holding her up as she slides to the ground.

'Let them help her now,' Clarke says to her, but she strains against him, trying to move towards Sally, afraid to let go.

'I love you. I love you. I love you,' she shouts towards Sally, more frightened than she's ever felt.

'Ciara,' Clarke reassures her, his voice calm and low. His words ground her in the spiral she is experiencing. 'You need to let them do their job now. Come on.'

With an anguished cry, Ciara releases Sally's small fingers and steps back. A nurse takes her by the elbow and leads her out of the small room. 'We need you to wait here,' she says, voice low and firm.

'No, I need to be with her,' Ciara begs, thick panic in her chest. Because Ciara knows how this goes. She knows that nobody should ever be there when people are pounding on their child's chest, shocking them, sticking tubes down their throat. There are some things in life we shouldn't see. 'Please,' the nurse says kindly. 'We'll take care of her as best we can.'

Clarke puts a steading hand on Ciara's shoulder, but she barely notices. Her eyes are locked on the doors Sally disappeared through.

Clarke insists she's checked over herself. Ciara is freezing cold and in shock, and her head wound deep. They promise they'll send someone to triage her and they give her a gown to change into and some blankets.

Sitting on a plastic chair in the waiting room a few minutes later, Ciara can't stop thinking about the last vision she had of Sally through those doors.

Every time the door opens, she jumps to her feet, a wave of anxiety washing over her.

Outside, the world carries on – footsteps in the corridor, the low hum of the vending machine, the clink of the dinner trolleys – oblivious to the fact that her daughter's life is teetering on the edge. Ciara pictures the crash cart surrounding her daughter. Then suddenly, she can't help it. She leans forward and retches and retches until she throws up. Tears and saliva mix with grief as Clarke jumps up to help her, calling for someone to get a bag and handing her tissues.

She barely registers his presence as she continues to throw up until the door opens a few minutes later and a young doctor walks in. Ciara tries to sit up.

'Sally is stable,' she immediately informs them. Beautiful words that take Ciara a moment to absorb. 'She's a tough cookie that girl of yours.' The doctor smiles, glancing up from her notes. 'We are not out of the woods by any means yet, but she's in the right place.'

Ciara closes her eyes and sags back into the chair, her heart feeling as if it's about to explode.

–

The following twelve hours are a blur of blood tests, assessments, chest X-rays, meetings with consultants – a haematologist, cardiologists and paediatricians – their words a fog of unfamiliar medical terms.

In the hospital ward, Ciara sits holding her daughter's hand as Sally lies motionless in the bed. Ciara is refusing to leave the room or eat. She is never leaving her daughter again.

She knows nothing of the Bergs, only that Clarke informs her that the family have agreed to compatibility tests to determine donor suitability.

'But don't they want to see her?' Ciara says, her tone careful.

Clarke explains that they won't know until later.

Meanwhile, the nurses skirt around the issue, skittish and nervous. They know this isn't a straightforward case. They don't mention the Garda now stationed outside in the hallway, keeping an eye on Ciara's movements.

Later that night, a group of hospital porters do a tour of the wards with someone dressed up as Santa, reminding Ciara that it's now officially Christmas day.

It's just before eleven when her daughter finally stirs and tries to opens her eyes.

'It's okay, darling,' Ciara says, jumping up from the chair she's been sitting in for hours. She's wearing clothes the hospital found for her after they'd stitched her head wound and given her a boot for her ankle. Ironically, it's a similar grey tracksuit to the one she'd been issued at Logan. She's also been treated for dehydration but refused to stay in the ward. Nothing would stop her being there with Sally when she woke.

'Mom?' Sally croaks. 'You're here.'

Ciara climbs up onto the bed beside her daughter and tells Sally that she's safe now and that everything is all right.

'Merry Christmas,' she kisses her daughter gently. 'Mummy's here now. Shhh, rest.'

They fall asleep together, Sally's head resting on her mother's shoulder, her fingers tucked into Ciara's neck, like she had done when she was a baby.

–

The next morning, despite her exhaustion and overwhelm, Sally smiles at the festive-wrapped gift tucked in beside her. Ciara helps her open it. It's a small white bear with a red scarf around its neck. 'Happy Christmas, darling,' Ciara whispers, and the bear accompanies Sally to even more blood tests and scans as Ciara paces the room waiting for updates, hating having her daughter be away from her even for a moment.

Clarke Casey arrives that afternoon. Sally is at yet more tests when he knocks gently on the door of the hospital room. Ciara's napping, too, head down on the bed, sitting in a chair. She looks up blearily but when she sees it's him, she sits up fully.

'How is she?'

'She's okay,' Ciara replies. 'Confused and scared. As am I,' she adds.

Casey pulls out a chair. 'Okay to sit?' he asks gently. 'Or would you prefer to go to the cafe?'

'I want to be here for her, when she gets back,' Ciara explains, knowing she will probably have to leave her child soon enough anyway.

'How are you holding up?' Clarke asks softly. 'Some couple of days...'

Ciara nods wearily.

'I wanted to give you some updates,' Clarke suggests. 'As you probably know, Morgan was declared dead at the scene at Glenavon,' he tells her.

'And Gabe has given a statement saying Morgan tried to kill you, so he shot him with one of your father's guns. Is that right?'

'Is he in trouble?'

Casey shrugs. 'If you corroborate the story then, as a trained security professional, Gabe Long was keeping you safe from someone who confessed to be a killer. No charges will be brought.'

'So no jail time for Gabe?'

Clarke shakes his head and one of the many knots in Ciara's stomach loosens. Gabe's perceived debt to Jimmy was more than paid. She marvels, for a moment, at Gabe's loyalty. *He saved our lives...*

'Yes, that's how it happened,' she confirms. 'What does Courtney say?'

'Courtney didn't see what happened. But in her statement, she says that Morgan admitted killing his twin brother to her. Plus, we have his fingerprints in Jimmy's car. That could well have been from anytime over the past few weeks before the murder, back before any of this happened, but it's the fingerprints and evidence of Morgan's that were found in Lana's home that has really swung this case on its head.'

'I told you my dad's death couldn't have been suicide,' Ciara points out. 'That was lazy policing.'

She glances up at him. 'Sorry.'

'Wasn't my case.' He shrugs. 'We can't always get it right.'

A flair of anger surges through her then, cutting through the endless worry for Sally that has been occupying her thoughts. 'I didn't kill Morgan. But I was sent to prison for it.'

'I understand, Ciara. But this case wasn't straightforward.'

'You are telling me...'

'It means that you can't be charged with murder if the victim was alive all that time. And if we had the wrong victim, the prosecution needs to start all over again with making a case and bringing charges.'

She shakes her head in disbelief. 'I shouldn't have had to fucking escape in order to prove my innocence.'

'I know,' he nods. 'But in fairness, it was an unusual case.'

'Do you know what I've been through?' Tears glisten in her eyes, but she shakes them away. 'I almost lost my daughter.' She glances at Sally. 'This system tore me away from her when she needed me most.'

Clarke frowns and shifts uncomfortably. 'There'll be an investigation,' is all he manages. It's all he can say.

Then the questions she needs to ask. 'Are the Bergs here? The nurse says they'd agreed to testing to see if they can match for donation.'

Casey's expression shifts slightly. 'Well, it's complicated,' he says.

'The consultant on the case said a stranger's match could be possible, but it was much riskier. The preferred option was a family member.'

'Angela Berg died two years ago,' Clarke says, and something inside Ciara releases – guilt, fear, sorrow? A devastation for that young mother she'd cared for ten years ago.

'Oh, my God' she breathes. 'How?'

'Drugs,' he confirms.

'Her husband, Roger Berg, doesn't want to be involved in any of this. His solicitor was in touch to say he's not interested in pressing charges and was most unhelpful.'

Ciara remembers him as a strange young man. She'd put it down to the problems he's faced with addiction, but it was always Angela who had expressed any interest in baby Rosie. The problem was that fondness and affection just hadn't been enough to be a good parent.

Ciara exhales.

So, there can be no family match.

Ciara's knee bounces up and down. 'What happens if she doesn't get a match?' she asks softly. Clarke frowns. 'I think it's better that you speak to the consultant about that,' he says quietly.

But Ciara knows already. Reading between all the lines of what the medical professionals had told her, Sally was unlikely to survive without a match. A transplant had been their only hope.

'But I thought you said they'd agreed to testing?'

Clarke pulls his chair forwards. 'This is what I wanted to tell you. Sally has older siblings – she has two sisters.'

Ciara frowns, then remembers the two little girls that were there at the Berg house in Brighton one day, around ten and twelve, poking noses around Angela Berg's bedroom door in the gloom, confusion in their eyes as their mother remained motionless in her bed, out of it. Emmet shepherding them away.

'Beth and Hannah Berg are both here. They have both agreed to try and help Sally.'

Tears flow down Ciara's cheeks. A bittersweet overwhelm. After all, it was her actions that contributed to their loss. The loss of their sister for all those years…

'Can I… do they want to meet me? Meet Sally?' she asks nervously.

Clarke nods. 'They were so happy to have found their sister and, according to the doctors, siblings are even better candidates.'

'What?' Excitement bubbles up in Ciara. 'So they might be able to save her?'

'I'm not a doctor, Ciara, but I believe she's in with a fighting chance if the match is strong enough.'

She hugs her arms around her torso, feeling incredibly grateful.

'They seem really nice. I've arranged for a meeting with them for you later today, if it suits—?'

'I'd love that,' she says softly.

'What will this mean for me?' Ciara asks Clarke in a small voice. 'Can they press charges?'

They both glance over at the Garda on duty outside the glass door of the room.

'Child abduction is a serious offence, and we have a duty to invest-igate such cases and pursue charges if deemed appropriate,' Clarke explains. 'The law is intended to protect the welfare and safety of the children and the state will take the responsibility of enforcing those laws seriously.'

Ciara nods, nerves jangling in her stomach. She'd known this.

'But,' Clarke continues, 'in this case, and at this time, the family have chosen not to proceed with criminal charges and without that, it's extremely hard to build a case, especially as Emmet Berg has since passed away too.'

She barely has time to register this when a knock on the door interrupts them. Sally's bed is wheeled into the room alongside one of the consultants. 'Mrs Duffy, may I have a moment of your time?'

Ciara stands up. Clarke nods at her. 'I'll speak to you later,' he tells her and leaves the room, closing the door gently behind himself. It's only then that she notices that he's brought Sally a small Christmas gift; a book of fairy tales with a red bow around it. Ciara grasps the book in both hands and smiles.

Just the day before, they'd spoken about this – about the notion of happily ever afters. It was after Sally was stable and Ciara was waiting on the doctor. 'After my mum died when I was so young, I stopped believing in fairy tales,' she'd admitted. 'I felt robbed somehow of those magical stories of a happy family, two parents, all of that, you know what I mean?' She pauses. 'I suppose, in a way, I wanted to give Sally that story and look what happened...'

'There was a time in my life when I stopped believing I deserved that kind of happiness too,' Clarke had replied. 'But then someone walked in. Not in a grand, movie-scene kind of way – just real, quiet, like she just... belonged. And suddenly it wasn't about getting through the day anymore, it was about coming home. Finding peace in small things – the way someone waits up for you, even when you tell them not to.' He had glanced over at her, his gaze soft at the mention of his wife. 'You can fight it all you want, Ciara. You can tell yourself the world is too messy and too mean for fairy tales, and I don't blame you for thinking like that. Look what's happened to you. But one day, you'll find your happily ever after. It won't be perfect, nothing ever is. But it will feel right to you. It will fit. When that happens, I hope you are brave enough to believe it.' She runs her finger gently over the illustrated book and sets it down for Sally to enjoy.

The consultant, Dr Moore, stands across from Sally's bed, opposite her as Ciara strokes her daughter's face. 'I'm very pleased to tell you that we have confirmed that Hannah Berg is a good match for Sally's bone marrow needs. We can now go ahead and schedule the transplant.'

Ciara's heart soars.

The consultant continues to talk about 'long roads ahead' and 'potential setbacks,' but Ciara tucks the little white bear into the bed next to Sally and silently asks her own mother and father to shine their positive vibes down to them.

Once Dr Moore has gone, Ciara pulls the chair as close to the bed as she can. She rests her forehead on her daughter's warm folded hands.

'We are going to be okay,' she whispers. 'Pinkie promise'.

And for the first time in weeks, Ciara starts to believe it.

Chapter 37

Beth and Hannah Berg stand up as Ciara walks towards them, in the small cafe at the hospital. There's a glass-fronted deli counter with sandwich ingredients and the hiss-chug of a coffee machine with a harried-looking barista taking orders.

Ciara knew it was the Bergs the moment she looked into the cafe. She herself was conspicuous by virtue of the officer accompanying her. Suddenly the room is far too hot. She wonders if the sisters will berate her, break down crying or do something dramatic to express how terrible a deed she'd carried out – stealing their beloved baby sister.

Ciara stops just short of the table and they all regard one another. Ciara pushes her hair back self-consciously, painfully aware she needs a shower and looks completely dishevelled.

Beth is like a younger version of Angela Berg, which startles Ciara as she studies the younger woman. She has shoulder-length fair hair and the same upturned nose as Sally. Hannah is much more similar in appearance to Sally – she even has the same dimples. With a jolt, Ciara gets a sense of what her daughter will look like as an older version of herself.

'Hi,' is all Ciara can manage, overwhelmed, exhausted and grateful.

Beth chews her lip. Then, after a beat, Hannah Berg reaches her hand towards Ciara. 'I remember you,' she says, tears glistening in her eyes. 'You were kind to us. You played hide and seek with us.' Ciara remembers the two little girls in scruffy, dirty pyjamas despite the family's wealth and status. She'd helped comb out their matted hair and even read them a bedtime story when baby Rosie – Sally – was napping the day they came to visit from foster care. Truth be told – she'd wanted to take them with her too. It was clear they'd been neglected by their young, troubled parents.

Ciara takes Hannah's hand in hers and finds tears running down her own face. For a moment, she can't speak. Then, she whispers, 'I'm sorry.' She sinks into the chair, overcome completely, her past jumping back out at her so intimately. This was the life she'd lived in Brighton before everything – before Sally was hers, before Morgan and the arrest and her father's death.

What if she'd never taken on the job with the Bergs? What if she'd refused when Beth and Hannah's grandfather had begged her to take the child and offered her money to give Alex a chance and Rosie a better life. What if she'd just said no? Would their lives have been better? Ciara wipes her eyes as the two girls sink into their chairs opposite her and wave the waitress over. Ciara knew she'd go to jail a million times over just to have Sally in her life. It wasn't a perfect scenario – not by any means – but the happiness and love she'd had with her daughter – their sister – was immeasurable.

Ciara tries to pull herself together. She blows her nose. 'I remember you both too,' she admits quietly. 'I remember your excitement over your baby sister. I'm just so sorry how everything happened.' She stares down at her hands, her voice breaking.

Her accompanying officer, a lanky man in his thirties, scrolls on his phone a few feet away. The waitress comes to take her order and Ciara risks a glance at the young women in front of her.

'I can't tell you how overjoyed we were to get the call about Rosie,' Hannah begins. 'And how devastated we were to hear how sick she was. We dropped everything to come.'

Ciara nods miserably. She'd denied Sally the joy of sisterhood on top of everything else. 'Thank you so much for that,' Ciara blurts out. 'I'm so grateful.'

Hannah puts her hand over Ciara's. 'It's us who are grateful.' She glances at her sister, who nods. 'We were already in the foster system when you came to look after Rosie,' Hannah explains. 'We'd only get the odd weekend with our parents, but even then, we knew they weren't well, and our grandfather... he couldn't really take care of us.' Hannah looks wistful. 'We were fostered separately and then found one another when we were a little older. There were ups and downs, as you might imagine, but we never felt that sense of home that we'd once had when Mum wasn't using.' She runs a hand over her face – still so young to have lived this pain. 'In some ways, we are still looking for that sense of home.'

Beth leans over and squeezes her sister's hand. 'You taking Rosie and being a mother to her meant our sister was loved and taken care of. I'm afraid to think what would have happened if you hadn't taken her.'

'I think about that day – the day I left with her – all the time,' Ciara admits, wrapping her fingers around her mug, shakily. 'It was the hardest choice I've ever made in my life. But I also didn't want Sally – sorry, Rosie – to be put into the care system.'

Hannah nods vigorously. 'Not when there's an alternative person who is determined to love them.' Hannah holds Ciara's gaze. 'And it sounds from what that detective told us that you love her a lot.'

'With every piece of my heart,' Ciara confirms, her voice cracking, thinking of her frail little girl upstairs.

'The spotlight on our family from the media about the missing Brighton Baby also meant that they, Mum and Dad, had to really step up and get the help they needed. They didn't get their act together until much later – my mother never really at all, but, and I'm sorry if this hurts you, my mother really always felt she'd find Rosie someday. In fact, she made me promise when I last saw her that I'd find her and we'd be reunited.'

Ciara's heart aches at the thought of poor Angela pining for her lost daughter because of her. 'And we probably never would have until we got the call. So in a way...' Hannah smiles. 'You helped us fulfil a promise.'

'You are saving her life,' Ciara says, choking on the emotion that spills out.

And in turn, saving mine, she thinks to herself.

–

Later, back in Sally's room, Ciara tries to square the circle of Sally and the Bergs, but her brain grows tired of the guilt-heartbreak cycle. She decides she's going to view this reunion as a positive, for all of them. Once Sally pulls through.

She glances at her daughter's delicate features and dark-ringed eyes. Nothing else mattered besides her getting healthy.

Don't be under any illusion that finding a match is fait accompli, the consultant had warned her. But she had to have hope.

A rap on the door startles her out of her thoughts. 'Mrs Ciara Duffy?' Two uniformed Gardaí enter the room. 'Would you have a moment, please?' one says, curtly.

So this is it.

She'll have to say goodbye all over again.

Ciara takes a deep breath and strokes Sally's hand. Her daughter will wake up and she'll be gone.

'Can I please have a moment?' Ciara begs, anxiety gripping her stomach. 'To say goodbye?'

The officers exchange glances.

'Oh…' says the first one, stammering. 'No, well…'

She can tell they are afraid she'll escape again. 'I'll be quick,' she lies. She'll take as long as possible with her precious girl. Who knows when she'll see Sally again.

'Actually,' the second officer explains, 'we've been examining the evidence you've put forward in relation to Jimmy Mooney's death. That, along with the statement from Gabriel Long and Courtney Duffy, means we have certain doubts over your responsibility when it comes to killing your husband on October the seventh.'

Ciara blinks at them, uncomprehending, her mind reeling.

'That said, we can't ignore the fact that escaping from custody is a serious offense,' he adds.

'However, given the extraordinary circumstances, you won't be detained while the process to overturn your conviction moves forward.' He pauses as she stares at him in shock.

'I don't understand,' is all she can manage.

'There are certain conditions, Ms Duffy. You'll need to surrender your passport and remain within the jurisdiction. This is non-negotiable until the legal process is complete. But for now, you are free to go.'

'Free to go?' Ciara repeats, her hands flying to her face.

'An internal review is underway to determine how this mistake happened, and we are taking it very seriously,' the second officer says. Then, muttering: 'We are sorry for what you've been through. It's not something anyone should have to endure.'

After they leave, she sits by Sally for a while, the officers' words ringing in her head. She still can't believe what they said.

A second chance.

Free to go.

She looks at her daughter's sleeping face.

Please get well, Sally, she prays. *We are so close, baby.*

Just before it gets dark, Ciara ventures out into the hallway. She notices there's no garda stationed at her door. Her feet propel her towards the doorway outside, the familiar feeling of having to sneak around so hard to shake.

Nobody stops her. There's no alarm, no angry shouts, no one chasing her.

A nurse nods at her as she passes Ciara, arriving onto the evening shift.

Outside is dusky golden, where shadows are long and the air is crisp. Ciara sits on a bench in the small garden next to a religious statue, its dark arms spreading against the amber sky.

She talks silently to her father first. Then her mother, watching the first stars emerge sparkling, signalling night. A million more suddenly appear.

Ciara drinks it all in. All the endless possibilities.

Free, she thinks, a fizz of something deep in her stomach. The skip of her heart.

I'm finally free.

Chapter 38

Two years later

Every shell Ciara hands to Sally, she throws into the surf at Brighton beach. For someone else to find, she tells Ciara, her toes sinking into the sand next to hers.

Ciara finds it hard to let go of her daughter's hand. Months of delicate recovery have resulted in a robust little girl with a positive future.

Ciara feels so lucky. She feels guilty sometimes too.

She slips some of the broken shells, still gritty with sand, into her pocket, enjoying the jiggle of them against the fabric of her jeans.

Her keepsakes.

She pictures all the drawings Sally sent to her in prison, now adorning her fridge at home in Kinloch. They sit alongside dozens of other keepsakes: Sally's report card from her new school; birthday cards from Courtney, Clarke Casey and Gabriel Long among others; Ciara's gym timetable; even the exciting letter that arrived in the post the other day is stuck on with a magnet – the formality of it no match for the thrill she felt when she'd read it. A job offer, at a new private clinic just fifteen minutes' walk from their home. She'd be back with her mother and baby patients three days a week.

Ahead of them, the churning sea teases Sally as she jumps over the waves and tries to skim stones.

The sea doesn't care what it holds. Or what it discards.

For so long Ciara has been the keeper of other things too. Of secrets – of her decision to take up Emmet Berg's offer to rehome Sally. Or her decision to use extra pain medication to let Alex go a day or two sooner than he would have anyway.

She questions why she made the decision to stay in a marriage to someone like Morgan, where too often she had to fold herself small.

She has creased her happiness over and over into the smallest version of herself for too many years. Her silence betraying her own self-respect.

But she's owning this now.

She's spent many months in a chair opposite a therapist trying to understand who she really is. Trying to quell the horror of what she's lived through. Finding compassion for the little girl with the blonde bob whose world was turned upside down after her mother died from cancer.

Ciara feels freer now in so many ways, trying to surrender to the possibility that she's more than an escapee, she's a fighter. She's someone worth fighting for.

In the stacking-doll history of her life, she's all of those things: Mother, Midwife, Survivor.

Partner.

She watches as Derry crosses the road from the guest house and joins them on the beach. They are all here visiting for the weekend. His arms wrap tightly around her waist, his face open, ready. He tucks her scarf – her dad's scarf – gently into her coat where it's unravelled.

Ciara flicks her newly styled bob at him. 'Gosh, you smell amazing,' he grins.

They'd promised Sally a lot after her recovery. The first was to visit her sisters once Ciara was able.

They're here too, on the beach, skimming stones along the swirling sea.

Sally wears a cone-shaped orange hat – a birthday bonnet Hannah brought her, plus a chocolate cake with chocolate Smarties and twelve candles. They laugh as the candles refuse to light in the gusty salt air. They hold the candles one by one to Sally's face and cheer as she blows them out.

She is loved, Ciara thinks happily. And that is all she ever wanted for Sally.

'Literally THE best day,' Sally exclaims, and Ciara catches a flashback to the younger version of her daughter – carefree and healthy.

Beth has brought her a scrapbook with a pretty star stuck onto the front. Later, sitting in the sand with their birthday picnic, she helps her little sister glue in photos, cut-outs from newspapers – they even stick on some of the shells they've brought from the beach in Dublin near Kerryvale.

Ciara has told her daughter everything, in a way she can understand. She's explained who she is, who she *was*, in order for her to understand who she was going to become.

On the first visit from Dublin, last year, Ciara took her to Angela's grave. The mother Sally was born to. The mother Ciara thought she was helping. They stood there together, just the two of them, hand in hand, allowing the freedom of all the things they needed to express leave them and come to rest on the spray of flowers that surrounded the black marble.

It's easy now sometimes to look back and justify her actions. Sally is happy. She's healthy and they have their beautiful life in the place they are happiest. But it's also difficult to reconcile the hurt that Ciara caused.

Sometimes she imagines that she hears Angela's voice that day on the pier in the wind when Sally was little. Her screams for Rosie. Ciara usually whips around, her guts turned inside out, and realise it's in her own head.

Like the sounds of the prison. They are all part of her now.

Those stories are written into Ciara's life in indelible ink: Paula's friendship, Gabe's loyalty, Clarke's steadiness, her father's protection. Derry's love.

Derry kisses her and tells Sally that he'll race her to the end of the pier.

They run, side by side, Sally's hair almost fully grown back now, pushed back with a pink headband; Derry like an owl flying next to her. Protective and safe.

Those people who helped Ciara escape, that version of her life, they linger, like the dreams she has of being chased, of climbing walls and falling. The sounds of crows in a forest – black and feathery. Or gunshots and slamming doors.

She dips down and finds an ivory spiral among all the broken shells by her feet. It's surprisingly intact. So few things remain so. It glints up at her as she wipes it with the ends of her scarf.

She continues down the beach, waiting for the others, collecting the prettiest shells. Broken ones too, thinking about her mother's sea-shell frame at home on the mantle.

Ciara keeps what she wants now. The rest – the clutter, the chaos, the sins of her past – the tide pulls beyond her reach.

She sees the silhouettes of Derry and Sally in the distance on the pier and smiles as he swings her around in circles.

She can hear her squeals of laughter from over here. Now Sally's calling her to join them. They both are. Ciara pats her pocket gently, happy with her imperfect lot, and then walks quickly towards them.

Acknowledgements

One of the books that really stuck with me when I was a child was *Flight of the Doves* by Walter Macken. It follows Finn and Derval Dove, two orphaned siblings running from their abusive stepfather, making their way across Ireland in search of their grandmother. Their journey is driven by the fragile hope for a better life. They slip through unfamiliar places, hiding from authorities and doing whatever it takes to seek safety. That story stayed with me. And, years later, their courageous escape quietly worked its way into the heart of this one.

Like the Doves, midwife Ciara Duffy is thrust into a world she doesn't recognise. In *The Stranger Inside*, she's accused of something unthinkable: the murder of her husband. In an instant, Ciara is left to pick up the pieces of her shattered life. Writing Ciara meant stepping into what it feels like to lose your footing entirely – and then, inch by inch, start again in a way you never anticipated. Her story evolved into something beyond the question of guilt or innocence. It became about survival and the resilience that comes with self-belief.

I'm deeply grateful to Governor Mary Kennedy, Governor Martin Galgey, Assistant Governor Damian Harris, and Assistant Chief Officer Terry Murphy for generously sharing their insights into prison life. Your time and openness during the early research stages for *The Stranger Inside* were invaluable and any mistakes in this book are entirely mine. My fictional version of incarceration at Logan only scratches the surface of the complexities and nuances of real prison life and is no reflection of any real Irish prison.

I'm so grateful to my agent Diana Beaumont at DHH Literary Agency, my editor, Louise Cullen, as well as everyone at Canelo publishing for the incredible support in bringing this book to life and into readers' hands.

To my family, my wonderful friends, and my amazing writing community (you know who you are!): thank you for cheering me on throughout the writing of *The Stranger Inside*. Your belief in me and my capabilities means the world. Sincere thanks also to everyone who reads my books, reviews or champions my stories. It's such an honour to be the author of a story you chose to spend time with.

A special shoutout to Declan, Georgina and everyone at Deloitte Ireland for encouraging me to challenge the format, make zig-zags out of straight lines, and somehow still make our collaboration work so beautifully.

My biggest cheer, of course, is to Eva Valentina, Bobby, and Isabella. Thank you for your loud, wonderful, effervescent love that fills up every corner of my lovely, lucky life.

ⓒ **CANELO**CRIME

Do you love crime fiction and are always on the lookout for brilliant authors?

Canelo Crime is home to some of the most exciting novels around. Thousands of readers are already enjoying our compulsive stories. Are you ready to find your new favourite writer?

Find out more and sign up to our newsletter at canelocrime.com